CONSCIOUSNESS RETURNED TO CIMARRON SLOWLY

He was tied to a pinon pine, his arms circling the tree, his legs splayed out before him. Every part of his body ached but he was still alive, no thanks to Belinda and her brother.

Cimarron heard a sound and saw Belinda coming toward him, a smile on her face. She knelt down and placed her hand between his legs, unbuttoning his jeans. "You look a bit stiff," she observed. Her moist, pouty lips formed a soft circle and she lowered her head.

Belinda knew many ways to torment a man, and she was an expert in all of them. . . .

CIMARRON AND THE BOUNTY HUNTERS

SIGNET Westerns You'll Enjoy

(0451)

- ☐ **CIMARRON #1: CIMARRON AND THE HANGING JUDGE** by Leo P. Kelley. (120582—$2.50)*
- ☐ **CIMARRON #2: CIMARRON RIDES THE OUTLAW TRAIL** by Leo P. Kelley. (120590—$2.50)*
- ☐ **CIMARRON #3: CIMARRON AND THE BORDER BANDITS** by Leo P. Kelley. (122518—$2.50)*
- ☐ **CIMARRON #4: CIMARRON IN THE CHEROKEE STRIP** by Leo P. Kelley. (123441—$2.50)*
- ☐ **CIMARRON #5: CIMARRON AND THE ELK SOLDIERS** by Leo P. Kelley. (124898—$2.50)*
- ☐ **CIMARRON #6: CIMARRON AND THE BOUNTY HUNTERS** by Leo P. Kelley. (125703—$2.50)*
- ☐ **LUKE SUTTON: OUTLAW** by Leo P. Kelley. (115228—$1.95)*
- ☐ **LUKE SUTTON: GUNFIGHTER** by Leo P. Kelley. (122836—$2.25)*
- ☐ **LUKE SUTTON: INDIAN FIGHTER** by Leo P. Kelley. (124553—$2.25)*
- ☐ **COLD RIVER** by William Judson. (098439—$1.95)*
- ☐ **DEATHTRAP ON THE PLATTER** by Cliff Farrell. (099060—$1.95)*
- ☐ **GUNS ALONG THE BRAZOS** by Day Keene. (096169—$1.75)*
- ☐ **LOBO GRAY** by L. L. Foreman. (096770—$1.75)*
- ☐ **THE HALF-BREED** by Mick Clumpner. (112814—$1.95)*
- ☐ **MASSACRE AT THE GORGE** by Mick Clumpner. (117433—$1.95)*

*Prices slightly higher in Canada

Buy them at your local bookstore or use this convenient coupon for ordering.
THE NEW AMERICAN LIBRARY, INC.,
P.O. Box 999, Bergenfield, New Jersey 07621
Please send me the books I have checked above. I am enclosing $_____
(please add $1.00 to this order to cover postage and handling). Send check or money order—no cash or C.O.D.'s. Prices and numbers are subject to change without notice.
Name_____
Address_____
City _____ State _____ Zip Code _____
Allow 4-6 weeks for delivery.
This offer is subject to withdrawal without notice.

by
LEO P. KELLEY

A SIGNET BOOK
NEW AMERICAN LIBRARY
TIMES MIRROR

PUBLISHER'S NOTE

This novel is a work of fiction. Names, characters, places, and incidents either are the product of the author's imagination or are used fictitiously, and any resemblance to actual persons, living or dead, events, or locales is entirely coincidental.

NAL BOOKS ARE AVAILABLE AT QUANTITY DISCOUNTS WHEN USED
TO PROMOTE PRODUCTS OR SERVICES. FOR INFORMATION PLEASE
WRITE TO PREMIUM MARKETING DIVISION, THE NEW AMERICAN
LIBRARY, INC., 1633 BROADWAY, NEW YORK, NEW YORK 10019.

Copyright © 1983 by Leo P. Kelley

The first chapter of this book appeared in Cimarron and the Elk Soldiers, the fifth volume in this series.

All rights reserved

SIGNET TRADEMARK REG. U.S. PAT. OFF. AND FOREIGN COUNTRIES
REGISTERED TRADEMARK—MARCA REGISTRADA
HECHO EN CHICAGO, U.S.A.

SIGNET, SIGNET CLASSIC, MENTOR, PLUME, MERIDIAN and NAL BOOKS
are published by The New American Library, Inc.,
1633 Broadway, New York, New York 10019

First Printing, November, 1983

1 2 3 4 5 6 7 8 9

PRINTED IN THE UNITED STATES OF AMERICA

CIMARRON . . .

. . . he was a man with a past he wanted to forget and a future uncertain at best and dangerous at worst. Men feared and secretly admired him. Women desired him. He roamed the Indian Territory with a Winchester '73 in his saddle scabbard, an Army Colt in his hip holster, and a bronc he had broken beneath him. He packed his guns loose, rode his horse hard, and no one dared throw gravel in his boots. Once he had an ordinary name like other men. But a tragic killing forced him to abandon it and he became known only as Cimarron. *Cimarron*, in Spanish, meant wild and unruly. It suited him. *Cimarron*.

1

The early-morning sun glinted on the surface of the Arkansas River, and Cimarron, as he walked along Fort Smith's waterfront, closed his eyes momentarily against the glare.

He fervently wished he could clear his head of the giddiness whirling within it as a result of the previous night's debauchery.

He had sat up until nearly dawn on the opposite bank of the river where the deputies—those not married and living in Forth Smith—camped. There was whiskey. There was beer. And there was talk. He'd told his share of big windies, and his extravagant and boisterous lies about his amorous adventures and lawman's escapades were as good and often better than those told by the other deputy marshals.

But now he was paying the price for having drunk too much, talked too loud, and generally caroused, he thought, like a hobo in a whorehouse.

As he turned his head—slowly in order not to dislodge it—he saw her walking down A Street, looking, he thought, just as pretty as a picture. He turned—more of a haphazard swerve than a purposeful change of direction—and went after her.

When he caught up to Rose Collins, he took her arm and she gave him a dazzling smile that almost blinded him.

"Cimarron," she said sweetly. "How nice to see you. You're up early."

"Didn't get to bed down hardly at all last night, but don't let's us talk about that. A fool ought to forget his folly as fast as possible. Where do you happen to be headed, Rose?"

"Pritchard's."

"For breakfast?"

"Yes. And you?"

"Pritchard's," Cimarron answered, only then making up his mind to accompany Rose, although breakfast was the last thing in the world he wanted at the moment. He suspected that if he threw any down, his stomach would throw it all right back up again.

When they reached the restaurant, he held the door for Rose, and after she had glided past him, he went inside and sat down across from her at the table she had chosen.

The waitress appeared almost immediately, a plain girl wearing a clean white apron over her dark dress. "Yes, please?"

No, thank you, Cimarron thought as he took off his hat, placed it on the table, propped his head in his hands, and muttered, "Coffee. Black as the pit and strong as temptation."

"I'll have some eggs—scrambled," Rose declared brightly, and Cimarron groaned. "Fried potatoes." He swallowed hard. "Stewed tomatoes." He almost retched. "Bread and butter and, of course, coffee."

"Yes, Miss Collins."

"Cimarron, is something wrong?" Rose asked when the waitress had gone, and she leaned solicitiously toward him, a concerned expression on her face.

He started to shake his head, decided that he'd better not risk doing so, and replied, "Nothing a good pine coffin and a six-foot hole in the ground wouldn't cure."

"You poor thing," Rose cooed, patting his hand. "Hangover again?"

"The granddaddy of all hangovers."

"Pretty?"

Cimarron looked up. "This hangover I've got's not the least bit pretty."

"I meant the woman you were drinking with last night."

"I wasn't with a woman," Cimarron said sorrowfully. "Wish to hell I had been. Wish I'd been with you or at least a lady half as pretty as you. There was just a bunch of us deputies with not the sense of a Philadelphia lawyer to spread among the lot of us."

"I should chide you, Cimarron."

"You go right ahead and do that, honey. I know I deserve it. A man should know his limit where liquor's concerned."

"I'm not talking about your drinking habits. I'm talking

about the fact that you haven't been to see me in ever so long."

"I did start out last week, Rose—I truly did—but then I realized I didn't have the price to pay you and you know Mrs. Windham don't give credit in her parlor house. Another time—but before I could put one foot in front of the other, Marshal Upham sent me hightailing it out into Indian Territory to hunt for a jasper who held up the station master in Boggy Depot."

"What about today—tonight?"

"Maybe. I'm on my way to see Marshal Upham. If he'll take pity on me and won't make me work today, I'll come by Mrs. Windham's and you'll be sure to hear me coming."

"I will?"

"I'll have bells on and I'll be hollering your name out loud so you'll have time to get yourself ready for me."

"I'm not sure that I've ever really been ready for you, Cimarron. You're too unpredictable, not to mention passionate."

They were silent as the waitress placed their orders on the table.

As she was about to withdraw, Cimarron caught her wrist and, looking up into her eyes, asked, "Will you marry me?"

"Beg pardon, sir?"

"I've just now made up my mind to tread the straight and narrow path and you look like a lady who could keep me on it." He slapped the waitress' buttocks lightly and she fled, followed by Rose's gay laughter.

"I declare you are a caution, Cimarron. You've terrified the poor girl."

"She terrified me. Didn't you notice the disapproving looks she was giving me? You'd've thought she was the Virgin Mary and I was a horse thief trying to sneak into Heaven."

As Rose began to eat, Cimarron emptied his coffeecup and stood up shakily.

"Tonight?" Rose prodded with a pert smile.

"We'll see, honey. Glad to have run into you, Rose. You've made this man's mournful morning worthwhile and given me the will to live again."

Cimarron placed a coin on the table, clapped his hat on his head, and once outside the restaurant, he walked slowly down the street. When he reached the stone-walled compound that had been his destination, he entered it; minutes later, he was inside Fort Smith's courthouse and knocking on the door of Marshal Upham's office.

"Come in!"

Cimarron opened the door, to find Upham standing just inside it. As he dropped down into the nearest chair, Upham gave the door a shove, and as it slammed, Cimarron winced.

Upham walked behind his desk and sat down, studying Cimarron.

"Have I got my hat on backward?" Cimarron asked gruffly. "Or did I forget to button my fly? You're grinning like a jackass eating cactus, Marshal."

"When's the wake?"

"Do I look that bad?"

"Worse." Upham rummaged about among the pile of papers on his desk, finally found what he had been looking for, and thrust a document at Cimarron.

"Shit, Marshal," Cimarron muttered as he studied the paper Upham had given him, "you can't expect me to go out hunting a murderer, considering the condition I'm in. If he so much as spits at me, he'll knock me down for sure and be gone."

"Ernie Wilcox," Upham said, ignoring Cimarron's outburst, "is wanted for murder. The grand jury handed up an indictment and that warrant you've got in your hand authorizes you to bring him in dead or alive."

"Marshal, sometimes you talk like somebody straight out of the pages of one of those Beadle and Adams' dime novels. '*Dead or alive.*' Why would I want to bring in this"—Cimarron glanced at the warrant in his hand—"Wilcox dead? The only way I can collect the two dollars for him is if I bring him in alive. Which is not a munificent sum in any man's jeans, I can sure tell you—two dollars isn't."

"Judge Parker, as you know, has repeatedly asked the federal government to authorize higher fees for the work you deputies do."

"Two dollars," Cimarron fumed. "A ribbon clerk makes more money in a year than I do. Some drifters do."

"Ernie Wilcox killed a man in a shootout in McAlester. Witnesses testified to that effect before the grand jury— eyewitnesses. It's an open-and-shut case. He'll undoubtedly be convicted when he's tried and then Maledon will have his chance to hang the man."

"Two dollars's not enough even to pay for the company of Miss Rose Collins."

"Cimarron, you're not listening to me."

"Wilcox. Witnesses—*eye*witnesses. Warrant." Cimarron held it up and waved it. "I heard you, Marshal. Did you hear me?"

"If you mean did I hear you and your complaints, which have become close to habitual, not to mention tedious, lately, yes, I did. Why don't you stop by the Paris Emporium here in town?"

A puzzled frown appeared on Cimarron's face. "What the hell for?"

"They might have need of another ribbon clerk."

"I'm a sick man this morning, Marshal. It don't seem right that you should be taunting me when I'm on the verge of expiring."

"It's a damn shame about Wilcox," Upham mused, leaning back in his chair and folding his hands across his ample stomach.

"What is? That he killed somebody?"

"The somebody he killed, as you'll learn if you'll read that warrant you're holding, was named Louis Labrette, a fur trapper in his early days, a gambling man of late. Yes, the murder itself was a shame, but that's not what I was referring to. Witnesses estimated Wilcox's age as no more than sixteen or seventeen. It's a shame to see a youngster like that end his life on the gallows before he's even had a chance to properly live it."

"A body—man or boy—who's quicker to draw a gun than he is to think—well, age don't make the difference. Hot blood's what does. Somebody once said—I read it somewhere—that you can take anything you want just so long as you pay the price for it. Well, this Wilcox fellow went and took what he wanted—a man's life—and now he's got to pay the price for it . . . if I don't die of a bad case of having no common sense before I can lay hands on him. Reminds me of that other murder case you sent me out on last year. The Fairfax case. Cele Fairfax was a woman and you'd've thought butter wouldn't melt in her mouth, but she went and killed two of her boarders up near Fort Gibson. A man can never

11

tell about people, including sixteen-year-olds, and I reckon he'd best not try to."

"If you have quite finished your heartwarming homily, Cimarron, may I suggest that you set out at once for McAlester."

"Well, the spirit's sure willing, Marshal."

"But the flesh is weak?"

"More like at death's door is what it is. I swear I'll never touch another drop of the ardent."

Upham threw back his head and erupted in laughter. "That reminds me of the time you swore you would never lay hands on another woman as long as you lived."

"I sincerely meant it at the time."

"Beth Clinton gave you a run for your money."

"You got it all wrong, Marshal. She ran *with* my money."

When Upham's laughter had subsided, he commented, "You're incorrigible, Cimarron."

"I'm warning you, Marshal. I'm fixing to buy me a dictionary one of these days, and when I do, I'm going to look up every last one of those names you're always slapping on me; and if they turn out to mean what I think they mean—well, you'd best watch your step 'cause I'll come after you with a bar of soap to wash out that nasty mouth of yours. Why, the idea! Calling me things like 'obstreperous' and 'intractable.' And what was that last one? Incor-what?"

"Incorrigible. It means that you are incapable of being reformed."

"How the hell do you expect me to ever be reformed," Cimarron inquired innocently and with a faint grin, "when you're all the time sending me out to keep company with murdering men like this here Ernie Wilcox? They're a bad influence on me, Marshal, and I thought an educated man like yourself ought to be able to see that clear as day."

"Cimarron," Upham said soberly, rising from his chair, "you be careful out there now. Wilcox is a desperate and therefore a dangerous man. He has threatened to kill any lawman who comes after him. Several people heard him make that threat and they are convinced that he is perfectly capable of carrying it out. I wouldn't want to lose the best damned deputy this court has ever had working for it."

Cimarron rose and started for the door. Before he went through it, he turned and said, "Don't you go worrying none about me, Marshal. I'm always careful. Got to be. With the small-size brain that the good Lord saw fit to dole out to me—well, being careful's my only ace in the hole. Be seeing you, Marshal."

Cimarron rode into McAlester the following morning after having camped out the night before under a cloudy sky that was occasionally illuminated by flashes of heat lightning.

He headed for the depot, and when he reached it, he got out of the saddle and wrapped the reins of his black around the hitch rail in front of the wooden building that had a sign above its entrance: LUNCH AND HOT COFFEE.

Once inside the building, he sat down at a table near the door, and when a man with a handlebar mustache approached him and asked him what he wanted, he answered, "Information, Hastings."

"The sign outside says we serve lunch and coffee."

"Read it. It happens I don't want neither your lunch nor your coffee. Been here before, you may recall, and had both, but I recovered. Where can I find—"

Hastings turned and began to walk away from the table.

Cimarron sprang to his feet, kicked a chair out of his way, which crashed to the floor, and seized Hastings by the shoulders. He spun him around and sent him hurtling into the wall.

"Hey, damn you—"

"Sit down, Hastings." Cimarron pointed to a chair and Hastings slid into it, his eyes wary. "Now, then. I'll just resume my seat right here beside you and you can tell me where I'm liable to find Ernie Wilcox, who's a citizen of your fair city."

"I don't know where he is. Haven't seen him in days."

"You know I'm a deputy marshal, don't you, Hastings?"

"I know. You were wearing your badge the last time you came barging in here."

"I'm here to bring Wilcox to Fort Smith for trial on a murder charge. Now maybe you'd like to tell me what you know about this fracas between him and Labrette."

"It happened in the alley that runs alongside the livery stable. Wilcox and Labrette met and they got into an argument. There were people on the streets and some of them saw Wilcox shoot and kill Labrette."

"What was the argument about?" Cimarron asked, hoping

to learn something—anything—that might give him a lead concerning the present whereabouts of Ernie Wilcox.

"Esther Lane."

"Who's Esther Lane?"

"A girl."

"Figured as much, since I never have yet met a man named Esther." Cimarron's face darkened and he reached out and seized a fistful of Hasting's shirt. "I'm going to shake you till your teeth rattle if you don't stop leading me all the way around the barn and do start getting directly to the point. Who's Esther Lane?"

"She was Ernie Wilcox's girl. Labrette had his eye on her, though, and Wilcox didn't like it. He'd told Labrette to stay away from her. Labrette didn't. They had words. You know the rest."

"I don't know much of anything yet. This Wilcox, he was a gunslick?"

Hastings shook his head. "Just a kid head over heels in love and hot under the collar about what he thought was Labrette's moving in on what he claimed as his territory—on Esther. Why, that boy was hanging around her house every spare minute he had, looking like a lovelorn loon. An armed posse couldn't have chased him away from her. The funny part, though, is that Wilcox didn't know that Esther had taken a shine to Dan Packer and not Labrette."

"Where might I find this Dan Packer?"

"He lives with his mother—she's a widow—on the east side of the tracks."

"Much obliged." Cimarron rose and left the building. He crossed the tracks of the Missouri, Kansas, and Texas Railroad, leading his black, and asked the first man he met where the Widow Packer lived. When the house had been pointed out to him, he went up to it and, leaving the black with its reins trailing, knocked on the front door.

The door was opened by a man Cimarron was sure wouldn't see thirty again. "Dan Packer?"

"I'm Packer. Who are you?"

Cimarron pulled his badge from his jeans, displayed it, and then pocketed it again. "I'm hunting Ernie Wilcox. You happen to know where he is?"

"No."

"When's the last time you saw him?"

"Some days ago. He seems to have left town."

"Which leaves you sitting in the catbird seat where Miss Esther Lane's concerned."

"My relationship with Miss Lane is none of your business, Deputy."

"Maybe you're right about that. Where do you suggest I start looking for Wilcox?"

"Couldn't say. But he'd better not come back here to McAlester and start pestering Miss Lane again."

"You'll run him off if he does?"

"I will."

"You do that, and from what I've heard, you're liable to wind up as dead as Labrette did when he started cozying up to Miss Lane."

"I'm not afraid of any fool kid."

"Maybe you should be. Guns in the hands of fool kids can cause one helluva lot of grief, as Labrette found out. Where can I find Esther Lane? I want to have a talk with her."

"She can't tell you anything."

Cimarron sighed. "Packer, will you do me the favor of letting Miss Lane tell me herself that she can't tell me anything?"

When Packer had given him directions, Cimarron led his horse down the street and tethered it to the picket fence that enclosed the small yard in front of the Lane house. He went up on the porch and knocked on the front door.

"Good day," he said to the young woman who opened the door. He touched the brim of his hat to her, thinking that she wasn't much more than a girl. "Would you happen to be Miss Esther Lane?"

"Yes, I am. But I don't believe I know you."

"My name's Cimarron. I'm a deputy marshal out of Fort Smith. I—"

"You're after Ernie."

"I am." Cimarron noticed that Esther's face had paled. "If we could step inside, maybe you'd be able to tell me something about him that will help me run him to ground."

Esther stiffened, her arms rigid at her sides. "I'll tell you nothing." She began to close the door.

Cimarron thrust out a boot and blocked it. "I know how much you hated him, so I thought—"

His ploy worked.

Esther's eyes widened. "Hated Ernie? I didn't. I loved him. I still love him! Oh, I'm so ashamed of myself!" Tears glistened in her eyes.

"You're ashamed of yourself on account of you let Labrette come calling on you, which led to Wilcox gunning him down?"

"No, that's not it. Mr. Labrette was no problem as far as I was concerned. He did make himself objectionable for a time, but I was finally able to discourage him. It was the way I behaved with Dan Packer that has made me so ashamed of myself. When he first came to town, I thought him rather charming, and then he asked if he could call on me and I said he could. He'd been to Saint Louis. Even to New Orleans once, he told me. I know he's somewhat older than me—I'm seventeen—but it's the way that two people's spirits touch that's important, not their ages, however different they might be."

"How old is Ernie Wilcox?"

"Eighteen."

"Just a boy."

Esther's eyes flashed. "He's a man, a real man. I know that now. I thought Mr. Packer . . . He seemed so sophisticated and Ernie, well, he's not seen much of the world and—Oh, I was a fool!"

"It's a good thing Wilcox didn't know about your interest in Dan Packer or he'd have like as not gone and gunned Packer down too."

"Don't you dare say a terrible thing like that! Ernie didn't kill Mr. Labrette."

"Witnesses say he did."

"I know they said they saw him shoot Mr. Labrette. But—"

"It's hot out here," Cimarron interrupted. "Couldn't we step inside?"

With obvious reluctance, Esther stepped back and Cimarron entered the front parlor of the house. When they were both seated, he said, "A woman in love's likely to believe all sorts of things about her man. She might even believe he didn't kill a man when other people saw him do it."

"Ernie couldn't kill anybody."

"But he did."

"You said you were a deputy marshal, not a judge."

Cimarron cleared his throat in faint embarrassment. "That picture over there on the table. That Wilcox?"

Esther reached out, picked up the framed photograph in both hands, and stared at it for a long moment before handing it to Cimarron. "That's Ernie. Oh, how I do wish he would come back." She paused and then, as if she were speaking to herself, added, "He will someday. He promised me he would."

"When there's no likelihood of a man like me being on his trail. Is that what you mean, Miss Lane?" Cimarron returned the photograph to her.

"It was a group of men like you—deputies—who made him run off in the first place. They were coming through town with their prison wagon and Ernie thought for sure they were after him, so he came here and he told me he had to leave and—"

"Where'd he say he was going?"

"Do you really think I'd tell you even if I knew? You want to see him hang. You've already decided that he's guilty."

"Whoa there, Miss Lane! You were right before when you said I was no judge. I'm just a lawman with a job to do."

"And that job is to place Ernie Wilcox in the hands of the hangman."

"My job is to take him to Fort Smith," Cimarron corrected, "to stand trial."

"How much do they pay you to do your dirty work?"

"Not near enough."

"How much?"

"Two dollars if I bring him in alive. Nothing if I have to kill him."

Esther gasped. Then, recovering, she jumped up and ran from the room.

Pretty little thing, Cimarron thought, and here I've gone and scared the living daylights out of her.

When several minutes had passed and Esther didn't return, he rose and started for the door. He was opening it when she called his name. He turned, to find her holding a small purse in her hand. She snapped it open and pulled out a coin, which she held out to him.

"Take it," she said sharply. "Take it and leave Ernie be."

Cimarron's shoulders slumped as he stared at the double eagle Esther was holding out to him. "I can't do that, Miss Lane."

"You can."

"I admit I'm tempted to. I could sure use twenty dollars about now, but—" He studied her face. "You love Wilcox a whole lot, do you?"

Esther nodded, tears sliding down her cheeks.

"He's just liable to take a notion to shoot at me when I catch up with him. I'll have to shoot back. You could help him by telling me where he's holed up, so I could maybe get the drop on him and avoid—"

"I can't!" Esther wailed, and then began to sob. "I can't because I don't know where he is. Oh, please, Cimarron. If you do find him, don't kill him. Please don't, I beg of you!"

"I'll try my best not to, but I can't promise you anything. Now, I've got one last question to ask you, Miss Lane. How long's Ernie been gone exactly?"

"Four days."

The sound of Esther's sobs followed Cimarron outside, where he stepped into the saddle of his black and rode slowly south along the railroad tracks, considering what he had learned. He knew it wasn't much and he also knew it wasn't enough to put him on Wilcox's trail. He was planning his next move when he noticed the wagon parked behind the depot and the crowd of men gathered around it.

He rode up to the wagon and dismounted, shaking his head. He strode over to the elderly man with the jug in his hands and said, "Pops, you old codger, you never do learn, do you?"

"Cimarron! It's good to see you again!"

"Is it, Pops? You know I got to fine you and then run you off just like I did the last time I caught you up in North Fork Town, where you were selling whiskey the same as you're doing here in McAlester right now."

"Selling whiskey? Me? Cimarron, I'm not selling whiskey. What in the world makes you think old Pops Clancy is selling whiskey?"

"That." Cimarron pointed to the Creek who had just handed money to Pops, after which Pops partially filled a glass from his jug and then handed the glass to the Indian, who promptly emptied it.

"Let me tell you something, Cimarron," Pops said as he reached into the bed of his wagon, took a potato from it, and handed it to the Creek. "You lawmen are always mighty quick to jump to conclusions. You judge a man far too fast."

"Pops, you're telling me you're *not* selling whiskey? You're telling me my eyes have went and gone bad on me?"

Pops accepted money from another Creek and poured whiskey from the jug into the man's glass before answering Cimarron. "You read the riot act to me up in North Fork Town about how selling whiskey in the Territory's illegal. So I paid the fine you levied on me—though five dollars struck me as a pretty steep price to pay for such a petty offense—and I went and turned over a brand-new leaf."

"You stopped selling whiskey, did you?" Cimarron asked in disbelief.

"Sure, I did." Pops handed a potato to the Creek he had just given the drink. "I'm selling potatoes now, Cimarron. Four bits apiece. Anybody who buys a potato off me gets a free drink. Nothing illegal about selling potatoes, now, is there, Cimarron? Or giving my customers a free drink?"

Cimarron exploded in laughter and slapped his thigh. "No, Pops, you old reprobate, I got to admit you're right. It's sure enough legal to sell potatoes in Indian Territory."

"Want to buy one?"

"Sure." Cimarron dug down in his jeans and came up with four bits, which he handed to Pops, who filled a glass to the brim, handed it to him, and then gave him a potato which he had taken from the bed of his wagon.

As Cimarron sipped the whiskey, Pops asked, "Are you still wandering about the Territory looking for evildoers and miscreants?"

"I am, Pops. Thought I'd just caught me my first miscreant on this trip when I spotted you, but like you said, I can't fine or arrest you for selling potatoes."

"Who you out after this time?" Pops asked as he filled another glass and handed over another potato to one of his customers.

"Man named Ernie Wilcox."

"Never heard of him."

Cimarron emptied his glass and handed it to Pops. He tossed the potato he was holding in his other hand back into the wagon. "It sure does my heart good to see how you've reformed, Pops. Good luck with your next potato crop. Be seeing you."

Leading his black, Cimarron walked on down the street until he noticed the livery stable on his left. He halted and stared up the alley that ran along one side of the building. He could almost see Wilcox and Labrette standing there and facing each other, their guns drawn. A question suddenly occurred to him.

He went into the livery stable, and when a man approached him, he said, "I'd like my horse rubbed down real good and fed. Grain. A mix of oats and barley."

"We'll take good care of him for you, mister. Fine animal, looks like. Looks like you've been riding him hard."

"I have been—all the way from Fort Smith. I'm a deputy marshal. Looking for Ernie Wilcox. Heard he shot a man in the alley next door."

"He did. I saw him do it. Too bad, too. Ernie was always such a nice boy."

"Would you mind showing me just how it happened?"

The man, after placing the black in a stall, led Cimarron outside and said, "Ernie he was down there near the end of the alley by those rose bushes that have gone wild. Labrette he was up here at this end. Ernie told Labrette to draw. He did, and then both of them fired at each other. Labrette was killed."

Cimarron looked up at the building next door and then at the livery stable.

"Labrette was gut-shot," the stableman said. "You'd have thought Ernie would have plugged him in the lungs."

"Why would you have thought that?"

"Why, because Labrette was such a little fella. Dapper but small of stature."

"Much obliged to you for taking the time to talk to me. I'll be back to pick up my mount and pay you what I owe."

When the stableman had disappeared, Cimarron leaned back against the wall of the livery, folded his arms, and was soon lost in thought.

Hastings' words came back to him. He recalled Hastings having said that Wilcox had been hanging around Esther's house every chance he got, and Esther, he remembered, had said that Wilcox had been gone for four days.

Several minutes later, he made up his mind about the course of action he would follow.

That night found him in a field with his back braced

against the trunk of a tree, his eyes on Esther Lane's house at the far end of the field. Time passed. The lamps in the Lane house were extinguished. More time passed.

Finally the night ended, and Cimarron rose, stretched, and went in search of breakfast.

But the following night he was back in the field watching the Lane house again. Long before midnight the lamps were extinguished and Cimarron continued to watch the house and surrounding area.

He estimated that an hour had passed, judging by the position of the polestar, when he heard a faint sound in the distance. He strained his eyes to see who or what had made it. It had been a harsh scraping sound. He knew where it had come from—the vicinity of the Lane house. He rose, flattening himself against a tree in order not to be seen by anyone who might be sharing the seemingly empty night with him, and watched the house, his eyes narrowed.

A shadow that was not a shadow moved across the overhang behind the house on its way toward the single open window facing Cimarron. The upper half of the window, a glassy paleness in the light of the half-moon, suddenly disappeared. When it reappeared, Cimarron loped toward the house, and once behind it, he climbed up on the rain barrel and then onto the overhang, moving carefully in order to make no noise.

He drew his .44 and remained motionless on one side of the window, listening.

Whispers.

A woman's voice. A man's.

He crouched down below the windowsill and, propping his gun barrel on it, said, "If you've got a gun, Wilcox, drop it. If I have to shoot at you in the dark, Esther's liable to get hit. Esther, you light a lamp and be quick about it."

When the lamp had been lit and the man in the room—who was, Cimarron was pleased to see, indeed Wilcox—had dropped his revolver, he climbed over the sill.

"Esther," he said, "you get over there against that wall so you won't get hurt." Cimarron bent down and picked up Wilcox's .31-caliber Colt and placed it in his waistband.

"How'd you know I was here?" Wilcox asked him.

Cimarron, aware of Esther's eyes on him, answered, "I kind of figured you'd be showing up here sooner or later.

Hoped I'd be here when you did, and as it turned out, I was."

"But how—" Wilcox persisted.

"I'd been told you spent a lot of time here and Miss Lane told me you'd left town four days ago. I figured that was a long time for a man in love to be away from his woman. I figured you just might sneak back and try to see her. You did, and I spotted you. Now, then, Wilcox, did you come here on foot or aboard a horse?"

"I rode in," Wilcox replied, fear twisting his features as he stared at the barrel of Cimarron's gun. "You're a lawman?"

"I am."

"Cimarron!" Esther cried. "Don't take him away from me!"

Cimarron ignored her plea. He gestured with his gun toward the window. "Wilcox, you're going out the same way you came in. I'll be right behind you. Bear that in mind. You run and I'll put a bullet in you. Maybe more than one."

"Ernie!" Esther cried. She ran to him and threw her arms around his neck.

Cimarron reached out, seized her arm, and threw her down on the bed. "Move, Wilcox!"

When Wilcox had gone through the window, Cimarron followed him out onto the overhang. He waited until Wilcox had climbed down onto the rain barrel, and then he leaped down to the ground. "Where's your mount?"

"I picketed him over there on the far side of the field."

"Let's go get him."

When they reached the horse, Cimarron waited until Wilcox had freed the animal, and then marched him, on foot and leading the horse, to the livery stable, where a yawning boy turned Cimarron's horse over to him and Cimarron paid his bill.

As both men rode out of McAlester, Wilcox said plaintively, "I didn't shoot Labrette, Deputy."

Cimarron said nothing.

"I just meant to maybe wound him. Scare him some to keep him away from Esther."

"You'll get to tell your story at your trial," Cimarron said bluntly. "There's no point in your telling it to me. My job's just to bring you in. The rest is up to Judge Parker and the jury."

* * *

Marshal Upham looked up as Cimarron strode through the open door of his office. "Did you get Wilcox?"

"I got him. I just turned him and his gun and his horse over to Charley Burns, who's got him locked up by now in the jail down in the basement, no doubt. Charley said you had a letter for me."

"Letter for you? Oh, yes, I do. I have it somewhere here. It was hand-delivered the other day—the day after you rode out, as a matter of fact. Now where did I put it? I know I put it somewhere for safekeeping. The question is where."

Cimarron watched Upham search through the papers on his desk, open drawers, and then slam them shut again. Grinning, he commented, "You sure ought to get yourself organized one of these days, Marshal."

"Here it is!" Upham announced gleefully, pulling a letter out from under his desk blotter. He handed it to Cimarron.

Cimarron took it from him and glanced at his name written on it. He tore the envelope open and took out the single sheet of paper that was inside it.

"What is it?" Upham asked. "Another bill you neglected to pay?"

"Listen to this, Marshal. *Whooeeee*, just you listen to this, Marshal D. P. Upham!"

Cimarron began to read the letter aloud. " 'I have heard extraordinary things about you, Cimarron. I have heard that you never fail to get your man and that—' "

"You didn't ever catch that owlhoot—what's-his-name—who tried to rob the Katy railroad."

"Your memory's slipping, Marshal. What's-his-name, it turned out, fell under the tracks and got run over by the locomotive, which nobody thought to tell us when they reported the attempted robbery. Now, don't interrupt me again or I'll be leaving and you never will learn what this lady has written to me."

"Lady?"

"She signs herself Harriet Becker. Now, where was I? Here we go. '. . . you are a fearless deputy marshal. I am offering you five hundred dollars to track down a murderer. The father of the murdered man will also pay you five hundred dollars if you are successful in your mission. If this matter proves to be of interest to you, please come to see me as soon as possible at the address listed below in Honey Springs.' "

Cimarron whistled through his teeth and thumbed his hat back on his head. "I'm going to be rich as Croesus, Marshal! Now, what do you think of that?"

"I think that letter raises a number of questions. For example, why didn't this Harriet Becker report the murder she mentions to this office? Honey Springs is, after all, in our jurisdiction."

"You're right. This letter does raise some questions and I'm going to find out the answers to them. But first, since it's near to night, I'm going to pay a social call before I set out for Honey Springs in the morning."

"Knowing you, that can only mean one thing. You're planning to visit Mrs. Windham's so-called boardinghouse—one of the girls there."

"You got it, Marshal, and the first time too. Me and Rose Collins are going to have us a lively little jamboree tonight!"

"That's what you call it—a jamboree?"

"What would you call it, Marshal?"

Upham blushed.

2

"What'll it be, Cimarron?" Mrs. Windham asked.

"Rose," he answered from where he sat sprawled in a wing chair in the gaudy parlor of Mrs. Windham's boardinghouse, a woman seated in his lap.

"No," Mrs. Windham said from behind her mahogany bar, "I—"

"I've got her price," Cimarron declared with faint annoyance. "Unless you just went and raised it again."

"Cimarron, be quiet and let me finish what I started to say." Mrs. Windham held up a bottle in each hand. "I mean, what will you have to drink, not who you came here to have."

"Whiskey'll be fine."

Mrs. Windham poured, patted her pile of auburn hair, and as the door to the parlor opened, cried, "Business is picking up! Or did you come to arrest us, Aaron?"

Cimarron nodded to Aaron Slocum as the deputy entered the room, his hat in his hands.

" 'Evening, Mrs. Windham," Slocum said, and returned Cimarron's nod. "I came to see Rose Collins."

"Doesn't anyone want *me* anymore?" wailed the woman who was still seated in Cimarron's lap. She put her arms around his neck. "I can teach you a trick or two, Cimarron. Want to learn?"

"He knows all the tricks, according to Rose," Mrs. Windham remarked as she handed Cimarron a glass of whiskey in which chips of ice floated. "Chances are he could teach you one or two, Lorrie."

"Will you teach me, Cimarron?" Lorrie asked playfully, running a finger over his lips.

25

Before Cimarron could respond, Slocum spoke. "Is Rose busy at the moment, Mrs. Windham?"

"No. She's upstairs primping. She'll be along any minute now. But you'll have to get in line—though the line's a short one."

"You?" Slocum asked Cimarron.

"Me," he replied.

"Whiskey," Slocum said to Mrs. Windham, and went over to the bar.

He was a tall man, almost as tall as Cimarron but thinner and not as heavily muscled. He was older than Cimarron, and the gauntness of his face together with its paleness seemed to add more years to those he had already lived. His bony fingers and deeply set dark eyes made Cimarron think of the grim reaper. Slocum was clean-shaven and his hair was neatly barbered. But there was something about the man, Cimarron thought, that seemed used up. Used up and on the verge of being worn out.

"Well?" prompted Lorrie.

"Not tonight," Cimarron said, and pinched her.

She squealed with delight and asked, "When, then?"

Rose appeared in the doorway and answered Lorrie's question by remarking, "When I'm through with him, Lorrie, you won't want him. He'll be good for nothing. Nothing that's any fun, at any rate."

Cimarron, studying Rose as she stood in the doorway with her hands folded demurely in front of her, eased Lorrie off his lap. She's like the sun on the rise, he thought, shiny and new and real bright. To him, Rose was both the new dawn and the provocative promise that midnight held in its dark hands. She sure makes me skittish, he thought. Not to mention lusty. Her and her golden hair and full lips. That gleam in her blue eyes, it's enough to turn a tame man wild and a wild one wilder. Those big breasts she's got. Remembering the taste of them, he grew hard. Small hips for a woman, he thought. Long legs. Slender arms. He remembered with pleasure how, in the past, her hands lit fires in him, which her full lips soon turned into raging conflagrations.

"I'm ready if you are, Rose," he said, and stood up.

She unclasped her hands and held them out to him.

"Two bits," Mrs. Windham said from behind him.

He took Rose's hands in his.

"Cimarron," Mrs. Windham said, "you owe me two bits for the whiskey."

Absently, he thrust a hand into his jeans and as absently handed Mrs. Windham a silver dollar.

She said nothing as he again took Rose's hands in his and let her lead him from the parlor.

"You forgot your change," Rose said as they climbed the stairs together to the second floor.

"What?"

"Never mind."

When they were in Rose's room with the door closed, she said, "I see you survived the hangover you had when we last met."

"Seeing you that morning kind of cured it—helped to."

"Unhook me, will you?" Rose asked, turning her back.

Cimarron did and her dress fell to the floor. She quickly shed her undergarments, shoes, and stockings, and then, turning back to Cimarron, she reached out and began to unbutton his shirt.

He reached for the buttons of his jeans and she whispered. "Don't. Let me. Sit down on the bed."

He did, and his hands roamed over her body as she pulled off his boots and then undressed him completely.

He took her in his arms and held her close to him as her fingers played teasingly along his thighs. She withdrew slightly, bent her head, and her tongue touched both of his nipples as her hands encircled the length of his erection. She squeezed it lightly.

He throbbed in her hot hands until he could stand it no longer. When she raised her head from his hardened nipples, he cupped both of her breasts in his hands and kneaded them gently. Then his right hand slid down her side and came to rest between her legs. But not for long. He inserted his middle finger and she responded by placing her hands on his bare shoulders and spreading her legs.

His finger continued its explorations for a moment and then he withdrew it and said huskily, "Let's lie down."

They did.

Lying on their sides and facing each other, they toyed with and teased each other's bodies for several minutes; and then, when both of them were breathing hard, Cimarron reached out and eased Rose down upon her back on the bed. As she lay there, he rolled over upon her, propping himself up with his hands, and looked down at her.

She smiled up at him, a brief smile, a tantalizing smile, and he accepted her unspoken invitation and eased into her. She was moist but not wet, so he bent and kissed her. When her teeth parted, his tongue slid between them and began to explore. Their tongues met briefly and then Rose began to suck on his and he found himself sliding back and forth easily inside her, felt the pressure building within him as his heart pounded, and then Rose suddenly moved and he was out of her and their lips had parted.

"What—" he began, but said no more as she gestured and he realized that she wanted him to lie down on his back. He did, and her fingers encircled the base of his erection. She squeezed and the intense but pleasant pressure he had been feeling gradually lessened. He was both sorry and glad because Rose was now fondling his testicles as the fingers of her other hand continued to squeeze him to prevent him from reaching a climax. She released him finally and bent down. She took him into her mouth and his back arched as her tongue flicked along the underside of his erection. Her firm lips held him prisoner as her head began to bob up and down along the length of him. His eyes closed. He groaned. He almost—

But she released him as if she had known he was about to explode, and her hand once again encircled and squeezed him and once again he was slowly descending, his erection gleaming wetly in the soft light of the lamp.

"Honey, I don't think I can stand it if you don't let me finish pretty soon."

"When you do, it will be a wonderful climax. Cimarron, that's a promise." She straddled him, her knees against the sides of his hips, and bent forward.

He took her left breast in his mouth and sucked it. He teased its nipple with his teeth, feeling it harden as he did so. She withdrew her breast and offered him the other one, which he eagerly took, and as he did so, he felt her grasp him, felt her adjust her position, felt her guiding him into her.

He groaned again, releasing Rose's breast as she began to ride him, slowly at first and then faster. And then still faster. He watched her breasts bounce as she rose and fell upon him, her eyes on his face, her fingers lightly caressing his nipples.

"Honey, I'm—"

She slowed her movements slightly but maintained an almost fierce intensity as she rose, fell, rose again. Suddenly, she plunged downward. Cimarron simultaneously thrust upward. She cried out—his name. He pulled her body down upon his. His arms embraced her as he ejaculated within her, his body shuddering as hers was shuddering, his heart pounding against hers, both of them moaning, both of them wrapped in an almost tangible web of rapture.

They lay there, silent, locked in each other's arms, their breathing slowing and gradually becoming normal once again.

Rose sighed and withdrew from Cimarron.

As she lay down beside him, one arm thrown over his chest, her head cradled on his shoulder, he said, "Honey, it gets better every single time. You do."

"It was good?"

"It was the best. You were—are."

Rose kissed his cheek.

"No wonder Mrs. Windham keeps raising your price."

"I wish—" Rose fell silent without having completed what she had been about to say.

Cimarron nuzzled her neck and whispered, "Tell me."

"What?"

"What you wish."

"Oh, that I was rich—so rich that I wouldn't have to work ever again."

"You don't like what you do?"

"Liking has nothing to do with it. I do it. Mrs. Windham lets me keep half of what I earn. Oh, I suppose I shouldn't be complaining. Or wishing I was rich either."

"No harm in wishing."

"If I were rich," Rose mused, "I'd have servants to wait on me hand and foot. I'd never do a lick of labor. I'd sit in the sun under a parasol in the summertime sipping lemonade and I'd dare any man or woman to point their fingers at me or whisper behind my back. In the winter, I'd have a fur coat and a little muff, and I'd never be cold and I would pay for everything I buy with cash money."

"You don't have to be real rich to do all that, honey." Cimarron's lips closed around Rose's right breast.

"I don't want to be rich just so I could buy things or never have to use credit," she murmured. "Being rich is being free. Free to do whatever you want to do. To go places. To see things. Wouldn't you like to see Paris, Cimarron? Wouldn't you like to live your life like other people do?"

Cimarron raised his head and looked down at Rose. "First off, I don't much care if I ever see Paris and I reckon Paris don't much care if it ever lays eyes on me. Second of all, I live my life like I want to, which may or may not be the way other people live theirs."

"But you're not a—you're a lawman. You're not—a whore."

So that's it, Cimarron thought. Fondly caressing Rose's cheek, he said, "People have called me lots of things in my time. Some of them were true, some weren't. None of the names they called me mattered to me much. They were like water rolling off a duck's back."

"That's because you're strong, Cimarron. I'm not strong. And I care about what people think of me. I want them to think well of me, think that I'm a lady, a real lady, not a—"

"Hush, honey. There's no little bit of use you pining like this. If you want to change the way you live—hell, change it. It's easy."

"It's not!" Rose exclaimed heatedly. "Everybody in town knows me, knows what I am and what I do for a living."

"You could go someplace else."

"Sooner or later somebody would show up who knew me here, so it wouldn't work. But if I were rich, my past wouldn't matter. Other people look up to rich people no matter what they do—or did. A fat purse is the surest way to guarantee respect."

"I'm not so sure you're a hundred percent right, Rose. Maybe you are. But it seems to me that with people who really count and who care about you—well, money's not the main thing, having it or not having it, I mean."

"It's different for a man and especially so for a man like you—a deputy marshal. People look up to you. They respect you. But me?"

"I respect you."

"I know you do, but you're not an ordinary man, Cimarron. You're not like Aaron Slocum and most of the other men who come here to me."

"I'm not so sure I follow you."

"Aaron uses me. Oh, I can't blame him. That's what I'm

here for—to be used by men. And now, it seems, I'm right back where I started from—wanting to be rich so I won't ever again be used by *anybody!*"

Rose's vehemence surprised Cimarron, almost startled him. He had never suspected until now that she harbored such a strong core of discontent within her. But looking at her now—at the angry expression on her face—and listening to the unmistakable note of despair that darkened her voice, he found himself looking at a woman he had never really seen before. She was not the lovely Rose Collins now. Nor was she the happy-go-lucky lady he thought he knew. She was— Who was she? He thought of a boy he had known when he was himself a boy. Bennie something had been his name. Bennie had had a birthmark that flamed scarlet on his left cheek and he had tried desperately to keep people from noticing it by constantly turning his head and as constantly shifting his stance. Rose's birthmark scars her heart, he thought sadly. But there's nothing much I can do about that. Only she can make herself learn to live with it—or learn to eliminate it, as Bennie never could with his disfigurement.

"Don't you ever dream about being rich someday, Cimarron?"

"Nope. I do dream, though, about having a comfortable nest egg in a bank somewhere, but I've not yet got one, though I may be on the verge of getting me one."

"How?"

Excitement began to grow within Cimarron as he thought about Harriet Becker's letter. "My jeans. Reach down there on the floor and see if you can find them. There's a letter in my pocket."

Rose scrambled over Cimarron, found his jeans, rooted through his pockets, and came up with the letter.

"Read it."

Rose began to read the letter, and as she read, her eyes widened and her jaw dropped. "One thousand dollars!" she cried when she had finished the letter. "Cimarron, that's more money than some small-town banks have in them!"

"Well, I'm hoping to have every last one of those thousand dollars stuffed into my jeans one of these days, and if they don't all fit, I'll take off my boots and use them for a bank, though going barefoot's not my idea of the best way to travel."

Rose laughed. "Oh, you are lucky! But then you're a man."

"You mean to tell me that women never get lucky like that?" he asked, pointing to the letter in Rose's hand.

"Harriet Becker never would have asked a woman to go out hunting a murderer for her."

"Reckon you're right about that."

"So, do you see?"

"Reckon I do."

Someone pounded on the door of the bedroom.

"Go away!" Rose shouted, snuggling up to Cimarron.

"Rose, dear," Mrs. Windham called out sweetly from behind the closed door. "Aaron's waiting."

"I'm busy!" Rose shouted back.

The door flew open and Mrs. Windham, hands on hips in the doorway, shouted even louder, "Cimarron, you get dressed and out of here by the time I count to ten or I'll— *Move!*"

"Yes, ma'am," Cimarron said, swinging his legs over the side of the bed and reaching for his jeans.

When he was dressed, he took the letter Rose still held in her hand as if it were some sort of magic talisman, and pocketed it. He paid Rose, who sat sulking on the pillows and then, as Mrs. Windham yelled down the hall, "Aaron, it's your turn!" he eased past her and went down the hall and then down the steps, passing Slocum, who was climbing them, and out into the night.

As Cimarron forded the shallow Arkansas River, it began to rain, lightly at first, but by the time he had reached the far side of the river, the rain was pouring down in torrents.

He quickly reached behind him for his slicker, which was tied with his bedroll against the cantle of his saddle. He slipped into the slicker and then took off his hat, creased it carefully, and put it back on. He kept his head tilted forward so that the rain poured off his hat and splashed against the already drenched neck and mane of the black beneath him.

Water seeped from his wet hair and ran in cold rivulets under his collar and down his back. The rain that slid off his slicker soon had soaked the uncovered parts of the legs of his jeans.

Lightning was racing back and forth across the sky as he came to the Rattlesnake Mountains. Thunder boomed like cannon as he rode through the foothills and then out onto the high prairie again.

He crossed the Texas Road and a little later, as he rode past the old Oktaha cemetery, he noticed the crude marker that identified the trench that was the grave of some one hundred and fifty of General Douglas H. Cooper's Confederate soldiers who had been killed in 1863 by General James G. Blunt's Union forces in an epic battle.

The Civil War, he thought. There'll be more wars. Men'll fight them. The world'll spin on and take no more notice of the dead than I'd take of a fish in the waters of Elk Creek up there to the north.

He was almost upon the tracks of the Katy railroad before he saw them because the rain, whipped by the wind, billowed like wet sheets in front of him. He crossed the tracks, turned south, and headed for the town of Honey Springs, the place he knew some people still called Oktaha after the famous Creek full-blood Oktarharsars Harjo.

Old Sands, Cimarron thought. Now, why'd they go and call you that, I wonder, Harjo? That name don't sound one bit like the bloody leader of a whole bunch of Indian risings that you were in the old days.

As he rode into Honey Springs, he peered at the stores and houses that were sprinkled haphazardly here and there on both sides of the tracks. Typical terminus town, he thought. It's just like Topsy. It just growed. And by the looks of it, it didn't care how or in which direction.

Thunder muttered in the sky above Cimarron. But it was moving off to the east now and the rain was slackening. Lightning still appeared, darting across the drab sky, but it was paler now. The fight's gone from the storm, he thought. Now, where's the Becker place? He remembered the address. Washington Street. Number ten.

Where's Washington Street? he asked himself as he rode directionless along the crisscrossing dirt streets. Nobody around to ask. They're all holed up inside on account of the rain.

He turned his horse and headed back toward the cluster of businesses near the depot, but before he reached them, a woman emerged from a house and peered from her dripping porch up at the clearing sky.

Cimarron asked her for directions and she cheerfully gave them to him. He went past the depot and then turned up a street that stretched westward. He stopped when he reached the large clapboard house with the number ten painted on one of the wooden pillars that supported the roof sheltering the wide porch.

No Uncle Tom's cabin this place, he thought as he tethered his black to a hitch post at the edge of the yard.

Mrs. Becker's well-to-do. Lace curtains in the windows. House freshly painted white as milk, probably this very spring. Brass knocker on the door.

He climbed the steps to the porch, lifted the brass knocker, let it fall.

The door was opened a moment later by a woman who momentarily took Cimarron's breath away. Beautiful, he thought. Is she ever! He took in her full figure, which made him want to reach out and draw her close to him. But it was her face that was even more striking than her body. Pale skin, almost translucent. A straight narrow nose. High cheekbones. Slightly slanted black eyes under long lashes that gave her a highly provocative look. She wore her hair loose and it, blacker even than her eyes, was a mass of natural waves.

"I'm looking for Harriet Becker," he told the woman.

"You've found her. I'm Mrs. Becker."

Her voice was faintly husky but decidedly feminine as was, Cimarron thought, the whole wonderful rest of her. His eyes dropped to the gold band on her finger. "Folks call me Cimarron, Mrs. Becker."

"I knew it was you the moment I saw you."

"You did? Well, sure, I guess you would, since you've been expecting me."

"I didn't know for sure whether to expect you or not. No, I knew it was you because of the hard—the almost cruel— look in your eyes and because you stand there looking at me like an animal of some kind about to spring. Please come inside, Cimarron."

He followed her into the house and found himself in a dim hall. A staircase on one side of the hall led to the second floor. She opened a door and ushered him into an equally dim and slightly cool parlor of substantial size.

"Please be seated, Cimarron," she said, and as he sat down, she went to a plush bell cord and pulled it.

A moment later, a woman wearing a starched white apron and white cap appeared in the open doorway. "Yes, ma'am?"

"Would you like some tea, Cimarron? Something a bit stronger perhaps?"

When he didn't answer immediately, Mrs. Becker said, "Dolores, bring tea and brandy, please."

When the maid had gone, Mrs. Becker sat down in an overstuffed chair and, because the windows in the room were behind her, her face was shadowed as she stared at Cimarron, the tips of her fingers touching just below her flawlessly carved chin.

"I got your letter," he said.

"Obviously. If you hadn't, you wouldn't be here. You found my offer satisfactory, I take it?"

"Yes, ma'am, I did indeed. Five hundred dollars is a lot of money."

"One thousand dollars. Mr. James Morris, Senior, I believe I wrote in my letter, will also pay you five hundred dollars when you have done what I've asked you to do."

"Right. One thousand dollars. I was thinking of *your* offer, not Mr. Morris'."

"Let's not split hairs, Cimarron. Or quibble over words."

"I didn't mean to—"

Mrs. Becker impatiently waved a hand and Cimarron fell silent. "I imagine you would like to know the details of what Mr. Morris and I want you to do."

"I would."

"Ah, the tea."

As the maid entered the room and placed a silver tray containing a teapot covered with a quilted cozy, cups, glasses, and a bottle of brandy on the table next to Mrs. Becker's chair, Cimarron looked around the spacious room.

There was a tall plant of some kind growing in a huge pot in one corner. On one wall was a stag's head with nine points on its rack. Bookshelves, filled, lined the opposite wall. The windows were bordered with heavy blue-velvet drapes.

"Brandy for the gentleman, Dolores."

Cimarron noticed that Mrs. Becker had made the decision about what he would drink for him. She evidently likes to run things, he thought. Well, no harm done.

When the maid handed him a delicate crystal goblet nearly, he thought, the size of a balloon, he took it and drank its contents. The brandy warmed him immediately and then began to make him feel slightly mellow.

"Nice-tasting," he said, and raised his empty glass to Mrs. Becker, who nodded to the maid, who promptly poured more brandy into Cimarron's glass.

"Now, what's all this about a murderer you want me to find for you?" he asked, settling back into his chair, the glass cradled in both of his large hands.

"That will be all, Dolores." Mrs. Becker waited until the maid had left the room and then said, "His name is Reuben Becker."

Cimarron stared at her shadowy features, trying unsuccessfully to make out her expression. "This Becker, he's—"

"My husband."

"He murdered somebody?"

"He did. A man named James Morris, Junior, the son of James Morris, Senior, who, as I said, will also pay you five hundred dollars, as will I, when you have done what we're asking you to do."

"Why'd your husband go and kill this Morris fellow?"

"Because he was jealous of Jim. You must understand, Cimarron, that my husband is a businessman—or was before he fled, following the murder. He owns a mercantile company in town—the largest, the best. He spent most of his time on the business. He was very skillful at making money. He was far less skillful at making a woman like myself happy, if you understand my meaning."

When Mrs. Becker paused and raised her cup to her lips, Cimarron nodded, not really sure that he did understand.

"Jim Morris was my lover," she declared, and Cimarron thought she had made the announcement as calmly as if she had been telling him the time of day.

"And your husband killed him because of what he—what you and him— You said your husband was jealous."

"My husband struck him on the back of the head with a large stone in a fit of fury one day not long ago. Jim was killed instantly. The right side of his skull was completely crushed. A crime of passion. If this were France, a jury might applaud his deed, since he was quite clearly a cuckold. This isn't France, however, and I want revenge for what my husband did to the only man I ever really loved. Oh, don't look so shocked, Cimarron. I married Reuben Becker for his money. I didn't ever love him. I did love Jim Morris."

"Were there witnesses to what happened?"

"Of course. Several. Foley Weeks, for one. Otis Shepherd, for another. And, of course, myself."

"Mrs. Becker, something's gnawing at me and I wonder if you could scratch the itch it's causing me." Cimarron thought her eyebrows rose, but because of the shadows, he couldn't be sure. "How come you didn't report the murder to the marshal in Fort Smith?"

Mrs. Becker put down her cup so suddenly it rattled in its saucer. "The marshal in Fort Smith!" she snapped, almost snarled. "What if his deputies failed to catch my husband?"

"They're good men, most of them. It's likely they'd have caught up with your husband sooner or later."

"You *will* catch up with him. I have no doubt about that. Now have I answered your question concerning why I sent for you instead of notifying the marshal in Fort Smith?"

"I reckon you have, yes."

"I wanted a man I was certain could do the job I want done, and you, I decided, are that man. I've heard talk about you."

"People tend to talk too much about other people and what they say . . . well, it's not always the unalloyed truth."

"If half of what I've heard about you is the truth, I have hired the right man. I'm sure of it."

"You said before that people saw the killing. Who's this Foley Weeks you mentioned?"

"He's a Negro who works at Becker's Mercantile. Otis Shepherd, whom I also mentioned and who also witnessed what Reuben did, is Reuben's partner in the mercantile business." Mrs. Becker paused a moment and then, "You want to talk to them?"

"I do. They might be able to tell me something helpful about your husband that will make hunting him easier."

"You can find Foley at the Mercantile. Mr. Shepherd might also be there, but he comes and goes. If you don't find him there, you can probably find him at home. He lives three doors west of this house."

"I hope you won't take it amiss, Mrs. Becker, if I say what's been on my mind while I was on my way here."

"Say it."

"I figured I might go and find your husband, bring him back, and then something might go wrong and I might not get paid."

"You think I would try to cheat you out of your fee?"

"I didn't say exactly that, but—"

"I'll give you two hundred dollars before you set out after Reuben. I'm sure Mr. Morris will also agree to advance you the same sum."

"Well, that's real nice of you, Mrs. Becker."

Mrs. Becker, after asking Cimarron to wait a moment, left the room. When she returned, she handed him two hundred dollars, which he pocketed. He set his glass down on a table and rose from his chair.

"You got a picture of your husband I could take a look at, Mrs. Becker?"

She pointed and Cimarron turned and saw the oil portrait hanging on the wall.

"That's him, is it?"

"It was painted last year by a gentleman from St. Louis. Yes, that's the bastard."

"What can you tell me about him that might be helpful? Who were his friends in town? Where do you think he might have gone to hide?"

"I don't know the answer to your last question. Wait." A grim smile appeared on Mrs. Becker's face. "Perhaps I do know. I can, at least, suggest to you that you talk to Miss Nell Cooper about my husband."

"She was a friend of his?"

Mrs. Becker's smile vanished. "You might say that. Reuben was in the unhappy habit of running to that woman when he was in need of—solace."

"She gave it to him?"

"I have no doubt that she did. Nell Cooper was employed at one time in the Mercantile. That's how Reuben met her. When I realized what was going on between them, I spoke to Otis Shepherd about her and he obliged me by sending the baggage packing."

"I'll have a talk with Miss Cooper and I'd best get started visiting her and the people you told me about, and then be on my way. There's just no telling how long it'll take me to track down your husband and get him back to Fort Smith."

"Cimarron, there is one thing that I did not tell you in my letter or during our conversation today."

"One thing? What one thing?"

"I don't want my husband taken to Fort Smith. I—"

"You don't want— Why not? I thought I was supposed to catch him and—"

"Don't interrupt me!" Mrs. Becker's voice and expression were both imperious. "Juries are fallible. So are judges. Both are capable of making errors and any lawyer my husband might hire to defend him would be clever, if not corrupt, I'm sure, so the net result might be that Reuben would escape hanging and go free. I don't want that.

"I want Reuben Becker dead, Cimarron," Mrs. Becker declared fiercely, her face darkening. "I want you to kill him for me!"

3

"You want me to kill your husband?" Cimarron responded, stunned by the request Mrs. Becker had just made.

"Yes."

He shook his head. "You've got the wrong man, Mrs. Becker."

"I think I've got the right man," she countered.

"I'm no killer."

"That's a lie and you know it is. I've heard about some of the men you've gunned down. There are undoubtedly others whom I have not heard about."

"Sure, I've killed men. Had to, or else they'd've killed me. But what you're asking me to do is kill a man in cold blood. I've never done that. Never will." He shook his head and started for the door.

"You could give my husband a chance to draw. I hear you're good with a gun—fast. Reuben isn't either—neither good with a gun nor fast. That way you could salve your conscience, if that's what's worrying you."

"If you want your husband killed, Mrs. Becker, I suggest you find somebody else to do your killing for you. Or do it yourself."

She held out her hand.

Cimarron looked at it.

"The two hundred dollars, please. Since you're not interested in the bounty I and Mr. Morris are offering for my husband, you will please return the down payment on it which I paid you."

Cimarron reached into the pocket of his jeans. His fingers closed around the wad of bills she had given him earlier. He hesitated.

Mrs. Becker, staring into his eyes, smiled faintly. "One thousand dollars is a lot of money, Cimarron. A sum not easily earned by a man in your profession."

She had him and he knew it. He wanted the money, wanted it badly. Rose's words came back to him. She had said that, to her, money meant freedom. He realized she was right, he had known it all along. The money would—it would do so many things, buy so many things, pay for good times. It could make life ease up on a man, stop it from crowding him, smooth out the rough ruts in the trail he was traveling.

"Well, Cimarron? I'm waiting." Mrs. Becker still stood facing him, her hand still outstretched.

"I'll get Becker for you," he said dully.

"Good. I thought you would. Money has a way of influencing people. It can make them be good. Or it can make them be bad, depending upon the particular circumstances and the amount of money involved.

"You really shouldn't look so downcast, Cimarron, because you are doing a favor for a lady. You are also ridding the world of a murderer. Killing my husband will be not only an act of justice on your part—'an eye for an eye'—but also a social good. Reuben might very well kill again."

"You're fixing to take on a new lover, are you?"

Mrs. Becker's eyes blazed. She raised her hand and slapped Cimarron's face.

I deserved that, he thought as he felt the flesh of his cheek stinging. That was a rotten thing for me to say. Her morals aren't mine to try and mend. "I'll go talk to those people you told me about—Weeks, Shepherd, Miss Cooper."

"I would very much appreciate it if you would let me know when you plan to ride out after Reuben."

"I'll be sure to do that, Mrs. Becker."

"How long will it take you to complete this mission?"

"Can't say."

"I will, of course, want some sort of proof positive that you have actually eliminated my husband."

"John the Baptist," Cimarron said softly.

"I beg your pardon?"

"You want your husband's head served up to you on a platter maybe?"

"I confess I would enthusiastically welcome such a sight."

"Reckon a bloodthirsty woman like you would at that."

This time when Mrs. Becker tried to slap him, Cimarron ducked. "Be seeing you, Salome," he said, and made for the door. "Soon I expect."

"Wait!"

He halted.

Behind him, Mrs. Becker said, "There is only one way in which I can be totally sure that you have indeed killed Reuben Becker."

He waited.

"I want you to bring his body back here. I want to see for myself that he's dead, indisputably so."

Cimarron left the room and then the house.

Outside, he freed his black and, leading the animal, walked west along Washington Street until he came to Otis Shepherd's house three doors down the street.

"Mr. Shepherd?" he called out to the man seated in a rocker on the porch.

"I'm Shepherd, yes. What can I do for you, stranger?"

Cimarron went up to him and said, "My name's Cimarron and I—"

"Aha! So you've come. Good, good. Harriet must be so pleased."

"She told me you saw Reuben Becker kill Jim Morris. That's true?"

"Yes, indeed, it is. Scandalous affair."

"You're talking about Mrs. Becker and Morris?"

"No. I'm referring to the killing. I thought that was obvious."

"What happened?"

"Reuben and I were on our way to our homes from the Mercantile late one afternoon. As we approached his house, Harriet came out of it, followed by Jim Morris. I guess by that time Reuben had stood about as much as he could. You see, it was common knowledge here in Honey Springs that Harriet and Jim Morris—well, Reuben had been the victim of snide remarks and the butt of so much ugly banter that, when he saw them together coming out of his own house in broad daylight, he just exploded. He ran up on his porch and he grabbed Morris and threw him down the steps. Then he bounded down the steps after Morris. He picked him up, hit him, and then hit him again. Morris went down. As he started to get to his feet, he stumbled. That's when Reuben, enraged as he was and close to being hysterical, picked up a stone and struck Morris with it, smashing the entire right side of Morris' head. The man died almost instantly."

"Nobody else besides you and Mrs. Becker saw it happen? Mrs. Becker said a man named Foley Weeks saw the killing too."

"He did. He was with Reuben and me at the time. I forgot to mention his presence. He's a Negro, you see."

"What did Mrs. Becker do when her husband killed Morris?"

"She ran to Morris and threw herself upon him. But she didn't cry. Harriet's not the kind to cry. She jumped up almost at once and attacked poor Reuben. She said she was going to get the law after him. I'm so glad she did."

"I'm not the law, not in this matter, I'm not," Cimarron said. "I'm"—he found it hard to get the words out—"what's called a bounty hunter."

"No matter," Shepherd declared airily. "The important thing is that Reuben Becker be brought to justice. Although he is a dear friend of mine and although we have been business partners for years, I want to see him punished as much as Harriet does, although I'll tell you quite frankly that I think she is going about this matter in the wrong way. I advised her to send word to the court in Fort Smith, but she wouldn't hear of it, although at first that is precisely what she intended to do. Harriet, though a lovely woman, is also a vengeful woman. Perhaps she can't be blamed in this instance. In any case, I'm not one who flings first stones."

"Where do you think Becker might have gone?"

"I've no idea, none. When Harriet, after the murder and with the body not yet cold, swore she would summon the law, Reuben simply fled. I don't know where he went. You may have your hands full finding him, Cimarron."

"I expect I will. Did he take anything with him—clothes or anthing?"

"Nothing. He just ran."

"Much obliged for your help, Mr. Shepherd."

Cimarron's next stop was at the Mercantile, where he found Foley Weeks sweeping the floor. "Weeks, Mrs. Becker hired me to find her husband." Why can't I say it straight out, he asked himself. Why can't I bring myself to say she hired me to kill the man?

"A shame," Weeks murmured, leaning on his broom. "Mr. Becker was a nice man. Awful nice to me, he was. Who would have thought he'd do such an awful awful thing?"

"I'm told you saw what happened."

"Yassuh, I did, and I wish I'd been born blind so I'd not never have to see such an awful thing, but, oh, Lordy, seen it I did."

"Tell me what you saw."

Weeks did, and his story matched Shepherd's account of the event in every particular.

"I'm just thankful to the blessed Jesus that my child, Martha, didn't see it. She might have seen it. Her and me and her mother, we all live in a shanty down to the end of Washington Street, and Martha, that chile does dote on her daddy. She likes to come to meet me when I'm on my way home from work. That day she didn't come, the saints be praised."

"Much obliged, Weeks."

"Yassuh, you're right welcome."

Cimarron was about to leave the Mercantile when a thought occurred to him. "I'm looking to have a talk with a lady—Miss Nell Cooper. Do you know where she lives?"

"Yassuh, Miss Cooper she live down near the depot."

After Weeks had given him directions, Cimarron left the Mercantile, boarded his black, and rode toward the depot.

As he passed the livery stable, he drew rain, hesitated a moment, and then dismounted.

Once inside the building, he spoke to the brawny man who was hard at work at the hot forge hammering a red-hot iron shoe.

"You know Mr. Reuben Becker, I imagine."

"Sure," the man said, looking up at Cimarron. "Everybody in town does."

"Did he happen to rent or buy a horse from you recently?"

The stableman shook his head and brought his hammer down, sending sparks flying from the shoe on the anvil. "Becker's been gone for a while now. Since the murder. You know about the murder?"

"I know about it."

"Why'd you ask if he wanted a horse from me?"

"I figured a fugitive'd rather ride than walk when he was heading out on the owlhoot trail."

"That's a fact, I guess. You a lawman? You after Becker?"

"I am," Cimarron replied, answering the last question and letting the stableman assume he had answered both questions. "Good day to you, Mr—"

"Burgess. Chet Burgess. Say, you've got me to thinking about that day Becker lit out. Now, let's see." Burgess put down his tongs and scratched his head. "Yep. It was the same day, all right."

"What was, Burgess?"

"The same day that horse was stolen. From in front of the Mercantile."

"You think Becker stole it?"

"I don't know who stole it. All I said is that you got me to thinking about that day—the day Becker murdered Morris. Maybe it was just a coincidence. Horses are always getting themselves stolen here in the Territory."

"True enough. But it's something to think on. Much obliged."

Outside, Cimarron stepped into the saddle again and made his way to Nell Cooper's small one-story house just east of the depot. He dismounted and knocked on the door, which was at ground level.

He had to knock a second time before the door was opened by a woman he considered plain, if not downright homely. "Good day to you, Miss Cooper. You are Miss Nell Cooper?"

She nodded and nervously patted her hair. "You're—"

"Name's Cimarron. I heard you were a friend of Reuben Becker's."

"What if I was?" she asked defensively, smoothing her skirt.

"Do you know where he is at the moment?"

"No."

"He ran off without telling a good friend like you were to him where he'd be hiding?"

"Reuben didn't kill Jim Morris."

Cimarron thought of his recent interview with Esther Lane. She'd been sure that Ernie Wilcox hadn't committed the murder Wilcox had been accused of. Well, it was good to know that there were still women in the world willing to stand by their men, come fire or flood, however mistaken their loyalties might turn out to be in the end.

"Reuben couldn't kill a fly," Nell declared emphatically.

"He tell you that?"

"No, of course, he didn't. I just know, that's all."

"You know a whole lot about him, do you?"

"We were—friends. I used to be employed by him, but—"

"Mrs. Becker got Otis Shepherd to give you the sack."

"How did you know that?"

"I wonder what Mrs. Becker did to the other women Becker was courting on the sly."

"There was no one else! There was only—"

"You," Cimarron interrupted, his face impassive.

Nell blushed. Her fingers fiddled with the buttons on her white blouse.

"He used to come here to see you, is that it? Or did you two meet somewheres else?"

"Oh, I'm so tired of pretending!" Nell exclaimed. "I love Reuben Becker and I don't care anymore who knows it! He loves me too. He said so. He *often* told me he loved me!"

"He came here?"

"No. We would meet each other in Eufala. At the hotel there." Nell turned her face away from Cimarron, biting her lower lip as she did so. "It was sordid. Almost ugly." She turned back to Cimarron, a defiant expression on her face. "I didn't care. I would have gone anywhere to be with Reuben. I love him so very much!"

"Much obliged for the information, Miss Cooper. You've been a big help to me."

"Wait a minute!" she cried as Cimarron went to his horse. "Who are you? Why did you ask me all those questions about Reuben? About Reuben and me?"

"Be seeing you, Miss Cooper." Cimarron swung into the saddle and turned his black. He headed back up the street, and as he approached the Becker house, he was surprised to see Chet Burgess emerging from it on the run.

When Burgess spotted Cimarron, a grin appeared on his face, and as he came abreast of the black, he stared up at Cimarron for a moment, his grin widening before he said, "I'm mighty glad you stopped in to see me today, Cimarron. I thought I'd better go tell Mrs. Becker that there was a stranger in town asking questions about her husband. Mrs. Becker, now she's a power here in Honey Springs and it serves a man well to stay on the good side of powerful people like her."

"You got a point to make, Burgess, go ahead and make it. I'm a busy man."

"You're going to be busier, from what I hear from Mrs. Becker. Busy hunting her husband, I mean. I never knew she'd offered a reward for him. When she told me, I volunteered to do all I could to kill Becker for her."

Cimarron's eyes narrowed as he studied Burgess' eager expression. "What'd Mrs. Becker say to your volunteering?"

"She said it was fine with her. She said she didn't give a damn who killed Becker, just so he was killed for sure."

Cimarron sighed and rode on until he reached the Becker house, where he dismounted, strode angrily up to the front door, and pounded on it.

Mrs. Becker opened it almost immediately. "You could have used the knocker," she said. "There is no need to destroy the door to gain admittance to this house."

"What's this about you sending Burgess out after your husband?" Cimarron barked as he brushed past her and moved on into the room he had been in earlier.

When Mrs. Becker had also entered it, she answered his question. "Chet Burgess was just here. He told me you had questioned him. I told him—"

"Why'd you tell him about the bounty? You hired me, didn't you? You think maybe I'm not man enough to do the job for you?"

"I think you're more than man enough, as a matter of fact. But I don't see any harm in having more than one man stalking my husband. It increases the chances, it seems to me, of my attaining my goal—Reuben's death."

Cimarron swore lustily.

He was still swearing, and as vociferously, when a knock sounded on the front door.

Mrs. Becker swept past him and out into the hall. Moments later, she reappeared and told Cimarron, "It seems that some friends of yours have come to call on me."

"Friends of mine? What friends of mine?"

Mrs. Becker turned and gestured, and as she did so, Rose Collins and Aaron Slocum entered the room.

"What the hell—" Cimarron exclaimed. "Rose, what are you doing here? Aaron, what—"

Rose said, "Cimarron, now don't let that terrible temper of

yours get out of hand. I just told Mrs. Becker that we'd come after you, Aaron and I, and—''

"Why?" Cimarron roared.

"To help you," Rose said, and Slocum, turning to Mrs. Becker, said, "We heard about the bounty you're offering to anybody who brings in the murderer you mentioned in your letter to Cimarron. So we thought we'd try to do what you want done."

"How'd you find out about the bounty?" Cimarron yelled at Slocum.

"Please!" Mrs. Becker said impatiently. "You needn't shout so, Cimarron. The neighbors—"

"Be damned!" Cimarron shouted. "Aaron, I want an answer and I want it now."

"The letter," Rose said in a low tone. "The one Mrs. Becker sent you, Cimarron. You remember, don't you, that you showed it to me? Well, I told Aaron about it when he visited me at Mrs. Windham's after you'd left."

"And I," Slocum said, "can scent a good thing when I smell it. So I decided to come here and see what I could do to assist Mrs. Becker."

Cimarron groaned and sat down in a chair, his legs thrust out in front of him. He pulled his hat down over his face and then let his arms hang over the sides of the chair.

"Who are you two?" Mrs. Becker inquired.

"I'm a deputy marshal, same as Cimarron," Slocum answered. "This lady here is a friend of mine who lives in Fort Smith."

Cimarron spoke.

"I can't understand a word you said," Mrs. Becker informed him. "Not through that hat that's covering your face."

"I said," he declared coldly, after removing his hat from his face and clapping it back on his head, "that you hired me and I don't need any help, dammit!"

Mrs. Becker spread her hands out in front of her in a helpless gesture. "I did hire you, Cimarron. And I'm sure you don't need any help. But what do you expect me to do at this point? Tell these people to simply go away?"

"Yes. Tell them to go away."

Mrs. Becker turned to face Rose and Slocum, her eyebrows raised.

"We're not going," Slocum announced firmly.

"We're going to catch—who is this murderer you want hounded down, Mrs. Becker?" Rose inquired.

Mrs. Becker explained and concluded, "But I don't merely want him hounded down, as you put it. I want him killed."

Rose glanced at Slocum, who was staring in disbelief at Mrs. Becker.

"You two in a killing frame of mind?" Cimarron asked them. "Well, speak up. Are you?"

"We . . . neither of us," Slocum said slowly, "had planned on killing anybody."

"Well, you heard the lady," Cimarron snapped. "She's bent on having her husband killed, and since you two aren't bent on making that kind of bargain, you can just clear on out of here."

"The bounty," Rose said to Mrs. Becker. "It really is one thousand dollars?"

"It is."

"Then we'll kill your husband for you," Rose declared stonily.

"With what?" Cimarron yelled at her. "That look you sometimes get in your eyes when the hating's on you?"

"With this," Rose replied soberly, and withdrew a .32-caliber Reid's knuckleduster from the reticule looped over her right arm.

Cimarron whooped with laughter, pointing at the revolver. "That thing's fit more for a bludgeon than a gun. It's not got any range worth talking about. You'd have to get up right next to your target with that thing before you'd have even the slightest chance of killing him."

"Maybe that's just what I'll do," Rose countered, pursing her lips seductively. "I imagine I could manage to get close to Mr. Becker. He is, after all, a man, and I am, after all, a woman. It wouldn't be all that terribly difficult. Not for me, it wouldn't be."

Cimarron's laughter died.

Slocum said, "Cimarron, the three of us could work together on this. You and me, we've worked together before and not done badly."

"No," Cimarron said. "I'm working alone on this one."

Rose hurried across the room and knelt beside his chair.

She put out one hand and lightly stroked his cheek. "Together, Cimarron, we could—"

"No," he repeated, shaking his head.

Rose got to her feet and turned away from him. "Aaron, *we'll* work together on this, then. We don't need Cimarron and he apparently doesn't want us."

"One thousand dollars split three ways," Slocum said, his eyes on Cimarron's face, "is still a hefty sum. Men like you and me, we don't always make that much in a whole year."

Cimarron stood up. "Your outhouse," he said to Mrs. Becker. "It's out back?"

"Yes."

"When you come back, Cimarron," Rose called out to him as he made his way out of the room and into the hall, "we can sit down and discuss this matter like the reasonable people we all are. I'm sure—"

Her last words were cut off as Cimarron slammed the front door behind him. He ran to his horse and swung swiftly into the saddle. A moment later, he was galloping down the street and then heading south as fast as the black would travel.

Night had fallen as Cimarron forded the north fork of the Canadian River and rode directly to the hotel, which faced the tracks; he dismounted and tethered his horse to the hitch rail. Glancing up at the weathered facade of the two-story building, he shrugged and went inside.

The interior was as rude as the exterior, he discovered as he walked across the worn carpet and up to the desk, behind which was a wall rack containing a number of pigeonholes. He slammed one hand down on the bell resting on the top of the desk, and before the ringing had died away, a thin man emerged from a door to the right of the desk.

"Yes, sir? A room?"

"I'm looking for one of your guests," Cimarron said. "His name's Reuben Becker."

"Reuben Becker," the thin man repeated, stroking his chin and eyeing Cimarron, who waited to be told that the thin man had never heard the name and had never seen the man. Becker, he supposed, had used some other name when he and Nell Cooper had registered at the hotel.

"He's not here."

Cimarron's face glowed with pleasure. So Becker hadn't

used a false name, after all. Probably figured he was too far south of home for anyone to catch up to him in the midst of his sexual shenanigans. "When do you expect him?"

"Well, sir, that would be hard to say."

"Try saying it. Bet you can do it."

"What I meant, sir, is that Mr. Becker is a drummer. He travels through the terminus towns along the Katy, and when he visits Eufala, he honors us by being our guest while he is in town."

"What you're telling me is that he comes and goes."

"Yes, sir, you've hit on it, you most certainly have. A sensible man, Mr. Becker, very."

"He is? How so sensible?"

"Why, he has a room reserved with us on a permanent basis. That way, whenever he comes to town, he is sure of accommodations. We are sometimes quite busy, you see, and that is the only way an itinerant merchant like Mr. Becker can be assured of finding a place to lay his head at night in an establishment such as ours."

"He pays you in advance, is that it?"

"Upon occasion. More often than not, however, he sends us a letter enclosing his payments. His account with us is impeccable. I wish to heaven I could say the same about some of our other guests. Some—would you believe it?—go so far as to climb out our second-story windows in order to avoid settling their bill.

"But Mr. Becker, as I said," the thin man intoned with the pride a man might show concerning a successful son, "always pays us in advance." He cleared his throat and inquired, "Is there anything else I can do for you, sir? Would you like to rent one of our better rooms while you wait for Mr. Becker?"

Cimarron shook his head. "What I'd like to do is use Mr. Becker's—my friend's—room till he shows up. Of course, I can use it only for tonight. If he don't show up by morning, well, I'm just out of luck this trip."

"Oh, sir, I really couldn't let you do that."

"Maybe you could send some whiskey up to the room a little later on."

"Well, yes, I could do that, but I really couldn't let you use a room that is reserved for one of our guests. Suppose he should arrive tonight and find that I've let you into his room—his private domain, you might say. I'm sure you see the difficulty, sir."

Cimarron nodded. "I see a couple or three things. One, Becker wouldn't mind if he found me flopped out in his room. We're bunkies from way back. Two, he's paid for the room—right?"

When the clerk nodded, swallowed, kept on nodding, Cimarron continued, "He'd not take it all that kindly if he learned you turned a good friend of his away. Three, selling whiskey in Indian Territory's illegal and I happen to be a lawman." Cimarron thrust a hand in a pocket of his jeans and then slammed his badge, face-up, down on the desk.

The clerk paled. He looked down at the badge and swallowed again. He looked up at Cimarron and a sibilant rush of air whistled through his store teeth.

Cimarron gave him a grin and nodded, tapping his badge.

"We keep whiskey—we—it's merely a service for our guests. You won't—you're not going to—"

"Arrest you? Not if you can see your way clear to oblige a weary representative of the federal law here in the Territory, I'm not."

"The key," the clerk said, flustered.

"The key," Cimarron repeated, still grinning, and held out his hand for it.

The clerk reached behind him, removed a key from one of the pigeonholes in the rack, and dropped it in Cimarron's outstretched palm. "Number six," he squeaked.

"The whiskey," Cimarron said, and winked at the clerk. "You'll send me up some a little later? I promise not to tell."

The clerk's head bobbed in an eager nod. "We try to keep our guests happy, Deputy."

"Number Six," Cimarron said, pocketing his badge. He turned and began to climb the stairs, aware of the clerk's awed eyes on him.

He found Number Six near the end of the hall, unlocked the door, went inside, and flopped down on his back on the bed.

He closed his eyes and yawned.

As a soft knock sounded on the door, his eyes flicked open and fastened on it. His hand went to the butt of his Colt. "Who's there?"

The door opened.

"Hello, mister," said the young woman who was wearing a low-necked, short-skirted red-silk dress with blue-velvet trimming on the bodice and hems of its sleeves and skirt.

Cimarron stared at her for a moment and then at the full bottle of whiskey she held in her hand.

She closed the door behind her and leaned back against it. "You're not very friendly, are you, mister?"

"Oh, I'm friendly enough. It's just that you took me some by surprise."

She crossed the room, placed the bottle on the table next to the bed, and sat down beside Cimarron. Her hand slid up his thigh and came to rest on his crotch. "That's nice."

"Is it?"

"I meant that you're friendly." She smiled. "But this is too." She squeezed him.

"I'm about broke," he lied, expecting her to leap to her feet and flee the room.

She didn't. Instead, she pointed to the whiskey and said, "Management told me to tell you this is on the house." She paused a moment, smiled. "So am I."

"Well, now!"

"Management said I was to be real nice to you because you're the law. Are you?"

"I am."

"There are folks who would like to see girls like me declared against the law."

"I'd sure like to see you against the law, if you can follow that, honey."

She giggled and squeezed him harder. Then she began to stroke Cimarron through his jeans. "My goodness!" she declared. "When's it ever going to stop growing?"

"You just let me get out of these duds, honey, and we'll find out." Cimarron quickly got out of the bed and as quickly stripped off his cartridge belt and then his boots and clothes as the woman beside him wordlessly slithered out of her dress, undergarments, shoes, and stockings.

He embraced her, and as he did so, she ran her fingers lightly along the length of him. He led her to the bed and eased her down upon it.

When he was kneeling on the bed, straddling her, she beckoned to him.

At first he didn't understand, but then, as her hands gripped his buttocks and pulled him forward, he thought he did understand. He got a grip on his erection and took aim.

"Hey, honey, hold on! I've gone and overshot my mark. I missed your mouth!"

"I'll take *that* later," she murmured from beneath him, her hand circling his left thigh and pushed him away so that she could grip his shaft. "For now, I'll just take a taste of these."

Her lips were warm as they enveloped his testicles, and her tongue, as it caressed them, was fiery. Cimarron gripped the brass headboard as the woman under him continued to suck his testicles, simultaneously stroking his stiff shaft with firm, deft movements of her hand.

He groaned with pleasure as her tongue, lips, and eager hand kept at it.

She suddenly released his testicles and eased herself up onto the pillow. Then, raising her head and supporting herself on both elbows, she lightly kissed his erection. A moment later, her tongue slid from between her lips and she began to lick it as it loomed wet and glistening above her.

4

Cimarron awoke, reached out . . .

She was gone.

But, he thought, she's not forgotten. How could a man forget the things she had done, and done so skillfully and sensually? She was, he thought, a woman to remember, and remembering, he began to stiffen again.

He'd look her up next time he was in town, he decided. But how'll I find her, he wondered. I don't even know her name. The thin man downstairs at the desk. That's how. I'll ask him where she's to be found.

He turned his head and glanced at the window. Light was beginning to creep around the corners of the shade covering it. He sighed. A new day dawning, he thought, and a wonderful night gone for good; just a memory now but one to hold tight to. He looked down at himself and forced himself to think of other things—of clouds in the sky, seeds sprouting in the spring, the way rain ran off a man's slicker and into his boots . . .

When he was limp and his thoughts no longer lusty, he swung his legs over the side of the bed and reached for the clothes he had flung into the nearby chair the night before.

Once dressed and with his cartridge belt circling his lean hips, he stood in front of the mirror above the dresser and ran a hand through his straight black hair to give it some semblance of order.

The man he saw in the mirror smiled faintly. He winked. His deeply set eyes, which were as green as grass, looked devilish beneath his broad forehead. He had a long nose, thin, wide-nostriled. His ears were invisible beneath the helmet of his hair. So was the nape of his neck. His cheeks were slightly sunken and his lips formed a thin, almost grim line above his square chin.

He was tall. Slender. Wide-shouldered and lean-hipped.

The only thing wrong with him, Cimarron thought, is that scar that cuts down along the left side of his face to mar it.

The man in the mirror winked back at Cimarron, who then poured water from the pitcher into the porcelain bowl that stood beside it on top of the dresser, after which he washed his face and hands. Again he ran his fingers through his hair and then he put his hat on.

His spurs clinking and his arms swinging, he left the room and made his way downstairs to the desk, where he told the thin man, who was still behind it, that he was leaving the hotel.

"I'll tell Mr. Becker you were here," the desk clerk said. "When I see him," he added.

"No need to do that. I expect I'll be running into him one of these days."

"Was the service satisfactory, sir?"

"She sure was. Much obliged. By the way, I didn't touch a drop of that whiskey you sent up to me. Never got the chance to. Had me a real busy night. By the way, what was her name?"

The clerk told him.

"She work the hotel regular?"

"Yes, sir."

"You ought to advertise that fact. You'd do a land-office business as a result, I can guarantee you. Now, I have a question for you."

"Sir?"

"When we talked yesterday, you mentioned the fact that Mr. Becker paid you his room rent in advance. You said, as I recall, that he often sent you the money by mail."

"That's so, yes."

"When did you get the last letter from him?"

"Yesterday. I have it right here."

Cimarron, as the desk clerk dropped down behind the desk, heard the clang of metal against metal and then the man reappeared with a letter in his hand.

"I've been holding it in our cash box until I can post his payment in our accounts-receivable ledger."

"Mind if I take a look at that letter?" When the clerk eased backward, Cimarron reached out and tore the letter from his hand.

"I say, sir—" the thin man spluttered.

Cimarron glanced at the postmark: McAlester. "Be seeing you," he told the still-spluttering desk clerk as he returned the letter and left the hotel.

After leaving his black at the livery to be cared for and fed, he went to the restaurant, which was directly across the street. He sat down at a small table after telling the man behind the counter at the far end of the room what he'd have to eat.

He was hungrily devouring the first of the two steaks on his plate when the door opened behind him. He didn't look up. Instead, he forked beef into his mouth and washed it down with some of the black coffee in his cup.

"You're a rascal, Cimarron," a woman said from behind him, and then her arms were around his neck.

He choked, coughed.

The hands withdrew and Rose Collins came into view.

A moment later, so did Aaron Slocum.

Both of them sat down at the table.

"What are you two doing here?" Cimarron asked, his appetite fading as he stared at them.

"The same thing you are," Slocum replied.

"Trying to earn that thousand dollars," Rose remarked casually.

"What makes you think Becker's here?"

"Oh, we know now he's not," Rose said. "But you are."

"You can't collect a thousand dollars by blasting holes in *my* hide," Cimarron muttered.

"Mrs. Becker," Slocum said, "told us about Nell Cooper. Miss Cooper told us about you having talked to her about Becker."

"She mentioned the fact," Rose added, "that she had told you about her trysts here in the hotel with Becker."

"I'm surprised she did. I'm surprised she didn't guess you were after him."

"She did," Slocum said. "Rose made the damn-fool mistake of telling her that Mrs. Becker was paying a thousand dollars to anybody who'd make sure her husband was dead."

57

"Then why'd Miss Cooper help you two out by giving you the information about her rendezvousing with Becker in the hotel here."

"Because," Rose said, "when I realized the mistake I had made by telling Miss Cooper about the bounty, I then told her a little fable about Aaron and I being brother and sister. I told her that you, a notorious bounty hunter known the length and breadth of the Territory, had shot and killed our father, who was a wanted man, though wrongfully accused."

Cimarron whistled through his teeth and stared at Rose with reluctant admiration. "You lie easier and better'n old Lucifer himself."

"When the need arises," Rose admitted with a faint smile.

"We asked around about you when we got here a little while ago," Slocum said. "The clerk in the hotel said you were in town. We did some scouting after we got here this morning and—"

"Here we all are," Rose cried gaily, spreading her arms wide. "All together again." She frowned. Her arms dropped to her sides. "You're not such a bad liar yourself, Cimarron."

"Me?"

"You said you were going to the outhouse back at Mrs. Becker's," Rose reminded him.

Cimarron pushed his plate aside, drank the last of his coffee, and beckoned to the man behind the counter. When the man arrived at the table, Cimarron paid him and stood up. "Be seeing you, Rose, Aaron."

They both stood up and followed him out of the restaurant.

"Where are you going?" Slocum asked him as he headed across the street.

"To get my horse."

Slocum sprinted after him, Rose following Slocum.

"You're not giving us the slip again, Cimarron," Slocum commented. "We're going to stick as close to you as two hungry fleas on a hound."

Cimarron ignored them as he paid the attendant in the livery and got his black. He led the horse out of the building and checked its gear.

"Those are our horses over there in front of the restaurant," Rose volunteered, pointing.

"Looks like you two came prepared for a long trip," Cimarron commented, tightening his cinch strap. "That pack horse of yours looks like his legs're about to buckle under that heavy load you've piled on him."

When he was satisfied that the cinch was tight enough but not too tight, he straightened and, turning to Slocum and Rose, said, "I'm riding out. Alone." He put a boot in the stirrup, a hand on the saddle horn.

Slocum seized his shoulder.

Cimarron turned his head slightly, staring at Slocum's hand. "Any man puts a hand on me, Aaron, he's asking for a peck of trouble."

"You're asking for trouble, Cimarron, if you've a mind to do what you just said you were intending to do. We're riding right along with you."

Cimarron slapped Slocum's hand from his shoulder and started to swing into the saddle. He was halfway up when Slocum seized his cartridge belt and yanked on it.

Cimarron lost his balance and fell at Slocum's feet. He was up in an instant, his right fist lashing out and landing squarely on Slocum's jaw. He followed up with a left hook that slammed into Slocum's chest and then another strong right to Slocum's head.

Slocum spun around and went staggering out into the middle of the street, narrowly missing being run over by a passing buckboard.

As Slocum regained his balance, Cimarron said, "I don't want to have to fight you, Aaron. But fight you I will, if I have to."

Slocum's reply was a lunge toward Cimarron. He delivered a smashing right to Cimarron's chin. He drew back his left fist, but before he could let it fly, Cimarron moved gracefully forward, knocked Slocum's raised right fist to one side, and landed a left that caught Slocum on the shoulder but did the man little damage.

Slocum swung his left fist, but Cimarron threw up his left forearm, blocking the maneuver, and hammered Slocum's face and body with a swift succession of blows that split Slocum's lower lip and left the man staggering in a kind of drunken dance in the middle of the street.

"Stop it, Cimarron!" Rose squealed, and grabbed his left arm.

He tried to shake her loose but failed to do so. He seized the fingers of both of her hands, which were gripping his upper arm, and pried them loose. He gave her a push and she went hopping backward away from him. As he reached again for his saddle horn, he was seized from behind by Slocum.

"You bastard!" Slocum yelled as one of his fists slammed into the small of Cimarron's back, sending pain stabbing into his kidneys.

Cimarron let go of the saddle horn, turned, and backhanded Slocum once, twice. His hand came away bloody as a result of Slocum's ripped lip. As Slocum made a grab for him, he threw a left jab and followed it up with a hard right to Slocum's midsection, doubling the man over.

Slocum seized his wrist before he could withdraw his arm and yanked on it.

Cimarron, jerked off balance, took several involuntary steps toward Slocum, who stepped nimbly to one side. As Cimarron went past him, Slocum put out one booted foot. Cimarron, tripping over it, went down, hitting the ground hard. Before he could get back on his feet, Slocum kicked out at him, but Cimarron had seen the heavy boot flying toward his face. He shifted position, reached out, seized Slocum's boot, and twisted it. Slocum let out a yell as he went down and the dust rose around him.

Cimarron quickly got to his feet, staring down at Slocum.

Rose, keening wordlessly, threw herself upon his back. She wrapped her legs around his legs. Her arms encircled his neck.

"Damn you, Rose," he muttered. "Let me loose!"

"No!" she wailed. "Cimarron, we were friends, the three of us. You and Aaron were. You'll kill each other!"

"Not likely. Hurt each other some's more like it."

"But why, Cimarron?"

"I could give you one thousand reasons why," he shouted. "Now, let go of me, Rose!"

"You're money-mad," Rose screamed at him.

"You're not?" he yelled back. "You mean you and Aaron aren't bent on getting those thousand damned dollars?"

Before she could answer him, he ripped her arms from around his neck, turned, scooped her up in both arms, and carried her over to the water trough in front of the livery. He dumped her into it.

She came up spitting water and obscenities, her hair dripping, her small fists flailing the air.

Cimarron, grinning at her as she climbed out of the trough, said, "Hell, I haven't had this much fun with my clothes on in a coon's age!"

Slocum's fists slammed down, catching Cimarron on the back of the neck. His head dropped down and then he was spinning around, his hand reaching out for his rifle in its boot. He came up with it and swiftly rammed its barrel into Slocum's heaving chest. "I'll shoot you, Aaron, if you so much as sweat. I'm bound and determined to have that bounty—all of it. I'm riding out of here now to get Becker, and I'm riding out alone. Don't you two try to follow me. You do, and I'll give you and Rose a whole lot worse than what I just did give you both."

He stepped into the saddle and, with the reins in his left hand, his rifle in his right, rode down the street, glancing back over his shoulder several times at Rose and Slocum, who stood staring after him. The last impressions he had of them before the dirt street gave way to grassland was the hard expression on Slocum's face and the alluring look of Rose's lithe body, which was the result of the way her wet jeans and shirt clung to her slick thighs and full breasts.

When Cimarron spotted the wild maize growing tall on the open plain, he stopped to make his nooning. He found more than a half-dozen ripe ears, which he picked, and then, using his flint and steel, he built a small fire. He poured water from his canteen into the dry dirt to make mud, which he smeared on the husks; then, when the fire had burned down to a bed of hot coals, he placed the ears on the coals and hunkered down to wait for them to roast.

Twenty minutes later, he kicked the ears from the coals, stripping them of their muddy husks, and began to eat his sweet-tasting and slightly smoke-flavored meal.

When he had finished, he sat down cross-legged in the grass and stared into the dying coals of the fire, thinking of the bounty that he was determined would be his in however long it took him to run Reuben Becker to ground. One thousand dollars was more money than he'd ever had at one time in his entire life. One thousand dollars was enough money to last him a long time and pay for a goodly number of high-priced whores and the best whiskey being bottled these days.

He was, he thought, on the way to being rich. Sure, it

wouldn't last, the thousand dollars. He knew it wouldn't. He'd spend it. Maybe even throw some of it away on who knew what kind of foolish fun and frolic. But the point was it would buy him some time. He wouldn't have to do any deputying for a long time. Wouldn't have to risk getting his ass shot out of his saddle for far more than a mere month of Sundays.

He could take a trip up to Dodge. To Jessica. Now there was a working woman who could curl a man's toes with just a touch of her slim white hands.

The thought made him want to whoop and holler. He remained seated, still staring into the dying coals.

He tried hard to hold on to his thoughts of Jessica, of what they'd done together on their infrequent meetings, of what they'd said, the pleasures they shared, but thoughts of Reuben Becker intruded, shouldering Jessica aside until she began to fade.

Becker.

The man, he thought, is as good as dead right now whereever he might be, with me on his backtrail. He took no pleasure in the thought, although he had expected to because of the bounty on Becker's head, placed there by his hating wife and the grieving father of the man he had murdered.

Cimarron laced the fingers of his hands together and propped his elbows on his knees. He rested his chin on his interlocked fingers and gnawed at his lower lip.

What the hell is it that's biting me, he asked himself. You've killed men in your time, he reminded himself. You'll probably kill more. Some of them were murderers.

Like Reuben Becker.

He knew what was wrong. I've never killed a man for money, he thought. That's what's wrong. I've killed only in self-defense, never drawing on an unarmed man, never back-shooting any man, always killing in a manner most men would have said was honorable. But Becker—this was different. Well, he'd give the man a chance . . .

He shook his head in unvoiced anger. It wouldn't work, wasn't working, and he knew it wasn't. No matter which way he turned or twisted it, this matter of bounty hunting had begun to leave a sour taste in his mouth and a definite uneasiness in his mind.

Why?

Because it was different than anything in his past.

Killing Becker wouldn't be a matter of self-defense, although it might, in the end, come down to that. No, killing Becker for the thousand-dollar bounty came real close to being what could only be called cold-blooded murder.

But Becker's a murderer, he thought, and I'm a lawman. Don't that make it right? I'm doing my job, even if I'm doing it unofficially. I've got me a right to gun down Becker. More of a duty, when you come right down to it. Who knows who else the man might take it into his head to throw down on—and maybe kill the way he killed Jim Morris?

"Shit," he said aloud, remembering his earlier thought: I've never killed a man for money.

"Shit!" he said, louder this time, and got to his feet. "Well, there's a first time for everything, and this is going to be the first time, old son, that you've killed a man for cash."

He stiffened as the ghost of a thought, wispy and not fully formed, drifted through his mind. And then, as the thought took shape and memory gave it color and sound, he heard the accusation that came from the suddenly remembered man's dead lips:

Liar!

The dead man was standing out there on the high plain pointing a finger at Cimarron, who heard the word the man had hurled at him from his lifeless lips, and he wanted to throw back his head and howl his anguish into the empty sky above him.

The bank—himself kneeling in the front of the open iron safe . . . He saw himself taking the money from it in the small Texas town all those years ago as the man out on the plain wept dry tears and watched him through them.

Himself again. On his knees. A sound from behind him. He swiftly turned . . . The sheriff! There—in the doorway of the bank, a gun in his hand, the light behind him, silhouetting him . . .

He got off a snap shot and the sheriff went down like a poleaxed steer, and he was running past the corpse and then halting—his mind erupting in awful images—and he was turning back, looking down . . .

The dead man was not only the town's sheriff but also his father. He heard the questions rumbling like late-summer thunder as he shouted them at the terrified patrons huddled in the bank. The father/sheriff he had shot, they told him, had come to town after the death of his wife. Good man. Responsible. They had offered him the job. He had taken it.

And then Cimarron was running out of the bank, tossing the money to one of the other outlaws he had been riding with, leaping into the saddle of his horse, fleeing . . .

Out on the high plain the dead man still pointed his accusing finger. The words he spoke so damningly were caught by the wind and delivered to Cimarron, who wanted only to escape them: "You killed me for money. For the money you were robbing from the bank that day."

The wind shifted.

The words were whirled away—almost all of them.

But not all of them.

". . . for money . . . for money . . . for money . . ."

The dead man abruptly disappeared with the awful echo of his words.

And was replaced by an oil painting that was no longer in the Becker home in Honey Springs but was instead now miraculously hanging on an invisible wall where the dead man who had been in life Cimarron's father had just been standing.

Reuben Becker's eyes gazed out of his painted likeness.

Cimarron swiftly turned his back on those indicting eyes he could not meet. He hastily kicked at his fire, unaware that it was already dead, and then climbed aboard the black and went galloping south toward McAlester.

Later, as he rode into the noisy terminus town, he asked one of the members of a team that was repairing a section of railroad track where the post office was. When he had been given directions, he followed them; minutes later, he dismounted in front of a wooden building that was little more than a shed and went up to the open window, through which he could see a man wearing a green eyeshade seated at a rolltop desk.

"I'm looking for a man named Reuben Becker," he told the man at the desk, who peered up at him suspiciously. "Thought you might be able to tell me where to find him."

"Reuben Becker?"

Cimarron nodded. "I happen to know he mailed a letter from here bound for the hotel in Eufala. Days ago."

"I know Becker. Not well, but I know him. He's not been in town long. He not only sends letters, he also gets them. He got one this morning, as a matter of fact. From Honey Springs. Must have been an answer to the one he sent to Honey Springs."

"Where's Becker staying?"

"Don't know."

"But you processed his letters. He must have put his return address on them."

"He didn't."

Cimarron considered the situation a moment before asking, "He writes a lot of letters, does he? Gets a lot?"

"About average, I'd say. He gets more than Johnny Doaks does."

"What's this Doaks got to do with it?"

"Nothing. Just a little joke. Johnny can't read—nor write neither." The man behind the desk began to laugh, a cracked, cackling sound.

Cimarron, as he turned away from the window, scanned the street in both directions. A tin shop. Feed store. Restaurant. Saloon. His eyes remained riveted on the saloon that was almost directly across the street. It would be a good place, he thought, from which to keep an eye on the post office. He headed for it, and upon reaching it, he tethered his horse to the hitch rail in front.

Once through the batwings, he made his way up to the bar, where he ordered whiskey. When a bottle and glass had been set before him, he poured some whiskey into the glass and then turned around, bracing his elbows on the bar behind him.

The few patrons in the saloon were all men. One of them was slumped over a table, his face buried in his folded arms. Through the window, Cimarron could see the window of the post office. For several minutes, he watched people arrive at the window, either to post or to collect letters. As a Katy locomotive whistle shrieked in the distance and the grating of wheels on rails invaded the saloon, Cimarron turned back to the bar. He picked up his glass and emptied it.

He was refilling it when someone behind him shouted, "More whiskey!"

"Damn drunken bum," the man behind the bar muttered

as he wiped the surface of the bar with a wet cloth, ignoring the man's demand.

"Hey, there, bar dog," the man called out. "I'm no deadbeat. I'm a cash customer. More whiskey!"

Cimarron looked up at the painting of a nude that hung above the bar, her arms and legs akimbo as she lay on a plush sofa, her long hair decorously hiding the nipples of both breasts.

Behind him, someone began to pound on the table.

"Cut that racket!" the bar dog yelled. "You've had enough for today—for this week, as a matter of fact."

The pounding continued unabated.

The bar dog made his way out from behind the bar and Cimarron turned to watch him deal with his unruly customer.

As the bar dog hauled the obviously drunken man to his feet, Cimarron's expression grew grim. He was about to turn his back on the pair when the man he had recognized as Chet Burgess shouted his name.

"Cimarron," Burgess yelled again. To the bar dog, he said, pointing a shaking finger at Cimarron, "That man's a friend of mine. He'll vouch for me!"

The bar dog glanced over his shoulder at Cimarron, who shrugged. And then, as a thought occurred to him, he picked up his bottle and glass, went over to the table, and told the bar dog, "I'll look after him. Keep him quiet."

"You do that," the bar dog grunted. "You don't, out he goes on his ass."

Cimarron put his bottle and glass on the table, eased Burgess down into a chair, and sat down himself. "What brings you to town, Burgess?"

"Same thing's brought you, most likely," Burgess replied.

"Becker?"

"Becker."

"What makes you think he's here in McAlester?"

"This!" Burgess crowed, and pulled a folded piece of paper from his pocket, which he handed to Cimarron.

Cimarron opened it and read the words written on it.

"Took it off Nell Cooper," Burgess said, reaching for the bottle that sat between him and Cimarron. As he poured whiskey into his glass, he added, "I went to talk to her—everybody knew she was sweet on Becker. Found her writing that letter to him. She was writing to warn him that you were out after him."

Cimarron looked down at the paper in his hand. The warning was incomplete, breaking off in midsentence. "You in the habit of stealing letters from ladies, Burgess?"

"I'm in the habit of getting what I go after in whatever way I can." He drank, almost emptying his glass.

"Have you—" Cimarron hesitated, afraid to form the question because he was afraid of what Burgess' answer might be.

"Have I killed him yet?" Burgess shook his head, blinking rapidly. "But I will when I find him. I've been staking out the post office from here. He'll show up sooner or later, and when he does—" Burgess thrust out a hand, thumb up, index finger pointing at Cimarron, his other three fingers folded against his palm. "Bang!" he said, grinning. "Bang, bang, and Becker's dead!"

"Becker could have come and gone while you were passed out in here."

Burgess' eyes narrowed. "You mind your business and I'll mind mine, Cimarron. I don't one bit like your holier-than-thou attitude. You're worse than my two kids, you are."

"Just making an observation, Burgess."

"Don't know which one of them's the worst," Burgess muttered as he emptied his glass and wiped his lips with the back of his hand. "My daughter, she thinks she's a real prim and proper lady and her old man's a disgrace to her good name. My son, he thinks his old man's worth less than a pile of horse shit steaming in the middle of the street."

Cimarron leaned back in his chair, poured whiskey into his glass, and sipped it as he watched Burgess rub his big fists into his bleary eyes.

"I tried my best with them," Burgess continued. "Always gave them everything they wanted when I could afford it, which wasn't as often as I would have liked. Trouble with those two is they're takers, that's what they are. Take, take, take, and don't give nothing in return. Not to me, they don't. You'd think all that giving of mine would have earned at least a little bit of love on their part for their pa, now, wouldn't you?"

Burgess looked up, his eyes boring into Cimarron's. "Wouldn't you?"

"Can't say. Don't know your son, nor your daughter neither."

"What's knowing them got to do with it? What's fair's fair and what's right's right, that's all there is to it. Even a lout like you ought to be able to figure that out for himself."

Burgess drank, filled his glass, drank again. He jabbed a finger in Cimarron's direction and, slurring his words, said, "I tried my best to do for them, both of them. If Jesse wanted new boots, I worked my fingers to the bone and bought them for him. If Belinda wanted— What the hell, it doesn't matter. But I'll fix them this time! Once I've got that bounty money tucked safe in my pocket, I'll go back to Honey Springs and split it between the two of them.

"Oh, that will be a day to dance and sing, you can bet your bottom dollar. They'll look up to their old man then! There'll be no more talk then about how the old man likes his liquor better than he likes his life. There'll be no more snooty looks or cuss words, because they'll both know then that their old man has finally amounted to something!"

Burgess dropped his head in one hand, but not before Cimarron noticed the wetness in his eyes. "They'll shower me with loving then, when they've each got five hundred dollars, thanks to nobody but me!"

Burgess lowered his head to the table and Cimarron looked away from him and then out the window.

"They will, won't they, Cimarron?"

Burgess half-raised his head, trying to focus his eyes. "Won't they love me then?" he whimpered. "When I hand over five hundred dollars to each one of them?"

As Burgess' head dropped to the table again and his eyes slid shut, Cimarron leaped to his feet. He threw coins on the table and went sprinting for the batwings, for he had just seen Reuben Becker ride up to the post office across the street.

5

Outside the saloon, Cimarron stood stiffly, watching as Becker got down from his bay and went up to the window of the post office.

The man looked exactly like his portrait, Cimarron observed. Becker was a wiry man, slender of face and body. His eyes were brown and mild, his hair black and curly. His face was pale but not weak. He had a sharp slice of a nose, flat cheeks on either side of it, a broad unlined forehead, and full lips beneath a thick mustache as black as his hair. He was a man, Cimarron thought, who looked like he could move fast if the need arose. A man who would mince no more words than were absolutely necessary. Reuben Becker struck Cimarron as a man to be reckoned with.

Cimarron freed his horse and led it across the street. As Becker turned away from the post-office window, he said, "Becker, let's you and me ride out of here together."

Becker's brown eyes fastened on Cimarron's face, his stance stiff and his right hand easing almost unnoticeably toward the six-gun in the holster that hung from the cartridge belt strapped around his hips.

Speaking softly, Cimarron said, "Don't go for your gun, Becker. I'll outdraw you. That's a promise. One I can keep."

Becker's hand froze. "Cimarron," he said, his tone as soft as Cimarron's.

"You know me?"

"Nell wrote to me to warn me that you were after me. You and Chet Burgess. I know Burgess by sight, so it was easy to guess who you were."

Becker's well-modulated voice betrayed no sense of alarm and no sense of fear.

"We'll get aboard our horses now, Becker. We'll ride north. I'll be a little bit behind you. Don't you go getting any nonsensical notions. This black of mine's fast. So am I—on the draw."

Without a word, Becker stepped into the saddle of his bay, and when Cimarron was astride his black, Becker moved out. Cimarron let him ride a few paces away from him and then he followed behind. Neither man spoke.

The whistle of a locomotive screeched loudly from the tracks, which were behind the row of businesses that lined the right side of the street down which the two men slowly rode.

None of the people on the street paid them any attention. Riders passed them, barely noticing them.

Cimarron hooked the thumb of his right hand in his cartridge belt, letting his palm rest against the butt of his Colt.

The sound of the locomotive leaving the depot was one of iron biting iron, a noise to set a man's teeth on edge, Cimarron thought as he rode on behind Becker.

A buckboard was coming down the street toward them, and at a fast clip, and Cimarron automatically gave a tug on his reins to move the black to the left in order to get out of the wagon's way. "Becker!" he barked when he saw Becker turn his horse to the right. "Becker!" he shouted, and was about to turn the black but he was too late.

Becker headed his horse and went galloping into an alley as the buckboard careened past, separating Cimarron from his quarry.

The instant the wagon was past him, Cimarron went galloping across the street and into the alley after Becker. It wasn't long until he was out of it, to find Becker galloping across an open expanse of grassland. The man was hunched low in the saddle and he was using his reins to whip the bay as he tried to make good his escape.

Cimarron spurred his black as he continued his pursuit. He was shortening the distance between himself and Becker when the Katy locomotive, pulling a string of passenger and freight cars, rounded the southern edge of the town.

He spurred the horse again as Becker changed course and headed at a sharp angle toward the locomotive. Damn fool, Cimarron thought as his horse pounded across the grassland. He's liable to get himself killed with what he's trying to do.

Cimarron muttered an oath a moment later as Becker cut

across the tracks only feet away from the oncoming locomotive, which a moment later hid him from sight as it gathered speed and thick clouds of smoke poured from its funnel.

Cimarron drew rein and sat in his saddle, cursing, as the train went past him, seeming to take forever to do so.

When the caboose finally went pounding past him, Cimarron spurred his horse and went racing across the tracks, spotting Becker's horse off in the distance, but no Becker. Had the man fallen from his saddle? He knew at once that that was not what had happened. He thought he knew what had happened, and as he turned to look north in the direction the train was heading, he spotted Becker clinging to one of the metal ladders on the side of a freight car.

He turned his black and went galloping after the train, his eyes on Becker, who, as he watched, climbed to the top of the freight car and then, on hands and knees, made his way along the top of it.

Cimarron kept up his pace, knowing that he couldn't keep it up too much longer. The horse under him was panting, its sides heaving, great strings of saliva being torn from its mouth as it galloped gamely on toward the train.

Becker, he saw, was climbing down another of the iron ladders now, one that was fastened to the side of a passenger car.

The train, as it rapidly gained speed, began to lengthen the distance between itself and Cimarron, who saw Becker suddenly disappear between two passenger cars. Minutes later, as the train went swiftly up a steep grade, he gave up the chase, slowing his horse and finally and reluctantly drawing rein. He got out of the saddle and stood beside the black, absently running one hand down the animal's sweat-slick side as its body heaved and trembled and its head dropped down as it fought for breath.

He watched the caboose top the grade and then disappear, his eyes cold, his expression a tortured blend of fury and disappointment.

He turned his horse and rode slowly back into McAlester, turning over in his mind his next move, uncertain of what he should do and equally unsure of exactly how to go about doing any of the several things that did occur to him. None of them offered, in his opinion, any guarantee of success. But he was sure of one thing, he would get Becker. The man had just made a fool of him and he wanted Becker for that reason almost as much as he did for the thousand-dollar bounty on the man's head.

He rode to the post office, dismounted, and went up to the window.

"You again," the eyeshaded man behind the desk commented as he squinted up at Cimarron.

"Becker was here a little while ago. He gave you a letter to mail. I want it."

"You'll not get it. Not from me, you won't. A man's mail is private. The government's got to protect it and I'm a government employee charged with looking after the mail here in McAlester."

Cimarron stepped to one side, opened the door of the post office, and moved swiftly in on the man behind the desk. He picked up the chair and the man sitting in it and set it down next to the wall.

He reached out and began to pull letters from the pigeonholes in the freestanding rack on the desk. He quickly shuffled through them, dropping those of no interest to him, until he came to the one addressed to Miss Nell Cooper in Honey Springs.

"Put that letter back," the clerk yelled, getting out of his chair and starting for Cimarron.

Cimarron said nothing, merely slapped the man's reaching hand away, and carrying the letter, left the post office.

"Stop!" the clerk yelled after him from the doorway. "Stop, thief!"

Cimarron spun around and stepped up to the man. He displayed his badge and said, "I'm a federal lawman out of Fort Smith. This letter's confiscated by the federal court as of now, and if you don't stop your yelling—and stop it right now—I'll fill your craw so full of dirt it'll be next year before you can get it cleaned out enough to speak again."

The clerk backed up, his eyes wide, his hands waving wildly in front of him, and when he was once again inside the post office, he slammed the door.

Cimarron grunted his approval of the man's action and then tore open the letter in his hand. He read it quickly, pocketed it, and then headed for his black. Before he reached it, Burgess came out of the saloon across the street and, when he saw Cimarron, walked unsteadily toward him.

"There's a man in the saloon after you," Burgess said when he reached Cimarron. "A man wearing a badge."

"Has he got a woman with him?" Cimarron asked, thinking of Slocum.

"No."

Cimarron, his curiosity aroused, led the black across the street and wrapped its reins around the hitch rail before entering the saloon, to find Aaron Slocum seated at a table just inside the door.

"Cimarron!" Slocum exclaimed. "Glad I caught up with you."

"I'm not glad you did."

"Did you catch up with Becker yet by any chance?"

"I just did."

"Where is he, then? You killed him?"

"Nope. I didn't kill him. Didn't even get much of a chance to try, since I ran into him at the post office across the street and I don't think the people in this town would look kindly on me gunning down one of their number in cold blood. He got away from me."

"Slick as a whistle too, sounds like," Slocum commented when Cimarron had finished his account of Becker's escape. "You going south after him now?"

Cimarron, instead of answering the question, asked one of his own. "Where's Rose?"

"Her and me shacked up for the night after you ran off on us—which reminds me. Cimarron, you shouldn't ought to run out on your friends like you seem to be in the bad habit of doing. Not on this friend of yours anyway you shouldn't. We've been through a thing or two together, some thick, some thin, in the past. That ought to count for something between us, don't you figure?"

"Where's Rose?"

"Who knows?"

"She went back to Fort Smith?"

"I said I don't know where she is. When I woke up the morning after our night together, she was gone, and so was her horse and the pack horse we'd brought along. Sit down, Cimarron. Have a drink."

Cimarron sat down at the table but refused the drink Slocum had offered him. "How'd you know I was here?"

Slocum took a drink and replied, "Talked to the desk clerk

in the hotel Becker sometimes stays at up in Eufala. He told me it seemed to him that a whole lot of people were all of a sudden interested in Reuben Becker. When I asked him what he meant, he told me you'd been badgering him about Becker. One thing led to another and he wound up showing me Becker's letter that he'd showed to you—the one Becker had mailed from here in McAlester. I figured you'd head here, so I did too, after Rose gave me the slip, which turned out to be a blessing in disguise."

"What are you getting at?"

"Hell, Cimarron, with Rose gone I figured the bounty split two ways is better than it being split three ways."

"What two ways did you happen to have in mind, Aaron?"

"Why, between you and me, of course." When Cimarron started to shake his head, Slocum hastened on. "I've got a deal to offer you. A sixty-forty split. How's that strike you?"

"No good. No deal."

"Seventy-thirty."

"I'm in this for a hundred percent. Don't plan on taking a penny less. Not for any reason."

Slocum stared into his partially filled glass for a moment before speaking again, this time in an almost inaudible voice. "Cimarron, I didn't figure on ever telling you this. But now—well, you being so damned adamant and all, I figure it's the last card I've got left to play. If it don't work, I'm out of the game for good."

Cimarron waited and, when Slocum remained silent, said, "Play your card, Aaron."

Slocum looked up at him and sighed. "I went to the doc in Fort Smith some time back." His right hand rose and his thumb and fingers caressed both sides of his jaw just below his ears. "Cancer," he said.

The ugly word drifted between the two men like acrid smoke.

"I'm dying, Cimarron." Slocum's hand dropped to the table. "I've only got me a few more months at most, according to the doc. I tell you it was a kick in the ass like I never took before, that bad news was. At first, I tried to pretend the doc was full of shit, that he didn't know what he was talking about. But it didn't work. I can feel myself being eaten up inside, Cimarron. The doc thinks it's probably spread from my lymph glands all the way through me.

"Well, I was just going along after that for a while, not knowing if I was going to get through the day or the night neither. It made me mad, being so sick did. I wanted to kill somebody or something. I even thought once about killing myself, cheating the reaper, so to speak. But I just kept keeping on from day to day. Then I heard about the bounty on Becker. That's it, I said to myself. Slocum, you may have bought yourself a one-way ticket to hell, but that thousand dollars is going to let you travel there in style, by Christ!"

Cimarron couldn't meet Slocum's gaze.

"I wanted the money," Slocum continued soberly, "to pay for one last real wild fling. Women. Whiskey. Clean sheets in the best hotel somewhere. New duds. I felt I was owed that much."

"Life don't owe anybody anything," Cimarron said. "A man just has to do for himself and hope for the best."

"You don't understand," Slocum cried. "I'm only thirty-one years old. I'm being cheated out of more than half the threescore and ten that's mine by right!"

"You're a dumb bastard, Aaron. You could be standing in a pile of shit up to your eyeballs and you'd think you were smelling roses. Nobody nowhere guaranteed you or anybody else threescore and ten. Nor anything else at all in this life. What a man gets out of life is sometimes what he's got the balls to take and sometimes the result of pure luck—either good or bad. And that's all, dammit, that there is to it!"

"Cimarron, I'm not as sharp as I once was. You remember how good a shot I was with a rifle? Why, I could shoot a gnat off a stag's nose at a hundred yards, maybe more. I'm slowing down fast, Cimarron. I can feel it. That's why I'd rather work this hunt with a good partner such as yourself. I'm not sure I can cut it on my own anymore. Hell, the fact is, I *know* I can't. I'll settle for—twenty percent."

Cimarron angrily slammed a fist down on the table, rattling Slocum's glass. "Fifty-fifty," he said without looking at Slocum.

Slocum's eyes widened. "You mean it, Cimarron? You really mean it, old son? You'll split the bounty with me on a fifty-fifty basis?"

"You and me, Aaron, we're going to Limestone Gap."

"After Becker?"

"After Becker."

"He's there? In Limestone Gap?"

Cimarron dug Becker's letter out of his pocket and handed it to Slocum, who took it, read it, whooped happily, and tossed his hat and the letter into the air.

But then, his whoop dying as he caught his hat and let the letter fall heedlessly to the floor by his chair, he sobered. "You know what you're doing, do you, Cimarron? I mean, that letter Becker wrote to Nell Cooper said he was planning on heading down to Limestone Gap for a spell in case you came looking for him here, but you told me before that he jumped on a train and took off for God alone knows where."

"It was a southbound train. Maybe I didn't mention that fact. So it suited his plans. Now, he won't have the least idea that I got my hands on that letter he wrote, so he'll figure I don't know where he's headed."

"Wait a minute. He knows you saw him on the train, so he knows you know in which direction he was headed."

"Aaron, will you stop trying to think this thing to death? We've got to get a move on. We know Becker's headed south. We know he intended to head for Limestone Gap. He'll just get there sooner than he expected to and he won't be expecting us to show up there looking for him, because he'll figure we know only that he's headed south, which could mean just about anywhere down there in Choctaw Nation. Now, let's go, Slocum. We're wasting time here."

Slocum rose when Cimarron did and said, with a wry smile, "And me, I've got no least bit of time to waste and that's a fact."

Slocum paid his bar bill, and once outside, as both men boarded their horses, Cimarron noticed Burgess standing in front of the restaurant across the street watching them. They rode out of McAlester, traveling along the tracks of the Katy railroad in a southerly direction.

"That Remington of yours," Cimarron said after a stretch of time during which neither man spoke. "It's the only iron you're packing?"

"Had to sell my Henry rifle," Slocum said with a sad shake of his head. "Do you have any idea how much doctors charge you to so much as look down your throat or peep into your ears these days?"

"Us deputies can't afford a whole lot of things, seems like, doctors very much among them."

"But think of it, Cimarron. When we both have five hundred dollars in our jeans, we'll be able to afford all kinds of things. The pair of us, we can go back to Fort Smith once we've disposed of Becker and take over Mrs. Windham's whorehouse for maybe as long as a week. We'll set up the girls in two long lines and have at them, one after the other, until we get to the end of the lines, and then we'll switch lines and start in all over again."

Slocum laughed heartily.

Cimarron couldn't help smiling. "What you're proposing, Aaron, 's liable to kill you quicker'n than—" His lips snapped shut and he silently damned himself for what he had been about to say.

"Ah, but think on it, Cimarron. What a truly wonderful way to die. With your boots and a hard on!"

Cimarron couldn't help himself. He hooted loudly and then let out a wild yell, taking off his hat and slapping it against his thigh.

He put it back on and pointed to a nearby tree. "Look there, Aaron."

"At what?"

"See those blazes up there on the trunk of that tree? The same blazing's on that other tree farther along. Made by a buck jackrabbit."

"You sure?"

"Sure, I'm sure. Those old bucks like standing up on their hind legs and rubbing their chins on tree bark. They mark their range that way by sight and scent. There ought to be tracks—there you go! See them? In there between those two trees?"

Cimarron drew rein and dismounted. He walked along, following the tracks in among the trees, and when Slocum had joined him, he said, "It's a black-tailed jack. It takes a whole lot longer hops than the white does. See there—that space between the tracks? He made a high scouting hop there to see what he could see of the world. Let's try to find him and turn him into our supper."

Cimarron moved cautiously through the trees, following the diagonal tracks of the jackrabbit, which were dotted here and there with a blurred impression where the animal's tail had touched the ground. Slocum was a few paces behind him.

"There!" he said and halted.

"Where? What?"

"There's his bed—under that clump of plum brush." Cimarron bent down, picked up a piece of a broken branch, and threw it.

The jackrabbit, its black tail bobbing, darted out of its thick bed and went bounding into the trees.

"Go after him, Aaron," Cimarron commanded. "Quick, now!"

As Slocum went racing after the jackrabbit, his gun drawn, Cimarron stood his ground. He drew his .44, waiting. He could hear Slocum, but he could see neither the man nor the jackrabbit now. Still, he waited and, while waiting, thumbed back the hammer of his Colt.

His patience was rewarded when the jackrabbit came bounding in nearly twelve-foot-long hops out of the trees toward him. He took careful aim and fired.

The jackrabbit, hit in midhop, spun in the air and then plummeted to the ground, blood staining its fur.

Cimarron went up to his kill and was picking it up when Slocum came racing toward him, breathing heavily.

"I lost him, Cimarron!"

"I got him," Cimarron said, holding up the dead animal by the hind legs like a trophy. "Thanks to you," he added.

"I—"

"You made him double back to get away, which is a trick of these black-tailed jacks. That's why I waited here. I figured he'd show up, and he sure enough did."

"Fat fellow, isn't he?" Slocum smiled.

"He's been eating good. Getting himself ready for the lean times ahead, come winter."

"I'll build a fire," Slocum volunteered.

"In there," Cimarron suggested, pointing into the trees. "The smoke'll get all mixed up in the leaves overhead, so it's not likely to get noticed by anybody who might be passing by."

As Slocum built the fire, Cimarron pulled his knife from his boot and began to skin the rabbit. He gutted it and then sliced off the head and legs. He had it spitted by the time the fire was burning steadily, and after hunkering down beside Slocum, he held the carcass over the flames, slowly turning it.

Fat fell into the flames and sizzled there as he continued

turning the spit in his hands. The flesh of the rabbit turned gold and then tan and then a deep brown, glazing slightly as it did so.

When he was satisfied that the rabbit was thoroughly cooked, Cimarron took his knife and sliced the carcass in half, spearing the severed portions with a stick, and handing one to Slocum.

Both men ate in silence as the shadows deepened around them and it was completely dark by the time they had finished.

"Are we moving on," Slocum asked, "or are we going to spend the night out here?"

"We can't do much good scouting Limestone Gap in the dark," Cimarron mused. "Seems to me we'd do just as well spending the night here and then starting out fresh in the morning. That suit you?"

"Suits me fine."

"Good. Because I'm feeling about as stalled right now as a tired horse facing a tall fence. Spent most of last night entertaining a lady and it's finally caught up with me, all that frolic has."

Both men rose and made their horses ready for the night in an expanse of wild clover growing thick not far away. Leaving them to graze, they returned to the fire and sat down near it, their gear piled beside them.

Slocum took out his sack of Bull Durham and packet of papers and proceeded to build a cigarette. He offered the sack to Cimarron, who shook his head and observed, "That's about the only bad habit I never did pick up."

Slocum took a wooden match from a metal container, struck it on the sole of his boot, and lit up. He sucked deeply on his cigarette, its lighted end glowing red, and blew smoke out into the shrouding darkness.

"You planning on deputying some more?" Slocum asked. "I mean, after we collect the bounty. You could use the money to lease a small spread in any one of the Nations and start stocking it."

"Don't rightly know just what I'll do with the money," Cimarron replied dreamily. "I think I like anticipating having it as much as I'll enjoy spending it on one thing or another later on."

"I never did settle down. Meant to. Sometime. Somewhere.

But now—'' Slocum was momentarily silent and then, "How come you never took root anywhere, Cimarron?"

"Couldn't say for sure. It seems I'm a drifting sort of man. Oh, I guess I wouldn't mind lighting somewhere more or less permanent someday, but not just yet. I'm always yearning to find out what's on the other side of the next mountain, what's around the next bend. Once I've found out, well, I'll probably hang up my guns, get out a rocker, and just sit and watch the sun rise and set day after slow and easy day."

"Maybe you'll get married."

"Maybe I will."

"You didn't ever?"

Cimarron shook his head. "Came close, though, once. Her name was Lila." Memories rushed through Cimarron's mind—bright, gay, tender. And then came the pain with the final memory as it always did—cruel and crushing.

Slocum blew smoke from between his lips, holding his cigarette pinched between thumb and index finger. "When I think of all the things I never did and won't do now— A man oughtn't to put things off. He ought to do them soon as he gets the notions."

"Maybe that's why I never settled down," Cimarron said thoughtfully. "Too busy doing with no time allotted to so much as slapping the dust out of my hat or letting the horse I happen to be riding trot past the same tree twice."

Slocum took a final drag on his cigarette and then flipped it out into the night, a small fiery beacon. "Me, now, I—"

He never completed his sentence. It was cut off by the report of a rifle firing, and as a bullet whined past him, he leaped to his feet, let out a startled yell, and took cover behind the tree he had been leaning against.

The instant the shot had been fired, Cimarron seized his saddle, threw himself on the ground, and using the saddle as a shield, scrambled backward on his belly until he too was behind a tree that he wished were thicker—at least as thick as his own body, which it was not.

"Who the hell's out there?" Slocum whispered nervously, peering into the darkness.

"Becker, maybe," Cimarron answered.

"But you said he jumped aboard a Katy train, so how could he—"

Slocum's words were interrupted by another report and a flash of fire in the night.

Cimarron, his rifle in his hands, took aim and fired at the spot where the flame had so briefly flared.

"You missed," a male voice shouted.

"Burgess," Cimarron muttered, recognizing the man's coarse voice.

"What the hell are you shooting at us for?" Slocum yelled.

"Once you two're out of my way," Burgess yelled back, glee brightening his voice, "that thousand dollars'll be all mine."

His third shot tore bark from the tree behind which Cimarron crouched. He returned the fire without much hope, feeling that he was shooting into the mouth of a deep dark mine with little hope of hitting his target.

"Been trailing you two," Burgess shouted. "Spotted your fire. Now, it's come round to killing time."

"Burgess," Cimarron yelled, "I'm going to get you before this night's many minutes older. I'm going to fill your hide so full of holes it won't even hold hay!"

Burgess' reply was another round, which did no damage.

"Aaron," Cimarron said, "I'm going to circle around and come in behind Burgess. You keep him busy from here. Keep firing. Shift your position from time to time, but don't expose yourself to his fire. That way, he'll think both of us are still here."

"Got you," Slocum said, and fired two shots in quick succession.

Cimarron moved out, his body belly-down on the ground, through the wild-plum brush, making as little noise as he could and thankful that the sound of Slocum's firing drowned out what little noise he did make as he crawled along. Several minutes later, when the sound of the shooting had dulled slightly, he decided he had gone far enough. Springing to his feet, he began to lope through the trees until he was out of them. He turned left and ran a course parallel to the one he had just crawled. When he judged that he had run far enough, he turned left again and began to move cautiously in among the trees. The sound of the firing continued ahead of him and he almost smiled as he listened to the number of shots that came in rapid succession. Aaron's keeping Burgess busy, he thought, pleased.

But then, suddenly, the shooting stopped.

So did Cimarron.

The sudden silence seemed ominous.

What now? he asked himself. He stood without moving, listening carefully. No sound reached his ear. Still, he waited. Then, determined to act to end this ugly matter, he began to move forward again to the spot where he was sure he would find Burgess. Moments later, as he neared it, his campfire, which was burning low now near the position he had left earlier, came into view. The thin light from the fire revealed no sign of Burgess.

Cimarron moved to the left, keeping the fire in his line of vision. No Burgess. He retraced his steps and continued moving to the right. Still no sign of Burgess. Where the hell, he wondered, was the man? The tree trunks were too thin to hide him. The underbrush—Cimarron scanned it carefully, looking for movement—wasn't that thick, not thick enough to hide a man of Burgess' bulk. Then . . . where?

He took a short step forward. He peered ahead of him and then looked on either side of him, the firelight flickering faintly ahead of him. No Burgess. He took a second step. And then a third.

The shot that tore toward him from within the grove was a wild one. It hadn't even come close.

"Aaron," Cimarron shouted, "don't shoot. It's me!"

No reply. Neither in words nor in bullets.

Aaron must have heard me, Cimarron thought, moving slowly forward again. "Aaron, where are you?"

"Drop that rifle and drop it fast, Cimarron!"

Not Aaron, Cimarron thought. Burgess. He dropped his rifle.

Burgess rose, a dark and deadly apparition, from the underbrush beyond the fire and stood where Cimarron himself had stood not many minutes ago. He was smiling, his face a shifting mass of light and shadow as he walked up to the fire.

"The three of us," Cimarron said, his eyes on Burgess', "could split the bounty—you, me, and Slocum."

Burgess slowly shook his head. "I told you back in McAlester. I intend to earn it all. Five hundred for Belinda, five hundred for Jesse. Then let either one of them dare say their old man's nothing but a drunken old fool."

Cimarron tore his eyes from Burgess' and looked down. At

the sound of Burgess levering his rifle, he hit the ground, seized a piece of kindling near the fire, and used it to uproot the fire and send some of its flaming tinder flying toward Burgess.

As the man let out a startled yell, Cimarron leaped across what was left of the fire and made a grab for Burgess' rifle.

But Burgess, who had leaped backward and escaped the embers Cimarron had flung at him, swung the barrel of his rifle, catching Cimarron on the side of the head and sending him stumbling to one side, wondering as he struggled to regain his balance where Slocum was.

He unholstered his .44, but before his finger could touch its trigger, Burgess fired and the gun was torn from his hand and sent spinning into the underbrush.

Unmindful of the pain in his bloody fingers, the result of Burgess' shot, he leaped behind a tree as Burgess fired again. Cimarron began to run through the trees, dodging first one way, then the other, Burgess' shots ringing in his ears.

"Aaron," he yelled. "Bring Burgess down, man!"

Slocum made no response.

Cimarron turned and ran toward his horse. He leaped aboard its back, dug his spurs into the animal's sides and, holding tightly with both hands to the black's mane, got the animal galloping away from Burgess, guiding it with only his knees.

He listened for the sound of shooting but heard none. All he could hear now was the noise the black was making as it went crashing through the underbrush and low-hanging branches.

Then he heard the sound of another horse behind him, making fully as much noise as was his black.

"Aaron?" he called out. "That you?"

A shot *pinged* past him.

Burgess, he thought. And the bastard's gaining on me.

He suddenly rammed one knee into the horse's ribs and it went galloping at a sharp angle to the right. Cimarron leaped from its back and, shoving the animal with his shoulders, managed to maneuver it into a heavily overgrown patch of ground, where he threw the animal to the ground. He quickly removed his bandana from around his neck and tied it over the horse's eyes.

The blindfolded horse, breathing heavily, lay quietly beside Cimarron as he silently and gently stroked its heaving body, trying to slow his own heavy breathing as he listened to the sounds Burgess' horse was making as it came closer to his refuge.

6

Cimarron continued stroking his horse with the fingers of his bloody right hand—the black's body still heaving as a result of its recent exertions—and listening warily as Burgess came closer to where he was lying.

Would Burgess turn? he wondered. He hoped not. He doubted that the man would because it was too dark to make out any trail.

He sighed as he heard Burgess move steadily on past his position. He didn't move until the sound of Burgess' horse had died away and silence had returned to the region. Only then did he rise to his knees and remove the bandana covering his horse's eyes. As the black lumbered to its feet, he stood up, tied one end of his bandana around the animal's lower jaw, and began leading it back the way he had come, loping through the trees and the night, the horse trotting briskly behind him.

When he reached the spot where he had camped with Slocum, he found Slocum's horse there but no sign of its rider. His Winchester lay where he had dropped it and he picked it up, booted it, and then saddled and bridled his black. After placing its gear on Slocum's horse, he searched for his Colt; when he finally found it buried in the underbrush, he holstered it and then went in search of Slocum, walking in ever-widening circles.

When he found Slocum's body sprawled on the ground some distance from where he had last seen the man, he stared down at the bloody hole in the back of the deputy's skull and knew what had happened.

Burgess had tried the same trick that he had tried, but more successfully. Burgess had evidently circled around behind

Slocum and killed him before the deputy became aware that Burgess had shifted position. That's when the shooting had stopped, he thought. And that's how come I walked right into the barrel of Burgess' rifle when all the time I thought I was coming up on the jasper from behind.

He bent down, lifted Slocum's body, and tossed it over the saddle of the deputy's horse, his arms hanging down one side of the animal, his legs down the other, his body already beginning to contort and his features twist grotesquely as a result of rigor mortis.

Cimarron climbed into the saddle of his black and, leading Slocum's horse, rode west, the blood dry and crusted now on the fingers of his right hand. He had covered, he estimated, a good three or four miles before he turned his horse and headed south. When he came to a small stream, he rode into it and through it for some distance before finally leaving it on the side opposite to the one from which he had entered the water.

Maybe Burgess is good at stabling horses, he thought as he cantered along through the darkness. It's not all that likely he's a good tracker. Hope he's not, anyhow. Even if he is, he won't be able to spot my sign till after first light at the earliest. But a thought nagged at him. Burgess had trailed him and Slocum, so he knew they had been heading south. Well, hell, he told himself, there's lots of places down south we could have been going. Even Texas is down south . . .

He rode on until he came to a stretch of sandstone ridges. He rode up along one of them and then down its far side to avoid skylining himself for the benefit of anyone approaching from the north or east—both directions from which Burgess would be most likely to come after him if the man hadn't abandoned his hunt by now.

Dawn found him not far from Limestone Gap. Tired and fighting the weariness that threatened to put him to sleep in his saddle, he jerked alert at the sound of a rider on the far side of the ridge. He eased his black farther down the slope and continued south, walking his horse now, aware that it was at least as tired as he was, if not more so.

A moment later, he heard a scream—a woman's scream.

He halted his horse, listening.

No sound of the rider now.

But he did hear something. At first, he wasn't sure what it

was he was hearing, but as he continued listening carefully, he was finally able to identify the sound of a woman sobbing.

He got out of the saddle and walked up the slope. He flattened himself just below the ridge line, took off his hat, and peered down the steep escarpment at the woman seated on the ground far below him. A horse stood beside her, its left front leg hanging useless.

As he watched, the weeping woman, whose face was buried in her hands, got to her feet and, with her arms rigid at her sides, threw back her head and let out a piercing wail.

"Rose!" The name slid from between Cimarron's lips. He stared at her in disbelief, but there was no mistaking the fact that it was Rose Collins down below him on the plain.

He was about to return to his horse when Rose suddenly crumpled to the ground and lay there motionless.

He watched her for a moment, silently swearing, and then turned around and sat down on the slope. He clapped his hat on his head and placed his forearms on his bent knees.

He didn't want to have anything to do with Rose. Not now. Not until he had the bounty in the pockets of his jeans. Later, he'd have a whole lot to do with her back at Mrs. Windham's parlor house, if she ever found her way back there. He'd move on, let her fend for herself the best way she could. All she'd be likely to do was bring him trouble if he were to let her hook up with him.

He got up and went to his horse. But after stepping into the saddle, he didn't continue journeying south. Instead, leading Slocum's horse, he rode up the slope and then started down the escarpment, his black slipping and sliding until they reached the plain, and then he rode up to the still-supine Rose.

He got out of the saddle and hunkered down beside her. "Rose?" He reached out and, gripping her shoulder, turned her over.

Her eyes opened. She blinked. She raised a hand to shield her eyes from the glare of the sun that had risen above the horizon. "Cimarron!"

"You all right?"

"Yes. I think so. What happened to me? Did I faint?"

Faint.

Cimarron groaned. So she'd only fainted, he thought, and I figured maybe she was bad hurt. Hell, I could have been the best part of a mile away from here by now if only I hadn't stopped and . . ."

"Oh!" Rose cried, her eyes wide as she caught sight of Slocum's body as his horse ambled up from behind Cimarron's. "Is Aaron—dead?"

Cimarron nodded and told her about Burgess' attack on him and Slocum.

"What if this man Burgess gets to Becker before we do, Cimarron?"

"He won't." Get to him before *I* do, he thought. "Rose, what in the name of all that's holy are you doing here, will you tell me that?"

"Oh, Cimarron!" Rose got to her knees and threw her arms around him. She pressed her cheek against his chest and hugged him fiercely. "I'm so very glad to see you. I was so afraid."

"Of what?"

"Everything," she answered, looking up into his eyes, her expression wistful. "Wolves. Getting shot. Or raped by some saddle tramp on the prowl. Wild buffaloes."

"That's some list of fearful things. Who'd shoot a pretty little thing like you?"

"Reuben Becker."

"Why would he shoot you?"

"Because I told him I was going to kill him when I ran into him in Limestone Gap. I recognized him because I saw that painting of him that his wife has hanging on her wall back in Honey Springs and he—"

"Hold *on!*" Cimarron clapped one hand over Rose's mouth. "Now, when I take my hand away, you answer each and every question I ask you only; don't go babbling on again like you've just been doing. You promise?"

Her eyes wide above Cimarron's hand, Rose nodded and he removed his hand from her mouth.

"How'd you get down here?"

"I took a train."

"Why'd you take a train down here?"

"Because of the letter."

"What letter?"

"If you'll just let me tell you everything in my own way, you'd understand."

"Tell me. Only tell me slow."

"All right." Rose sat down on the ground, and as Cimarron continued to hunker down with his buttocks resting on his boot heels, she took both of his hands in hers and said, "I ran out on Aaron Slocum. I took my horse and our pack horse after Aaron and I had found out from the hotel desk clerk in Eufala that Becker had sent a letter to the hotel from McAlester.

"I started out for McAlester, but I got lost and it took me forever to find my way there. Finally, though, I did. But I couldn't find Becker anywhere, although I met a man who knew where he lived. So I went to the boardinghouse the man told me about, but Becker wasn't there and he never showed up while I waited for him.

"Finally, I gave up and went to the saloon. By that time, let me tell you, I was ready for a good stiff drink. Well, I had one. I was on my second one when I noticed the piece of paper lying on the floor. A name written on it caught my eye—Reuben Becker's name. His signature."

Cimarron suddenly remembered Becker's letter, which he had taken from the postmaster and later handed to Slocum in the saloon; Slocum had then tossed it into the air before he and Cimarron had hurriedly left the saloon to head south to Limestone Gap after Becker.

"Did you hear me, Cimarron?"

"Nope. What'd you say?"

"It was pure luck my finding that letter that Becker had written to Nell Cooper. He must have been in the saloon and dropped it there without knowing that he had done so."

"So you found out from the letter that Becker was planning on coming down here to Limestone Gap."

"Yes. Well, I was ever so excited and fairly leaped out of my chair and ran to the livery and made a deal with the man there to buy my horse and pack horse, complete with supplies, and then I ran lickety split to the depot, bought a ticket, and took the next train to Limestone Gap. I arrived very late last night and went immediately to the hotel and found that Becker was registered.

"I went to his room, but he wasn't there. I tried the saloon next." Rose smiled brightly. "He was *there*. Well, to make a long story short— Am I boring you, Cimarron?"

"Nope. You just go ahead and make your long story as short as you can, honey."

"We became quite friendly, Reuben and me. Later, back

in his hotel room, I told him who I was and why I was there with him. He had thought we were going to—you know—but I, of course, had other plans.

"Well, I told him that there were a whole bunch of people out looking for him and he said he'd already met one—'a scar-faced son of a bitch,' he said, and then I knew he was talking about you, Cimarron; and then, well, I got my gun, which was held tight against my thigh by a garter, and I pulled the trigger."

When Rose fell silent, Cimarron squeezed her hands. "You shot him?"

Rose dropped her eyes and shook her head. "No. The gun—it didn't go off. It jammed. It's an old gun. I've had it for a long time. I don't know anything about guns—how to clean them or anything like that."

"What'd Becker do?"

"He laughed at me, and the next thing I knew, he was out of the room and locking the door—locking me in his room. But I climbed out the window onto the roof and started screeching and pretty soon a young gentleman came and helped me down from the roof. But not before I got a good glimpse of Reuben Becker riding out of town.

"Well, I wasted no time, although the young gentleman was most courteous and did offer to buy me a drink, but I thanked him and told him another time because I had business to look after and he said—"

"Rose!"

She glanced at Cimarron. "Oh. I was going to make my long story—"

"Short. Do it, Rose. Please?"

"I stole a horse."

"You what?"

"Once I'd gotten rid of the young gentleman, I stole a horse from in front of the saloon. I *needed* it, Cimarron! I didn't want to lose Becker. Once I've caught and killed him, I promise you that I'll take that horse of mine back where I found it, so you won't feel you have to arrest me for being a horse thief."

"What did you scream for before?"

"That horse I stole put a foot in a prairie-dog hole. He fell and threw me." She released Cimarron's hands and began to rub her buttocks with both hands, a rueful expression on her face.

"I'm going to have to shoot him, Rose. He's gone and busted one of his front legs."

"No matter," Rose responded brightly, getting to her feet as Cimarron did. "I can ride Aaron's horse. He certainly won't be needing it."

"He'll be needing it till I get him into Limestone Gap and pay to have him buried."

"But, Cimarron, we don't have time for all that. Becker's already got a head start on us. Couldn't we bury Aaron right here and ride out after Becker?"

"You fixing to dig his grave with your bare hands?"

Rose looked at her hands and then at Slocum's body as Cimarron unholstered his .44 and went over to where Rose's horse stood unsteadily on three legs.

He put a bullet in the animal's brain and then, returning to Rose, he stepped into the saddle and held out a hand to her. "Climb up behind me."

She did.

Rose was waiting for Cimarron when he came from the mortician's. "Is everything settled?" she inquired in an appropriately mournful tone of voice.

"It is and I'm hungry. Let's eat."

"I'll buy. I have money," Rose chirped. "Some of my own and all of Becker's."

"Becker's?"

"I stole his wallet when we were together in his room. That was before I tried to shoot him. Come on, Cimarron. I'll buy breakfast for both of us and then we can go after Becker. We'll eat real fast."

Rose talked throughout the meal they ordered in a nearby restaurant.

"Oh," she declared between mouthfuls of roast beef, "I'm so looking forward to the future. When I've got my share of the bounty, I'm going to go to—to California. Or maybe to New Orleans. Saint Louis. Somewhere nice. I'm going to start a business—a respectable one. No more earning my living on my back, no, sir. I'm going to be a lady and a pillar of whatever community I finally decide to settle in."

Cimarron said nothing.

"I've so wanted to get out of the life, Cimarron, and for ever so long. It's a hard life, it really is. A woman in my business has to smile even if her heart's near to breaking. She has to laugh and dance and sing when her spirits are lower than well water after a summer-long drought. And the men! The things they do to you and want you to do to them. It can be awful. You just don't know. But *I* know.

"Well, I'll soon be free of all that. Free as the wind and as ready to roam." Her face grew solemn. "Cimarron, this may be my last chance to be somebody, not just a worn-out and cast-aside whore."

"You're far from worn-out, Rose."

"I'm getting on, Cimarron."

"Don't see any gray hairs." Cimarron emptied his coffee cup.

"Thirty's old in my trade. You're over the hill by then and starting down the other side. Forty's ancient in my profession."

"Rose, you know what you ought to do, don't you?"

"Invest the bounty money once I've got it?"

Cimarron shook his head. "What you ought to do is go on back to Fort Smith, where you belong."

"No!" Rose cried. "I'm never going back there, not ever! Cimarron, don't you think I want to get married someday? Have children? Nobody in Fort Smith would ever marry the likes of me. But when I get to wherever it is I'm going and nobody knows me or anything about my past and I have my first real chance to be somebody as good as anybody—then I'll have a chance to meet a decent man who might want to marry me. Don't you understand, Cimarron? I mean, don't you understand what that bounty money means to me?"

Cimarron understood and said so. The urgency of Rose's tone, the hopeful expression on her face as she talked— dreamed, really—had not escaped him. Neither had the light glowing in her eyes as she painted the bright picture of the life she believed the bounty money was going to buy for her.

"We should be going, Cimarron," she said, rising from the table.

Cimarron kept his seat. Looking up at Rose, he asked, "Did you know that Aaron was dying of cancer?"

She slowly shook her head. "Oh, the poor man!"

"Poor man is right, in more ways than one. He wanted a share of Becker's bounty too. Like you do. He had his reasons for wanting it, too, and they were every bit as good as yours are. But, Rose, the man's dead now, killed by another man who's got *his* good reasons for collecting the bounty. Don't you see where that leaves you?"

"You think I could be killed too—like Aaron was."

"I do."

"I won't be. I won't *let* myself be! I've got to get my hands on that money, and as God is my witness, I *will*."

"Get on the train and go back to Honey Springs, Rose. From there you can make your way east to Fort Smith and then—"

"I'm leaving now, Cimarron. I'm going after Becker. With or without you. What is it going to be?"

"You're welcome to try for Becker on your own, honey."

Rose suddenly dissolved in tears. "You know I can't," she said, sobbing. "You know I need help—*your* help! Do I have to beg you for it!"

Cimarron got up from the table, rounded it, and took her in his arms. "We'll ride together, you and me."

Rose looked up at him, her cheeks wet. Then, smiling happily, she kissed him and led him from the restaurant.

Later, as they rode along in silence beside the Katy's tracks, Cimarron scanned the countryside—the sandstone ridges on their left; the dense growth of rabbit brush on his right: spread out nearly as far as his eyes could see, it was interspersed here and there with stunted piñon pines. In the distance was a ragged line of low limestone battlements, and the uneasiness he had been feeling since leaving Limestone Gap suddenly intensified.

Lots of hiding places around here, he thought, his eyes narrowing. On the other side of those sandstone ridges. In the rabbit brush. Behind one of those piñon pines. Tucked up in one of the crevices on the side or top of those battlements.

And he was riding with a woman. A woman who had a gun that wouldn't fire. A woman hungering for money but with no real appetite for what she might have to do to get it.

Well, he thought, I told her we'd ride together, and ride together we will. Only I didn't say for how long or how far.

It wasn't just that he wanted the thousand dollars for himself, he reasoned. It was more than that: he wanted to be rid of Rose for her own good. If she didn't have even the sense God gave grasshoppers, then he'd have to fix it so that she wouldn't get hurt—maimed, maybe, or even killed.

Giving her the slip wouldn't accomplish what he had in mind. That ploy hadn't worked the first two times he'd tried it. No, he'd have to figure out a way to get her out of the area—somewhere safe, somewhere where she couldn't do herself or him any harm. And she could, he thought angrily, do both of them harm by being foolish, as she obviously was, and more than half-drunk on her dreams—dreams he doubted would ever come true even if she did manage in some freakish manner to collect the bounty.

The shot, when it came, took Cimarron by surprise. It missed Rose but came close enough to him to cause his black to try to bolt. He got a tight grip on the reins, reached out, tore Rose's reins from her hand, and then went galloping across the tracks toward the sandstone ridges, leading Rose's horse.

He was halfway to the nearest ridge when Reuben Becker's head and shoulders appeared above it. Becker raised his revolver and Cimarron turned his horse and went galloping to the left.

He leaped from the saddle, pulled Rose from her horse, and threw her down behind a dead piñon pine.

"We almost had him," Rose screamed.

"Sure, we did," Cimarron snapped sarcastically a moment before Becker fired a second time, his bullet striking a branch of the pine tree, causing it to snap and come tumbling down upon Cimarron, who shook it off his shoulders while simultaneously pulling his rifle from its boot.

He took quick aim and fired at the top of the ridge behind which Becker was now completely hidden.

The ground beneath him suddenly seemed to tremble, and a moment later he heard the distant wail of a locomotive's whistle.

He laid his rifle down on the ground and, crouching, seized the reins of both horses. He led them around a sandstone hummock and into a cut in the ridge; he left them there, their reins trailing.

Still crouching, he made his way back to Rose. "Get down," he ordered. "Flat on the ground!" When she made a frantic grab for his holstered Colt, he slapped her hand away. When she struck out at him in anger, he slapped her face hard, sending her toppling over backward to the ground. "Now, don't you move!"

But Rose did move. She got quickly to her knees and lunged at Cimarron, making another try for his revolver.

He struck her again, this time with his right fist, and he grunted with satisfaction when her body went limp and her eyes closed.

The Katy's locomotive shrieked a second time, closer now.

Cimarron glanced over his shoulder, saw the northbound train, turned, and looked down at Rose. Now, dammit, he told himself, is the time. It's now or maybe never. He scuttled along the ground on his hands and knees to the cut in the ridge, grabbed the reins of his black, and moved cautiously back to his former position. He booted his rifle, scooped Rose up, and tossed her facedown over his horse's withers.

He leaped aboard the black and spurred it savagely, galloping back the way he and Rose had come. Once he was sure he was out of Becker's revolver's range, he cut to the east. A few minutes later, slowing his horse, he glanced over his shoulder.

The Katy was coming, smoke puffing from its stack.

When the locomotive had passed him, he swung his right leg over his saddle, and then, with his right arm around the still-unconscious Rose, he sprang from the saddle.

He landed on the platform between two passenger cars and dropped Rose. Then, turning swiftly and whistling to his black, who was beginning to fall back as the train sped on, he got himself ready; when the horse came abreast of him, he leaped from the train, missing his saddle and landing on the animal's rump, causing it to break stride. He got a grip on the reins, and holding on to the saddle horn with his left hand, he drew rein. As the horse slowed, he eased over the cantle of his saddle, turned the horse, and rode south again, pulling his rifle from its boot as he headed back toward the sandstone ridges and Becker.

He almost let out a yell of pure joy when he saw Becker crest the ridge and come riding down it toward him. He was about to raise his rifle when Becker spotted him, turned the horse under him, and went galloping south.

Cimarron did let out a yell this time, the lusty sound of a man happy to be hunting and confident that his hunt would end in success.

He had almost reached the point where Becker had descended from the ridge when a second man appeared high on the ridge, a rifle in his hands aimed at the fleeing Becker.

Burgess!

And Burgess was about to bring Becker down.

Rage flooded through Cimarron, bearing on its turbulent tide an ugly image of the murdered Aaron Slocum. He fired once, but his shot missed Burgess because, at the instant he had fired, Burgess had dropped to one knee, taking aim at the now-distant figure of the fleeing Becker.

At the sound of the shot, Burgess turned, aimed his rifle at Cimarron; but before he could fire, Cimarron slid out of the saddle, and as the black veered to one side, he was running along the ground toward the sandstone escarpment as Burgess began firing wildly at him.

Seconds later, he dropped down behind a hummock, took aim through his rifle's backsight as Burgess searched for him, and thinking of Slocum, fired.

Burgess made no sound other than a wet gurgle when Cimarron's bullet ripped open his throat. Blood pumped from an artery Cimarron's shot had severed; Burgess crumpled to his knees, grasping his throat with ten suddenly bloody fingers. He pitched forward and fell facedown on the rough sandstone.

Someone unseen screamed.

Cimarron, who had been about to get to his feet, held his position as a woman mounted on a chestnut crested the ridge, got quickly out of the saddle, and threw herself on Burgess' body.

Who the hell's she? he wondered. Then, as she took up a position flat on the ground, using Burgess' body for cover, and began firing a pistol wildly in his general direction, he swore.

Another bounty hunter? Whoever the hell she was, he couldn't help thinking, she's one helluva well-built, big-breasted woman. She was of average height and she was wearing a Stetson over her short auburn hair, a man's shirt over her breasts, which were tantalizing full and firm, and jeans over lithe legs and provocatively curved hips. He was unable to make out the color of her eyes or the details of her features because the sun was behind her.

He looked back over his shoulder. His black wasn't far away. But to get to the horse, he'd have to travel over open ground.

He looked back up at the woman, who had stopped firing now, and then he decided to make a run for it. If he ran fast enough in a ragged line . . .

He was up and starting for his horse when the woman let out an enraged roar and fired on him again.

He danced backward and got down behind the hummock again, damning the woman, damning Burgess, and damning Becker, who would be halfway to Texas if the woman on the ridge succeeded in keeping him pinned down where he was for very much longer.

He braced the barrel of his rifle on his knee and, peering around the side of the hummock, squeezed its trigger.

Burgess' corpse lurched as the bullet entered it.

"God damn you, Cimarron," the woman screamed, and got off another volley.

Cimarron, stunned that the woman he didn't know knew his name, flattened his body against the hummock, wondering what the hell to do next. He didn't want to kill her. Didn't even want to wound her. But he had to do something or he'd be an old man if this Mexican standoff went on the way it seemed to be promising to do. He did, however, want to scare the shit out of her. So he put another bullet into Burgess' corpse and then was up and turning, ready to run.

He found himself facing a young man with a revolver in each of his hands and a sour expression on his face.

"It's over, Cimarron. Drop that rifle and do the same with that sidearm you're wearing."

Cimarron hesitated, his eyes on the face of the man who, he now realized, was even younger than he had at first thought. His hair was as auburn as the woman's up on the ridge. His nose was straight above firm lips. His forehead was broad and unlined, his cheeks two flat plains, his chin square and clefted, his eyes black. Good-looking kid, Cimarron thought, even though he does look like he's just been sucking lemons.

A bullet bit into the hummock on his right, sending splinters of sandstone showering into the air.

"Back off, Belinda," the boy shouted in a furious tone. "I can handle this."

"Then handle it, Jesse," the woman on the ridge behind Cimarron yelled back. "But don't kill him. Not yet!"

Cimarron heard her making her way down the escarpment

toward him. He dropped his rifle. He unholstered his Colt and dropped it as well.

A moment later, she was standing in front of him.

"You know my name," he said to her, noting that her eyes were the color of hazelnuts and her face beautiful in a sultry, pouting way. "Don't believe I've had the pleasure, miss."

"I'm Belinda Burgess." Cold voice. Colder eyes.

"You're Burgess' wife?" Cimarron asked, unable to believe that such a young and, he now saw, lovely woman would have married Burgess.

"She's his daughter," the boy said sullenly. "And I'm Jesse Burgess. His son."

"We're going to kill you for killing our pa," Belinda said.

"Slow," Jesse said.

"Real slow," Belinda said.

Cimarron, looking at the oddly lustful expression on Belinda's face and at the anger in Jesse's eyes, felt cold, although the sun was high and hot in the empty blue sky above him.

7

"Where'd you two come from?" Cimarron asked Jesse and Belinda, keenly conscious of the rifle in Belinda's hands and the two six-guns in Jesse's.

"Pa wired to me at our homeplace in Honey Springs to come help him kill Reuben Becker," Jesse replied, his eyes unwavering, his expression as grim as Belinda's.

"He wanted your help in getting the task done too?" Cimarron asked Belinda.

"I volunteered it," she replied, "although—"

"I didn't want her—"

"—to come," Belinda said, completing Jesse's sentence.

"Pa wasn't—" Jesse began, but Belinda interrupted him.

"—all that good with a gun or—"

"—at bounty hunting," Jesse concluded. "We met him in McAlester and then the three of us started south, but we got separated."

"When we heard the sound of shooting in the distance—" Belinda began, and Jesse explained, "—we rode here to see what was happening, and found you." A smile flickered briefly on his face before abruptly vanishing.

"If you'd come along a little earlier," Cimarron told them, "you'd have found Reuben Becker, who was taking potshots at me. That was the shooting you heard."

"Becker was here?" Belinda asked incredulously.

"Your daddy saw him from the top of the rise. He was about to shoot him. I shot at your daddy to stop him from killing Becker and then your daddy was about to try to take me, so I killed him in self-defense." He paused briefly and then, "You two look kind of young to me to be bounty hunters."

99

"I'm seventeen," Jesse said defensively, his face darkening, "and Belinda's sixteen."

"How old we are has got nothing to do with it," Belinda declared. "We intend to get Reuben Becker and then the bounty."

"After we've finished with you," Jesse said. "You shouldn't have killed our pa."

"He was trying to kill me," Cimarron pointed out.

"Pa," Jesse said, "wasn't much of a man—"

"He was a blunderer and a drunk," Belinda said, interrupting her brother. "But he—"

"—was our pa." Jesse's eyes drilled into Cimarron's.

"He was a murderer," Cimarron said flatly, and told them about the killing of Aaron Slocum by Burgess.

"I don't believe you," Belinda declared when he had finished. "Pa wouldn't have killed in cold blood like you just said he did. He was—"

"—too spineless," Jesse stated bluntly. "It's doubtful Pa could have killed anybody even in hot blood, seeing as how he hadn't the courage of a chicken."

"It's clear to me that you two didn't think much of your daddy when he was alive. How come you're both so concerned about him now that he's dead and gone?"

"He was of our blood," Jesse muttered.

"We've got a filial duty," Belinda said, her tone bitter, "to even things out with you on account of how you went and spilled Burgess blood."

"And we're going to settle our score with you, Cimarron."

Belinda moved up next to her brother and added, "In a way you won't like one little bit, I can promise you that."

"What way've you got in mind exactly?"

Belinda glanced at Jesse, who frowned and answered, "We're not sure yet. But—"

"We'll think of something," Belinda assured Cimarron.

"Mean," Jesse added as if it were the last word in his sister's sentence. "Belinda, you go get my horse over on the other side of the ridge. Bring yours down here too."

Belinda left, climbing back up the escarpment, and when she returned minutes later, she was leading her chestnut and a dun that evidently belonged to her brother.

"What are we to do about Pa, Jesse?" she asked.

"Cimarron here's about to bury him for us."

Belinda glanced from Jesse to Cimarron and then back again. "He's got no shovel. Neither have we."

"He's got hands," Jesse said. "Go get Pa, Cimarron. I'll walk along with you to make sure you don't try to scoot out on us."

As Cimarron climbed the escarpment, Jesse walked right behind him, his six-shooters in his hands. When he reached the top of the ridge, he bent down, picked up Burgess' bullet-ridden body, and tossed it over his shoulder. Jesse followed him back down the escarpment, saying nothing.

But when they were on level ground again, Jesse walked around Cimarron and pointed with the barrel of the revolver he held in his right hand. "Over there's as good a place as any."

Cimarron went to the spot Jesse had indicated and lowered Burgess' body to the ground. Straightening, he said, "I could fashion a digging stick out of part of that piñon pine over there. If I had a knife to whittle away at it, I could."

Belinda pulled a knife from her saddlebag, glanced at Jesse, who nodded curtly, and then handed it to Cimarron, who took it and strode over to the pine. He broke off a stout branch and then, sitting down on a flat boulder, began to whittle one end of it. He soon had a flat-ended tool that vaguely resembled a spade in his hands.

"Throw that knife over here," Jesse ordered.

Cimarron did, rose, went to the spot Jesse had indicated earlier, and began to dig. Sweat soon darkened his shirt as the sun continued trying to incinerate the land and all upon it. Sweat dripped from his face as he went on digging in the hard and rocky ground, the branch in his hand barely equal to the task of rending it.

He stopped, straightened . . .

"No funny moves," barked Jesse, who was seated in the shade of a pine beside Belinda.

Cimarron ignored the command. He untied his bandanna and then wrapped it around his forehead to serve as a sweatband. After knotting it at the back of his head, he went on digging.

He had dug only a shallow trench when the thirst that had been growing within him became almost overpowering. "I could use some water," he said. "My hide's about dried out and my insides are baking."

Belinda got up and went to her horse. She removed the canteen that was hanging from her saddle horn and walked over to Cimarron, stopping some distance away from him, her expression wary. Placing the stock of her rifle on the ground and letting the barrel lean against her thigh, she unstoppered her canteen.

When Cimarron reached for it, she flicked her wrist, sending water splashing into his face, before picking up her rifle and stepping quickly backward.

From behind her, Jesse's raucous laughter racketed from between his lips.

Cimarron's tongue tasted the few drops of water that had struck his lips, before he bent over to continue digging.

Hours later, he was still digging. His breathing had become ragged and the air he inhaled and exhaled burned his nose and lungs. His back seemed to be blazing as the sun beat down upon it and sweat ran down his cheeks and soaked the bandanna he had tied around his forehead.

The sun was not far from the western horizon when he finally straightened and, leaning against the side of the grove, said, "This suit you two?"

Jesse rose, went over to him, looked down. "It'll do. Put Pa down there."

Cimarron boosted himself out of the grave and suddenly swung his makeshift shovel. It caught Jesse on the side of his left leg, causing him to stumble to one side; and as he did, Cimarron lunged for him. He almost had him, but the bullet Belinda fired from her rifle stopped him in his tracks.

Jesse, cursing at the top of his indignant voice, brought one of his revolvers down to crack against the side of Cimarron's head, dropping him to his knees and then to his hands and knees as he fought to remain conscious, shaking his head in an effort to banish the pain that seemed to be about to sunder his skull.

"Get up," Jesse screamed at him. *"Get up now!"* He kicked Cimarron in the ribs.

Cimarron went down and then fought his way to his feet, to stand swaying drunkenly in front of Jesse, who pointed to the corpse of his father, muscles twitching in each of his cheeks.

Cimarron bent down. He picked up the body and unceremoniously dumped it facedown in the grave.

"Now, fill it up," Jesse ordered.

Cimarron picked up the pine-branch shovel and thrust it into the high mound of dirt beside the grave. He worked on mindlessly, in pain, unaware that the sun had slid below the horizon as he worked. Finished finally, he wearily dropped the pine branch, waiting for whatever was to come next.

"Belinda," Jesse called out. When she had joined him, he said, "Put that rifle up against the side of his head, and if he moves, drill him."

"Where are you going?" she called out as her brother picked up Cimarron's Winchester and Colt and walked away from her, but she received no answer to her question.

Cimarron watched Jesse place his Winchester and Colt beside a boulder near the horses and then remove a coil of rope that hung from the saddle horn of his dun, beckoning to Belinda as he did so.

She backed away from Cimarron, her rifle still trained on him, and stood unblinking as Jesse spoke to her in low tones. Suddenly, she began to giggle. Her giggles soon matured into ripe laughter.

Jesse left her and went up to Cimarron. He looped rope around Cimarron's wrists and bound them tightly in front of him. Then, pulling Belinda's knife from his waistband, he severed the rope, leaving several yards of it dangling from Cimarron's wrists. He knelt down and bound another length of rope around Cimarron's ankles. Again he severed the rope, again leaving yards of rope trailing.

He picked up the loose end of the rope binding Cimarron's ankles as Belinda brought his dun over to him. When he was aboard his horse, Belinda shoved her rifle into its boot behind her saddle, and picking up the free end of the rope that dangled from Cimarron's wrists, she stepped aboard her chestnut.

Cimarron watched her wrap the end of the rope around her saddle horn, the action causing his arms to rise slightly.

Behind him, Jesse let out a wordless yell and jerked the rope he was holding, sending Cimarron toppling to the ground and causing him to lose his hat in the process.

"Move out, Belinda," Jesse yelled

Belinda turned her horse and walked it away from Cimarron. Behind him, Jesse walked his dun in the opposite direction.

As the ropes tied to his ankles and wrists grew taut,

Cimarron's body was lifted up into the air to hang suspended horizontally between the two horses.

His shoulders shrieked with pain as his arms were almost wrenched from their sockets. Pain also ripped through his pelvis as his body was stretched between the two horses.

Belinda's horse, pawing the ground, took another step and Cimarron gritted his teeth to keep from screaming.

He did scream—an obscene epithet—as, behind him, Jesse's horse strained in the opposite direction and agony embraced every muscle, every tendon, every cell in his body.

He heard his bones begin to snap and crack as he struggled desperately to get a grip on the rope that bound his hands. He failed to do so because the rope's knot was tied above his wrists, leaving his hands below the rope that stretched between him and Belinda.

Suddenly, as he fought for breath, his body dipped and he managed to raise his head far enough to see Belinda's horse backing slowly toward him. But just before his body touched the ground, she dug her heels into the chestnut and it walked away from him again, jerking him upward, again stretching him taut between the two horses.

His wrists seemed about to snap but his ankles no longer pained him. They were numb now, nonexistent in terms of his ability to feel them. And then, when he was sure that he was about to have his limbs torn from his torso, he fell facedown on the ground, although his legs were still angled above it.

He raised his head groggily, and although his vision was blurred, he saw that Belinda had backed her horse toward him, removed the rope from her saddle horn, and thown it to the ground.

The great sense of relief that swept over him, almost counterbalancing the pain that still possessed him, was vanquished as he was dragged backward along the ground, Jesse's joyous whoops shattering the still air.

He rolled over and over as Jesse, galloping now, dragged him along the ground. His body bounced into the air. It landed on the ground. It rolled out of control, and as dust invaded Cimarron's nose and throat, he coughed, gagged, almost choked, could no longer see, could only endure the agony that had become his entire world to the exclusion of everything else.

A moment later, his head struck a rock that he never saw and the blow was a merciful one because it ended his agony, sending him whirling away from the world and into an oblivion where no pain lived and agony was not even a dream.

Consciousness returned to Cimarron slowly, accompanied by bright bursts of pain that erupted from his shoulders, his hips, his wrists, and his ankles.

Like sharp knives, the pains sliced through his flesh, to bury themselves in his bones.

His breathing, shallow and uneven, gradually deepened and became regular. The blackness in which he had been drifting swirled, shifted. He tried to move, but the effort brought him only more pain.

He opened his eyes and confronted more darkness, but not the utter black void he had been lost in—for how long? He blinked, looked about, and realized that it was night, realized that he was staring at the ground he could make out by the light of the moon drifting among the stars above him.

Tied. His wrists. Behind the piñon pine against which his back rested as he sat on the ground, his arms circling the tree, his legs splayed out before him.

He heard the sound of someone moving through the night and looked about, trying to locate the source of the sound. He saw her coming toward him, an almost dead campfire behind her, his hat in her hands, a small smile on her face.

Belinda knelt down between his spread legs and said, whispering, "Your hat."

Cimarron said nothing. He looked away from her, wanting never to have to see her again, wanting to forget what she and her brother had done to him earlier.

Belinda placed his hat on the ground beside him. "I imagine you're a bit stiff," she whispered, and when he made no reply, she continued, "I can make you stiffer." She reached out and placed her right hand on his groin.

He moved his legs, trying to free himself of her touch, but as he did so, his pelvis seemed to shatter and he was forced to let his legs slump back down on the ground where they stretched out around Belinda, whose hand remained where she had placed it.

"Does Jesse know his sister's a slut?"

Belinda's hand rose. She was about to slap Cimarron's

face, but then she glanced furtively over her shoulder toward the embers of the campfire. Then, looking back at Cimarron, she said, "Jesse's asleep and I don't want to wake him." Her hand returned to Cimarron's groin. Her fingers stroked him and the smile on her face widened as he began to stiffen.

"Let's get Jesse over here," he said, "and see what he has to say about all this."

As Cimarron was about to let out a yell, Belinda clapped her free hand over his mouth and held it there, although he twisted his head from side to side in an effort to dislodge it.

At the same time, she managed to unbutton his jeans. As he snapped erect, her hand went around him. It squeezed, relaxed, squeezed him again.

"I saw the way you looked at me when we first met," she said softly. "I knew what you were thinking." She continued to stroke him and he began to throb in her hand. "Do you really want to call Jesse and make me stop doing this?"

Cimarron leaned the back of his head against the trunk of the pine as the tension mounted within him and the pleasure Belinda was giving him increased, almost making him forget the pain that seemed to be everywhere in his tortured body.

Belinda removed her hand from his mouth and continued manipulating him, her eyes on his face, still smiling. "I knew you wouldn't want me to stop," she whispered.

He wanted to stop her. He wanted to call Jesse and put an end to this. But he also wanted her to continue what she was doing. He didn't want her to stop until . . . He looked down at himself, watching Belinda's fingers—her hand . . .

Her lips, as her head dropped down between his legs, took him and her tongue swirled wetly along the base of his shaft, teasing, teasing . . .

He couldn't help himself. Despite the pain his action caused him, he thrust himself up from the ground and deeper into her mouth, wishing that his hands were free so that he could grip her head and hold it right where it was until she had sucked him dry.

She withdrew from him suddenly. "Tell me when you're ready," she said, her voice husky, her hand encircling him again.

"I was—just then—almost—"

Down went her head and he was in her mouth again, and as her head bobbed rapidly up and down on him, he groaned, his body began to shudder. He felt the impending explosion building within him and a powerful, all-encompassing wildness centered in his loins as Belinda continued to work upon him, drawing him closer and closer to the climax he so eagerly desired, so desperately needed . . .

"Now," he moaned as the tension in his body reached a mute crescendo and he longed for its ecstatic release. *"Now!"*

She abruptly released him and stood up, her hands resting idly on her hips, her eyes on his long stone-stiff shaft, which throbbed moist and unsatisfied between his legs.

He groaned in frustration, breathing heavily. "Why'd you stop?" I was ready to—"

"There are all kinds of ways to torment a man like you," she declared, glaring down at him. "Jesse thought of one. A little while ago, I thought of another." She turned her back on him and walked swiftly back to the fire, where she lay down and wrapped a blanket around her.

Cimarron, hating himself for succumbing to her, cursed. Her. And himself. As his shaft slowly subsided and at last went limp, he continued cursing himself for having let his lust betray him so that his torment had become the temptress Belinda's triumph.

A new pain, one of desire unsatisfied and therefore needling, was born within him as he sat in the stillness, his eyes closed, his breathing finally slowing until it became normal once again.

A dense wave of weariness swept over him and he gave in to it, letting his body go limp and the back of his head rest against the tree behind him. Then, as sleep stole upon him, his head fell forward and his chin dropped down upon his chest.

A touch woke him—gentle, almost timid.

He crooked his right knee, intending to kick out at Belinda, unwilling to let her torture him again.

"Cimarron!"

The name was a sibilance in the darkness, and at first he was not sure where it had come from, although he knew it was not Belinda who had just whispered his name in the night.

"Cimarron, it's me."

Rose Collins!

Impossible, he told himself. He was imagining things.

"Are they asleep?"

The voice was real.

"Rose? Is that really you?"

The answer came to him in the form of Rose herself as she crawled out from behind the tree and into Cimarron's line of vision.

"How'd you get here?" he asked her, unable to take his eyes from her face, sure that if he did, she would disappear, vanish completely as dreams nearly always did.

"You son of a bitch!" she snapped.

"Hush, woman, or you'll wake those two imps of Satan sleeping over there by the fire."

"I should have let them finish you off," Rose said. "After what you did to me—dumping me on that train, *hitting* me!"

"Honey, I did it for your own good."

"That's what my pa used to say when he switched me— that he was doing it for my own good. Well, you and him were both wrong."

"Untie me, Rose."

"Look at you," she exclaimed, but quietly. She pointed to his crotch. "Even tied up you're not to be trusted to keep your pants on when a woman's around."

"It was her doing, though she didn't do near enough. Now, Rose, untie me, honey, so we can both get the hell out of here."

Rose scuttled around behind the tree and out of Cimarron's sight.

He felt her fingers fumbling with the knots in the rope that bound his wrists. He heard her swear and then he felt her teeth gnawing at the unyielding knots. He heard her swear a second time.

It seemed to him to have taken her hours—nearly an eternity—to free him, but free him she did. As he got quickly to his feet, his body betrayed him and he almost fell. Staggering, he turned and held on to the piñon pine for support, leaning heavily against it.

Rose's hand reached out and gripped his forearm. "Can you make it? I could go get your horse—"

"No."

"What does that mean? That you can't make it? Or that you don't want me to get your horse?"

He turned around, pressed his back against the tree, and

buttoned his jeans. He removed his bandanna from his head and tied it around his neck. "It means I intend to do for Jesse and Belinda before we leave here."

"You're going to kill them?"

"You stay here. I'll yell when I want you." He waved a hard to silence Rose's protest and moved unsteadily away from the tree, heading toward his horse, which was grazing with those belonging to Jesse and Belinda not far from the campfire. His legs felt as if they belonged to somebody else and it was that somebody else they obeyed, not him. He went staggering out into the open, and when he reached his black, he fell against it, clutching the animal's mane to keep from falling.

The horse stepped away from him, but he held on to it and then got his rifle, which Jesse had returned to its boot. He turned and started toward the fire, halting a few feet from it but close enough so that its light revealed his presence.

"Get up!" he roared.

Jesse was the first one to sit up, throwing off his blanket as he did so and reaching for his revolvers, which lay on the ground beside him.

Cimarron fired, putting a bullet into the ground only inches away from Jesse's desperately grasping hands.

Jesse sprang to his feet and backed away as Belinda, startled, jumped up, her eyes peering blindly into the darkness.

"How'd you—" Jesse began, but Cimarron shouted for Rose, drowning out the rest of his words.

"Cimarron!" Belinda exclaimed in disbelief when she finally recognized him.

"I want my forty-four. Which one of you's got it?"

Belinda picked up her blanket and pointed to the Frontier Colt lying beneath it.

"Toss it over here," Cimarron ordered, and she did. He picked it up and holstered it. As Rose ran up to him, he said, "You go get what's left of that rope that's hanging from the saddle horn of that dun over there, and then you tie these two up nice and tight."

Rose went racing toward Jesse's horse.

When she returned, she proceeded to obey Cimarron's command. She bound Jesse and Belinda both hand and foot, and when she had finished, she turned to face Cimarron. "What now?"

"Now, honey, you and me, we ride." He backed toward

his black and, upon reaching it, stepped painfully and therefore gingerly into the saddle. He held out an unsteady hand to Rose and helped her up behind him. Then, without a backward glance, he rode out of the camp, heading south.

"We'll get you, Cimarron!" Jesse yelled after him.

"We *will!*" Belinda screamed.

Cimarron merely grunted. "Why the hell didn't you stay on the train and then head back to Fort Smith?" he asked Rose.

"You know why. When I came to and realized what you'd done to me, I jumped off the train. I just started walking south and I caught sight of what those two were doing to you back there. Who were they?"

Cimarron told her. "Wish you'd come to my aid a bit sooner."

"How could I? I had no horse. I'd thrown my gun away, since it was useless. Where are we going?"

"Boggy Depot."

"Why?"

"Why not? You know a better or closer place to get aboard the Katy?"

"You're taking the train? Where to?"

"*You're* taking the train—the northbound train."

"I'm not!"

Cimarron did not pursue the argument, and when they rode into Boggy Depot just after dawn, he searched for a restaurant. He found one not far from the depot, got out of the saddle, and began to pound on its locked wooden door.

Finally, in response to his incessant hammering, a head appeared in an open second-story window.

The man peering down at Cimarron waved an impatient hand and said, "Go away. We don't open till six and it's not near that yet."

"You'd best come down and open this door," Cimarron told him, "or I'll bust it down. Then I'll raid your kitchen. You can save your door and receive payment for the two breakfasts we want, or you can be stubborn—not to mention stupid—and stay up there in your roost."

The man, muttering, withdrew his head; minutes later, he opened the door, still muttering.

Rose dismounted and followed Cimarron inside the restaurant, where he told its owner what they wanted for breakfast.

Both of them sat down at a table. Neither of them spoke before or during their meal. After Cimarron had paid the man, who was muttering something about "damned indecent hours," they left the restaurant. Once outside, Cimarron seized Rose's right wrist with his left hand and, leading his horse with his right, walked slowly toward the depot.

Rose struggled and tried to bite his hand.

He held on to her and, at the depot, asked the sleepy station master when the next northbound train was due.

"Not for nearly another hour," the stationmaster answered. "It's due in at six-ten."

Cimarron nodded and, after tethering his horse to the hitch rail next to the depot, sat Rose down on a wooden bench and then sat down beside her.

They waited, Cimarron silent, Rose sullen.

When the clock on the wall in the stationmaster's office read six o'clock, Rose said, "Let go of me. My arm's numb."

Cimarron released her.

She stood up and began to pace back and forth along the raised wooden platform, her arms folded in front of her.

Cimarron leaned back against the wall, crossed his booted ankles, and folded his arms across his chest. He tried to ignore the sharp pains in his body but they seemed to demand his attention. They seemed to be everywhere. In his ankles. His wrists. His—

He snapped erect when he realized that Rose was no longer on the platform. He jumped up and ran the length of it and peered across the tracks and then toward the town. No sign of her. He ran back to the other end of the platform and spotted her just before she dodged into an alley that ran between the restaurant at which they had eaten and a tin shop next door to it. He leaped down from the platform, ignoring the pain the action caused him, and went racing after her.

He had almost reached the restaurant when a woman came out of it carrying a tray covered with a white linen napkin.

Cimarron skidded to a halt and ducked into the shadows shed by the overhang in front of the saloon that was on the other side of the restaurant.

As the woman with the tray hurried across the street toward the hotel, he watched her. Several minutes after she had entered the hotel, he crossed the street and went inside it and up to the dozing clerk behind the registration desk.

"That lady who just came in here with a tray," he said sharply. "She's registered here?"

"Lady?" The clerk yawned, patting his thin lips. "What lady? I didn't see any lady."

Cimarron described her to the clerk.

"Oh, *that* lady. I must have dozed off. I didn't see her. But, yes, she is a guest of the Haven Hotel. Her and her husband."

"Her husband?"

"Mr. Cooper's been feeling poorly. He paid me to send a telegram to his wife in Honey Springs to ask her to come down here to look after him. Well, sir, she did. That woman is a saint, I can tell you. She waits on her husband hand and foot. He never leaves his room. She brings him his meals from the restaurant across the street, looks after him—"

"What room are the Coopers in?"

"Number one here on the ground floor. Right through that archway over there and then turn left."

"Much obliged."

Cimarron went through the archway, turned left, and walked down the corridor. A moment later, he was standing in front of the door that had the number one painted on its paneling. He could hear low voices coming from inside the room and he was about to knock; then, thinking that a knock on the door—an unexpected knock—might cause the occupants of the room to react in ways he would not welcome, he glanced down the hall, saw the window at its end, and went toward it. When he reached it, he opened it and stepped out onto the ground.

Unholstering his Colt, he made his way around the side of the building, counting the windows and halting when he reached the one that was his destination.

He flattened his back against the wall to one side of the window and then, reaching out, he used his gun barrel to slowly ease it open. He continued opening the window, the barrel of his .44 beneath the window frame now.

When the window was wide open, he stepped out in front of it, leaned through it, his revolver held tightly in both hands, and said, "Don't budge, Becker. Don't you neither, Miss Cooper."

He boosted himself up on the sill and swung his legs over it. Standing in the room with the window at his back, he stared at the startled Reuben Becker, who sat on the edge of the bed, Nell Cooper beside him, the tray she had brought him uncovered and resting on his lap.

"Cimarron," Becker breathed. His shoulders slumped.

Cimarron gave Becker a triumphant grin.

8

Despair was etched on Becker's pale and drawn face. He sighed mournfully and said, "I thought that by using Nell's surname instead of my own you wouldn't be able to find me. I guess I knew all along, though, that you'd catch up with me sooner or later. Still, I kept hoping that you'd give up the chase, forget about me, and—"

"*Never!*"

Cimarron stepped to one side and glanced at the window from which the voice had come, his Colt still trained on Becker.

Rose, clutching a broken barrel stave, climbed in through the window and went up to Cimarron. Taking up a position beside him, she put an arm around his waist and remarked, "Well, Cimarron, we finally got him!"

Cimarron groaned.

Rose gave him an affectionate hug and, brandishing the barrel stave in her hand at Becker, said, "I was looking for him, Cimarron, when I happened to see you skulking—"

"I wasn't skulking."

"—out there behind the hotel, so I figured you must be onto something. I crept up to the window and I listened. Do you want me to hit him with this?" She raised the barrel stave high above her head.

"No!" Nell cried. She threw herself at Rose, seized the barrel stave, wrested it from Rose's hand, and threw it out the window. Her hands fastened in Rose's hair, and as Rose screamed and battled Nell furiously, both women fell to the floor.

They rolled over and over, finally colliding with the bed. Rose, on top of Nell, began to choke her, her hands encircling Nell's slender throat. Nell let go of Rose's hair and tried desperately to pry Rose's fingers from her throat, gagging as she did so.

Cimarron bent down toward Rose's upraised buttocks and his strategically placed index finger caused her to give a shocked cry and snap erect, releasing Nell as she did so. He hauled her to her feet and sent her hurtling across the room; she landed, legs up in the air and arms akimbo, in an overstuffed chair.

As Nell scrambled to her feet and lunged at him, he raised his right foot and booted her in the midsection, toppling her backward onto the bed.

"Becker," he said, his eyes darting between the two grasping and frantic women, "we're getting out of here, you and me." He gestured toward the door with the barrel of his revolver.

"You're going to kill me?" Becker asked, his voice cracking on the word "kill."

"Well, I'm hell-bent on collecting the bounty your wife's offering for you."

As Nell started to rise from the bed, her eyes afire, Cimarron stabbed an index finger at her and said, "Sit down!"

She sat down.

"I didn't kill Jim Morris, Cimarron," Becker said in a hopeless voice as he placed his tray on the table beside the bed.

"People saw you kill him," Cimarron countered coldly. "Now, let's go, Becker."

Nell threw her arms around Becker's neck and practically climbed into his lap as if she were trying to shield her lover from the gun in Cimarron's hand.

He was about to reach out and pull her off Becker when Becker said, "I was coming home from the Mercantile one day—a day like any other day, or so I thought. When I was approaching my home, I saw Jim Morris run out of my house with Harriet right behind him.

"She was shouting at him. He called her a name—an ugly name. She bent down, picked up a stone, and hit him with it."

Cimarron's eyes narrowed. "You trying to shunt the blame for Morris' death onto your wife, Becker?"

"Harriet killed Jim Morris," Becker said, his voice and expression both sad.

"How?"

"I just told you. She hit him in the head with a stone—from behind. I think he might have been dead before he hit the ground. The whole right side of his head was crushed. I could see his brain, part of it, and—" Becker shuddered.

Cimarron, his thoughts racing, tried to sort them out. What was it, he asked himself, that was wrong? What was it that was bothering him about all this, not just about what Becker had said but what Harriet Becker herself had said to him back in Honey Springs.

"Your wife told me *you* hit him from behind," he said more to himself than to Becker as he continued trying to pin down whatever it was that was bothering him.

"I was merely approaching Morris when Harriet killed him," Becker said. "Cimarron, I'm telling you the truth."

"Your partner, Otis Shepherd, told me he was with you and saw you brain Morris."

"I was alone. Otis was not with me. I was coming home from the Mercantile—"

"You're saying Shepherd's a liar?"

"I'm saying simply that I am telling you the truth."

"Cimarron," Rose said from her chair, "let's get him out of here before—"

"Shut the hell up, Rose," Cimarron barked. "Becker, Foley Weeks told me the same story about the murder of Morris that Shepherd did."

"I don't care who told you what," Becker shot back. "*I'm* telling you the truth."

Cimarron pinched his eyes shut momentarily between the thumb and index finger of his left hand. When he opened them again, his gaze rested on the breakfast tray Becker had placed on the night table beside the bed. Something clicked in his mind.

Something about Reuben Becker. Something about the tray, about the way he had seen Becker place it on the table next to the bed. And something else. A memory, echoing faintly in his mind. Harriet Becker and something she had told him:

"*Jim was killed instantly. The right side of his skull was completely crushed.*"

But Becker, Cimarron thought, when he had picked up that tray . . .

Otis Shepherd's suddenly remembered voice reverberated in Cimarron's mind:

"*That's when Reuben, enraged as he was and close to being hysterical, picked up a stone and struck Morris with it, smashing the entire right side of Morris' head.*"

Foley Weeks, Cimarron remembered, had said the same thing as had Harriet Becker and Otis Shepherd concerning the blow that had killed Jim Morris.

"Becker," he said, "pick up that tray that's sitting there on the table."

"Why—"

"Do it, Becker!"

Becker reached out with his left hand and picked up the tray, holding it out toward Cimarron. "What am I supposed to do with this?"

"Put it back on the table," Cimarron ordered, and Becker obeyed. "Now, I want you to pretend that there's a six-gun lying on the floor just in front of your feet. I want you to bend down and pick it up."

"Oh, let him alone, for heaven's sake!" Nell cried, close to tears. "Stop tormenting the poor man."

Cimarron gestured peremptorily and Becker bent down and picked up the imaginary gun in his left hand, aiming it at Cimarron.

Cimarron nodded thoughtfully. "Becker, everybody I talked to about the murder—the ones who said they'd seen it happen—told me you brained Morris from behind."

"I didn't."

"Shut up, Becker! They said you were standing behind him and you smashed his skull."

"Harriet was standing behind him," Becker insisted wearily. "She did it, not me."

"Is your wife right- or left-handed?" Cimarron asked Becker.

"Right-handed. But what—"

"When you picked up that breakfast tray a minute ago and then that make-believe gun—you used your left hand both times. You're left-handed."

"Yes, I am, but I fail to see what that has to do with anything."

"It has to do with the murder of Jim Morris, Becker,"

Cimarron said, feeling some of the tension that had been stiffening his body begin to ease. "You said—so did Otis Shepherd and Foley Weeks—that Morris' skull had been busted on the right side."

"It was—because Harriet struck him on that side."

"There it is, as plain as pie," Cimarron said.

"I don't understand," Nell murmured faintly.

"Picture this," Cimarron said. "You've got somebody standing behind Jim Morris. This somebody's got a stone and this somebody slams the stone against Morris' skull, cracking it on the right side." Cimarron, almost smiling, waited.

"Right side, left side," Rose declared impatiently. "What difference does it make? Cimarron, let's *go!*"

He noted the puzzled expressions on Becker's and Nell's faces and then said, "A left-handed somebody would have smashed the left side of Morris' skull if that somebody was standing behind Morris."

Becker leaped to his feet, his left arm outstretched, a finger pointing at Cimarron. "I get it," he crowed. "I'm *left*-handed!"

"Darling," Nell began, reaching for him.

"If you'd've hit Morris from behind," Cimarron said, "you'd've opened the left side of his skull, not the right."

Becker sat down on the bed, his eyes still on Cimarron. "Then you believe me?"

"I believe you," Cimarron answered. "I believe it was your right-handed wife who killed her lover, Becker."

"She did," Becker said firmly. "She told me that she was going to accuse me of the crime. She said no one would believe that she did it because everyone knew they were lovers. They would believe, she said, that I did it because people knew I was jealous of Harriet, and I was until I met Nell here and we became—"

"Oh, Reuben," Nell cried happily and embraced Becker.

"Oh, hell," Rose exclaimed angrily. "After all the trouble I went to and now there's to be no bounty. There isn't, is there, Cimarron?"

He shook his head and Rose swore.

"How come, do you suppose," Cimarron inquired thoughtfully, "Otis Shepherd says you did it, Becker? Shepherd and Foley Weeks both?"

"Frankly, I have no idea. As I told you before, Cimarron, Otis wasn't there. Neither was Foley. I'd left Foley behind to lock up at the Mercantile and Otis had remained at home all that day nursing his catarrh. No one saw the murder, I'm certain, except Harriet and myself."

"But now Shepherd and Weeks claim to have been eyeballing the whole thing from start to finish," Cimarron mused. "And they both pegged you as Morris' killer."

"Reuben has told you the truth, Cimarron," Nell cried. "Just as he told it to me when I got here. I believe him. Can't you?"

"I said I believed him, Miss Cooper. It's just that I'd sure like to know why Shepherd and Weeks are lying about what happened."

"If I died," Becker said slowly, "or were killed, Harriet would inherit my share in the Mercantile, Cimarron."

"That'd make her and Shepherd partners, huh?"

"Otis has been wanting to buy me out but I wouldn't sell. Harriet, I think, would sell if she had control of my interest in the business."

"I reckon I see the trail you're traveling, Becker. But what about Weeks? What's he got to gain if you're dead?"

"Nothing, as far as I know."

"Must be something, though. Or is Weeks the kind of man who likes to lie a lot?"

"He's a decent man. Hardworking. God-fearing. No, there would have to be some compelling reason for Weeks to lie about what happened as he has done."

"Maybe we can find out what that reason is once we get back to Honey Springs," Cimarron commented.

Rose let out an anguished wail.

"What's the matter with you?" Cimarron asked her, but he realized he knew the answer to his question before she squalled, "I'll never see a single cent of that bounty money now!"

Cimarron holstered his .44 and went over to her. He squatted down in front of her as she sprawled weeping in the overstuffed chair and said, "You know what it says in the Bible, honey: 'The Lord maketh poor, and maketh rich; He bringeth low, and lifteth up.' Well, one of these days maybe He'll make us both real rich since He's seen fit to keep us so dirt poor so far."

Rose's wail increased in intensity, and as it reached a crescendo, she pounded her small fists on the arms of her chair.

"There's more," Cimarron said, reaching out and brushing the tears from her cheeks. " 'He raiseth up the poor out of the dust, and lifteth up the beggar from the dunghill, to set them among princes.' Now, that's something to look forward to, Rose, honey—the two of us hobnobbing with princes."

"What am I going to do?" Rose cried.

"You're going to go home to Fort Smith," Cimarron told her gently.

"But I came so far and I had such hopes, Cimarron."

"So did I, honey, so did I."

Rose reached out and placed both of her hands on Cimarron's shoulders. "Tell me something, and tell it true. Were you really going to kill him?"

"Becker?"

She nodded.

Cimarron cocked his head to one side. "I had me a mighty powerful hungering for that thousand dollars, Rose, same as you."

"That's not answering my question."

"I'm not so sure what I would have done once the game was almost over and I'd been called." He glanced at Becker, pondering Rose's question, knowing he had had doubts, from the very outset, about what he had set out to do. He looked back at Rose, leaned forward, and kissed her on the tip of her nose. "Sometimes it's best for a man to have an unanswered question or two in his life. This, I reckon—for me, at least—is one of those times. If I had the answer to your question, I'm not so sure I'd like it all that much."

He got to his feet and held out his hands to Rose. He lifted her to her feet, put an arm around her, and turned to Nell Cooper and Becker, who were still seated side by side on the bed. "I'm putting Rose on the train to Honey Springs. She has business to tend to back in Fort Smith, and the sooner she sets about tending to it, the happier the men there'll be." He hugged her and added, "Miss Cooper, I think you ought to take the train along with Rose here."

"I don't want to leave Reuben," Nell said, looking into his eyes.

"Cimarron's right, Nell," Becker said. "You take the train with Rose. Cimarron and I will ride north together as soon as I'm feeling better."

"You're sick?" Cimarron peered at Becker.

"He's feverish," Nell volunteered.

"You do look a bit peaked, Becker," Cimarron observed. "And I'm a bit tuckered out. I guess there's no real big hurry for us to head out to Honey Springs. We could hole up here in the hotel till your fever's gone and my bones stop feeling like they've every one been bent the wrong way."

"Cimarron," Rose said, "be careful. I want you to be sure to make it back to Fort Smith—to Mrs. Windham's—in one piece."

"I'll be careful, honey. Now, let's get you and Miss Cooper on that train."

In midafternoon on the day following the departure of Rose and Nell from Boggy Depot, Cimarron awoke in the soft bed in the room he had rented in the town's hotel; yawning, he stretched lazily.

He lay there naked on the bed staring up at the ceiling, feeling fresh and almost completely free of pain now. Tentatively he bent his ankles, then his wrists. They made no protest, nor did his pelvis when he maneuvered his hips.

I'm next to new, he thought, and ready to ride. He wondered if Becker was. The man's fever had subsided somewhat the night before, but he was still weak. Well, there's always the train, Cimarron thought. Becker could sell his horse and take it. He could lay low up in Honey Springs. Nell Cooper would be glad to help him do that, Cimarron was certain.

Eager to head north again, he got out of bed, poured water from the pitcher on the bureau into the bowl sitting beside it, and washed himself. When he was dressed, he started for the door, but before his hand touched the doorknob, someone knocked.

"Becker?" Cimarron called out, his hand reaching for his .44.

"Cimarron, let me in!"

Taken totally by surprise at the sound of Rose's voice on the other side of the door, Cimarron reached out, unlocked the door, and swung it open.

Rose hurried into the room and slammed the door behind her. "Cimarron, you've got to get out of here. You and Reuben Becker. Get him and get out of here, both of you. Now!"

"Hold on, Rose. What the hell are you talking about? And what the hell are you doing here?"

"Nick Hammond's gunning for you, Cimarron!"

"Hammond? Why's he after me?"

"Harriet Becker hired him after I went to see her." Rose's gaze lowered. "You remember that I told you I stole Becker's wallet when he and I were in the hotel room in Limestone Gap together?"

"I remember. But what's Becker's wallet got to do with Nick Hammond?"

"There's no time to explain," Rose insisted. "Not now. Maybe later. Cimarron, he'll kill you both."

"I need to know what's going on and why, Rose. Now, slow down and take your time, but tell me."

"All right. On the train on the way to Honey Springs, I did some thinking. I still had Becker's wallet, and thinking about it, I had an idea. When the train arrived in Honey Springs, I went to Harriet Becker and gave her the wallet. I told her I'd killed her husband—that the wallet was proof I had killed him—and that I wanted the bounty money.

"But she just laughed at me. She said she'd told me and Aaron when we first talked to her that she wanted Becker's corpse. That was the only proof she'd accept. I made up some cock-and-bull story about not being able to bring Becker's body to her because he had fallen down a ravine after I shot and killed him.

"She kept right on laughing at me. She told me she knew me for what I was the minute she first laid eyes on me. She called me a slut. Some other names too that were far worse. Well, I got mad then and I told her that she might fancy herself an upright and respectable lady but she would soon get her comeuppance. I told her that you had caught up with Becker here in Boggy Depot and that you'd figured out that it was her who had killed Jim Morris, not Becker. I told her you were coming after her to arrest her for murder.

"After that *she* got mad and she admitted that she'd killed Morris because he'd started seeing another woman and was going to leave her in the lurch. She said you'd never take her. She said she'd see to it that you and her husband would both be killed—by Nick Hammond. She said she'd heard he was in town and she was going to pay him to kill the two of you. She said he was a man she knew could do the job and one who would do it gladly because, she said, he'd killed over ten men since he first took to hiding out here in the Territory. She said she was going to double the bounty. She said she would pay Hammond one thousand dollars, and that, with Mr. Morris' five hundred, would make fifteen hundred all told. Cimarron, I took the train and came back here to warn you. You've got to run!''

"I've never run from a fight in my life and I'm not about to start running now. Hammond's a hard case, there's not the least little bit of doubt about that. He's wanted on a dozen or more charges, but no federal deputy's yet come even close to running him to ground."

"Maybe *you* don't run. But Becker had better. He's no gunfighter. Hammond will kill him and it will be your fault if he does."

Cimarron considered Rose's last statement. He wasn't particularly worried about Hammond. He was sure he could take care of himself where Hammond was concerned, and he even welcomed the potential chance to arrest the man and take him to jail in Fort Smith. But Becker was another matter altogether. Rose was right, he decided. He'd have to see to it that Becker was safe and then he could start keeping his eyes peeled for Hammond. Meanwhile, Harriet Becker would be sitting tight in Honey Springs, a plum ripe for his picking—when he was ready to do the picking.

"Well, Cimarron?"

He bent down and kissed Rose on the forehead. "I sure do thank you for coming all the way back here to warn me. Now, you stay right here in my room for a few minutes. I'm going to Becker's room downstairs and tell him what you just told me and then I'll be back for you."

"You won't be long, will you?"

"I'll be back faster'n you can get used to the idea that I'm gone." He left the room, hurried down the hall, and then bounded down the stairs to the main floor. He went through the archway and, a moment later, was knocking on Becker's door.

"Who is it?"

"Becker, open up. It's me."

Once inside Becker's room, Cimarron quickly told him about Rose's unexpected arrival and about what she had just told him.

"Nick Hammond," Becker exclaimed when Cimarron had finished speaking. "He's one of the worst outlaws in the entire Territory, from what I've heard."

"You heard right. I had a run-in with Hammond once—it was late last year—just north of Ardmore in Chickasaw Nation. He gave me the slip that time and I've not laid eyes on the man since, but I can tell you that Judge Parker would give a year's growth and the same amount of salary thrown in for good measure to see Hammond standing before his bench to answer for the crimes the man's committed since he came down here from Kansas."

"What are we going to do, Cimarron?"

"You feeling strong enough to take a train ride?"

"Yes. But I thought we were going to saddle up and ride north together."

"We were. But now, because of the chance that Hammond may be coming after your hide as well as mine, we'd best change our plans. You take the train to Honey Springs. Miss Cooper can hide you in her house there. Hammond won't be looking for you so close to home. He will, though, be looking for me—here, probably, since Rose told your wife that you and me were here in Boggy Depot."

"I can leave right away."

"You'd best to do that. I'll walk you down to the depot—no, I'll go get Rose first and then walk you both down to the depot. Once I've got the two of you safe on the train—"

Cimarron's words were cut off by the sharp sound that suddenly resounded somewhere inside the hotel.

"Was that a shot?" Becker asked him anxiously.

"Sounded like one." Cimarron opened the door, went down the corridor, and peered across the lobby at the knot of people who had gathered at the foot of the stairs and were staring up them. A sense of foreboding swept over him. He went back to Becker's room and said, "You stay here. Lock the door after me."

"Where are you going?"

Instead of answering Becker, Cimarron left the room and ran down the corridor.

"A shot," someone said as he shouldered his way through the growing crowd at the foot of the stairs. "It came from the second floor," someone else said as he bounded up the stairs, drawing his Colt as he did so.

124

When he reached the landing, he raced down the corridor and saw that the door to his room was open. As he reached the open doorway, he halted and holstered his gun. He reached out and placed the palms of his hands against the wall on either side of the door, staring down stricken at Rose, who lay on her back on the floor of the room near the bed, several men surrounding her and talking in low tones among themselves.

Cimarron drew a deep breath, entered the room, and elbowed his way in among the men, who made way for him. He stood staring down at Rose for a moment—at her closed eyes and at the blood soaking through the front of the shirt she was wearing.

"We're sure awful sorry," a man behind Cimarron told him. "Was she your wife?"

Cimarron shook his head. "She was a friend of mine."

"I saw him," another man said. "Lean, he was. Tall. Mean-looking. Reminded me of a half-starved wolf. He went out the window onto the roof after he shot her."

"He had black eyes," Cimarron said dully. "Black hair. A nose as crooked as a buffalo's back."

"How'd you know?" one of the men inquired. "You weren't here, were you?"

"His name's Nick Hammond," Cimarron said, bitterly regretting having left Rose alone.

The name was repeated in awed whispers by several of the men—*nickhammond, nickhammond, nickhammond*—a harsh and evil incantation.

Cimarron's body sagged. He sank to his knees. "Oh, Rose," he whispered, bending over her. "Rose, I'm so sorry. I shouldn't have left you." His right hand rose and covered his eyes.

His hand fell away when he heard Rose faintly whisper his name. "Rose! I thought you were—" He acted without thinking, acted on the basis of the feelings that the sight of her had stirred within him as he knelt beside her. He lifted her to a sitting position and held her close to him. "Get a doctor somebody," he snapped. "Get him quick, dammit!"

"Cimarron—no."

"Rose, you're going to be all right." His hands on her back were warm with her blood. "The bullet went right on through. You'll be—"

Rose, with her cheek pressed against Cimarron's chest as he held her tightly, shook her head, the ghost of a movement. "Hammond," she said.

"I know." Cimarron's right hand rose as her head rolled to one side. He placed it behind her head to steady it, continuing to hold her against him, wanting to swear, to strike out hard at Nick Hammond, wherever he might be in the world.

"I let him in, Cimarron. He said he was you. He said he followed me—took the train. Harriet Becker, he said, pointed me out to him."

"I'll put you on the bed, honey."

"No!" Rose said, her voice suddenly as vibrant as it had always been. "Don't let go of me. Not now, Cimarron." She drew a deep breath and Cimarron heard the bubbling in her throat. "Harriet told him I'd be likely to lead him to you, and I did."

"Rose—"

"He told me he got your room number from the desk clerk, Cimarron. He wanted to know—I told him I didn't know where you were. He said he'd kill me if I didn't tell him. But I wouldn't—" Rose's voice faded away before, with an obvious effort, she continued, "He shot me, he said, to make one less bounty hunter—and as a warning to you."

Cimarron glanced at the room's window, which had been closed when he left the room earlier and was now wide open.

"Cimarron?"

"I'm here, honey, right here."

"Almost every Saturday night when you were in town." Rose drew her head back slightly, looking up at him. She tried hard to smile and failed.

"Those Saturday nights of ours in Fort Smith, honey, they were as fine as any I ever had. Finer."

"Don't," Rose murmured, and managed to raise one hand to gently touch Cimarron's wet cheeks. "I said I wanted to be free. Remember?"

"I will be soon." Rose's hand dropped and her arm hung limply at her side. "Some Saturday night— Cimarron, where are you?"

He clutched her tightly and his head dropped. He buried his face against her shoulder.

"Some Saturday night when you're with some woman in some town somewhere—cheat, Cimarron. Think of me. Don't tell her. But think of me. Think of how wonderful it always was with us."

Cimarron looked up as he felt a hand come to rest upon his shoulder. "You the doctor?" he asked the man with the tired eyes who was standing above him.

"Let her down easy, son, so I can take a look at her."

Cimarron eased Rose to the floor and continued kneeling beside her, his arms hanging helplessly at his sides.

The doctor, on one knee, took her wrist between his thumb and index finger. He shook his head and turned to Cimarron. "Dead," he said in a voice that was as tired as his eyes.

The word thundered in Cimarron's mind as the doctor closed Rose's eyes and stood up. It cannonaded through his consciousness, but as it did, he knew it was a word he would use himself one day . . . and hopefully soon. When he spoke it, he knew it would be over the body of Nick Hammond. He vowed vengeance: it was a poor promise he made to Rose, but it was all he had to give her, all he would ever be able to give the woman whose lively laughter replaced the ugly word "dead" in his mind as he remembered other days, other times with her.

He slowly got to his feet. He backed out of the room, past the cluster of men who were still standing within it, his eyes on Rose, her blood still warm on his hands.

9

Cimarron and Becker made arrangements with the town's mortician for Rose's burial and then, upon leaving the man's grim establishment, made their way to the livery stable where Cimarron's black and Becker's bay were stabled.

"Rose and Aaron started out together from the same place," Cimarron mused as they walked along, "and they both ended up at the same kind of place."

"We'll be lucky if the two of us don't wind up in a similar place," Becker observed morosely.

"Well, there's no use in us sweating and fretting about that," Cimarron said, and clapped Becker on the back. "What we've got to do now is keep our eyes wide open. Our ears too."

"For Hammond."

"Him, sure. But there's two others we got to watch out for as well." Cimarron told Becker about Jesse and Belinda Burgess. "They were real upset about me killing their daddy and it's likely they'll still be prowling about ready and waiting to do me in. You too, Becker."

"Because of the bounty."

Cimarron nodded. "So we've got three people to steer clear of if we can. All three of them have awful good reasons for wanting you and me dead." Cimarron paused, thought for a moment, and then suggested, "Becker, maybe it'd be best if we split up. That way it might be that we'd each of us'd have a better chance. You could ride east or west a ways before heading up north again to Honey Springs. If I run into Hammond or the Burgesses, I could decoy them away from you long enough for you to reach Miss Cooper and hide out with her."

"I'd be a whole lot happier remaining with you, Cimarron. I'm not all that good with a gun and the only one I have is this Smith and Wesson forty-four-forty and it's a bit ungainly, if not downright clumsy, in a man's hand." He patted the holstered revolver that hung from his cartridge belt. "I am, after all, a merchant, not a gunslinger. I haven't got the stomach for killing, but I guess I could kill if I had to save my own hide."

"You didn't do so bad when you were shooting at Rose and me not so long ago."

Becker glanced at Cimarron, saw the grin on his face, and said, "I'm mighty glad now I didn't hit either one of you. If I'd killed—or even hurt—you, well, Cimarron, you're a man it's comforting to have on one's side. That's been plain to me for some time now."

"We'll travel together, then," Cimarron said flatly, ending the discussion.

After reaching the livery and getting their horses ready to ride, Cimarron and Becker each paid the stableman what they owed; ten minutes later they rode north out of Boggy Depot together.

As they rode, Becker talked of his life with Harriet, how good it had been when they were first married, and how bad it had become when he realized she was not a woman to be content with one man. He told Cimarron how hard he had tried to please her—to satisfy her insatiable sexual appetites and how, in the end, he had failed.

"Jim Morris wasn't her first lover," he commented ruefully. "There were others. Two I knew about. Probably others I never knew about. Nell Cooper was my salvation. She was kind where Harriet was cruel. Loving where Harriet had become hateful.

"Cimarron, how is it that things can go so sour between two people who once loved each other?"

"Can't answer that, Becker. Though I can speculate. When two people love each other a whole lot and the fire burning between them gets so hot—well, sometimes maybe it just burns itself out."

"I felt so guilty at first when I started seeing Nell on the sly, and even worse when I knew I was in love with her and she was in love with me. I'm no saint, but I was never all that much of a sinner either."

"Good and bad, right and wrong," Cimarron said, shaking his head. "They differ from time to time and from place to place. Sinning's what some people decide's going to disrupt things so that they don't run smooth, and that means trouble for the people who're trying to keep a lid on things and make other folks tow the line—their line."

"Preachers, you mean."

"They're in on it. So are politicians. Probably most of them have a notion they're doing the right thing, only I find it awful hard to see why it's wrong for a man like you or me to make love to a woman from time to time.

" 'Course, the pulpit pounders'd say that the good Lord frowns on such carrying-on. I suspect He doesn't mind it all that much, since I'm told He wants us to love one another. I do the best I can where that godly admonition and lovely ladies are concerned."

"I'm inclined to agree with you," Becker said. "Marriage is fine enough, but it's more a way of keeping people and society at large in line, like you said. Harriet and I were living totally destructive lives together. But Nell and I—we help each other along and we don't hurt anybody because of our relationship."

"A lot of what society calls sin I call having a helluva good time without hurting anybody."

Cimarron said no more, noting Becker's pensiveness, and the two men were riding through Limestone Gap before he spoke again.

"I'm hungry, Becker. How about you?"

"Ravenous."

"That place up ahead looks as good as any, and stopping to eat there'll save us having to shoot our supper."

The two men dismounted in front of the building above which hung a sign that said, TASTY MEALS SERVED CHEAP.

They went inside and ordered beefsteaks and boiled potatoes, which they washed down with black coffee that was strong but only lukewarm.

When they had finished their meal and paid for it, Becker, once they were outside again, turned to Cimarron and said, "There's a hotel down that way. We could stay the night there."

"We could. But I think we'd be better off out in the open. If Hammond comes looking for us, a hotel's one of the first places he'll look. I figured we'd ride on, camp out tonight for a few hours, and move out early in the morning. The sooner we settle this matter of your murdering wife, the better I'll like it. That suit you?"

"It does. Like you, Cimarron, I'm eager to see this matter brought to an early end, although I don't like the idea of seeing you cart Harriet off to jail."

"It's where she belongs."

"I can't argue that point with you," Becker said as he stepped into the saddle of his bay. "But it saddens me, I must admit. Harriet's a strong woman in some ways, but jail could kill her."

Cimarron boarded his black and moved out, saying nothing more about Harriet but marveling at Becker for wanting to save his wife from hardship even though the woman had tried to have him killed for a crime he didn't commit. He wondered whether Becker knew that something worse was in store for Harriet than jail, namely, one of George Maledon's stout ropes, which would go around her neck if a jury convicted her of the murder of Jim Morris. Becker, he decided, probably hadn't thought that far ahead. Probably didn't want to. Or maybe wouldn't let himself. A man's mind, he thought as he rode out of Limestone Gap with Becker beside him, plays him for a fool more than once in his life. It lets him see the world in a way that suits him whether that way's real or not.

The sun was down now and Cimarron, as he rode, searched for a place to spend the night. He wanted one with water, good graze, and some kind of shelter.

Purple shadows had claimed the land and were quickly becoming black shadows when he found what he had been searching for. He pointed to it and said, "See that crick running just east of us? We can camp beside it in the willows growing along its banks. Our horses can graze there easy. The grass is tall on account of the creek. It probably floods in heavy rains and when the snow melts in the spring."

They made for the spot Cimarron had selected, and once there, Becker saw to both of their horses while Cimarron walked about the area, looking first in one direction and then in another.

North of the spot was a stretch of rolling plain that appeared from his vantage point to be a series of rounded ridges stretching into the distance. To the east was open plain and to the west beyond the creek was more open plain, upon which grew occasional clusters of pin oak and loblolly pine. To the south the plain was flat and featureless.

Becker left the horses standing hock deep in the creek and drinking noisily. As he came up to Cimarron, he asked, "You want to bed down here?"

"I'll bed down here," Cimarron replied. "You'll bed down on the other side of the creek." He turned and pointed. "Over there. In among those scrub oaks."

When Becker gave him a puzzled look, Cimarron explained, "If somebody's out scouting for us, they'll like as not stumble on only one of us if we bed down in separate places."

"Good idea. I'd not have thought of it."

"I might not have thought of it neither, except that I've seen critters use the same tactic in my time. You take a pronghorn antelope doe, for example. Say she's got herself two kids. What she'll do is she'll hide one in the grass in one place and the other one some distance farther away, so that if some painter comes stalking her kids, it'll likely get one but the other'll have a chance to escape. Whereas it wouldn't, if it'd been snuggled up next to the first one. The painter'd take them both that way."

"You think Hammond might be around here someplace?"

"Don't know if he is or not. Don't plan on making things easy for him if he is. Now, I'm a light sleeper. If a grasshopper so much as spits or shits, I'll hear him. How about you, Becker?"

"I can't say I'm a light sleeper, no."

"Then try to stay awake as much as you can tonight, so nobody'll have a chance to sneak up on you. You can sleep in the saddle when we head out in the morning.

"And, Becker—take your horse and hide him in among the trees along with yourself."

Becker nodded and went down to the creek, which he forded on stepping-stones, leading his bay.

Cimarron stood watching until Becker had disappeared among the trees. Then he went down to the creek and led his black from it. He was starting back toward the willows that were growing not far from the creek's bank when he halted, his hand dropping down fast and coming up with his .44.

Belinda, who had just stepped smiling out from behind a

willow, threw up her hands and said, "Hello there Cimarron," in a light and decidedly seductive voice.

"Where is he?" Cimarron snapped, scanning the trees behind Belinda and the area on either side of him.

"Jesse? He went home after we managed to get ourselves untied."

"But you didn't."

"No, I didn't, as you can see."

"You should have."

"I really couldn't."

"Why not?"

"There was something I had to do first."

Cimarron frowned.

"You remember what I did to you, don't you?"

"I remember you and your brother tried to tear me limb from limb, if that's what you mean."

"That's not what I mean and I suspect you very well know it isn't. I was referring to what I did when you were tied to that tree the other night. You do remember?"

"I remember."

Cimarron did, and remembering now, he began to stiffen as he stared at Belinda, whose face was faintly visible in the light of the rising moon. As her tongue slowly licked her lips, his shaft grew, thrusting down along his thigh.

"Becker's not here," he said coldly, "so you wasted your time looking for him and me."

Belinda slowly lowered her hands and took a step toward Cimarron and then another, her hips swiveling, the smile still on her face.

Cimarron cocked his Colt.

Belinda kept coming.

He fired.

She didn't look down when the bullet tore up the dirt a short distance from her feet. "You don't want to kill me, Cimarron," she said softly. "You and I both know what you really want to do to me—and, Cimarron, I want you to do it to me."

She was only a foot away from him now and she raised her arms, an invitation. "I've not got a gun, Cimarron. I gave mine to Jesse to take home with him. I have only my horse, which I left back there in the willows when I spotted you a minute or so ago down at the creek."

"You're a night rider, are you?"

Ignoring the question, Belinda stepped up to Cimarron and her arms went around him.

"You're hurting me," she murmured, and reached down and pushed his revolver away from her ribs.

He holstered it as her hands slid down his body and came to rest on his thighs. He kissed her when she raised her face to him. He parted her teeth with his tongue and probed her mouth.

She drew away from him, her breathing shallow and swift, and said, "I want you, Cimarron. I wanted you the other night, but Jesse—if he'd known, he would have killed me for what I was doing, even though I only did it to torment you then. But now—I didn't come searching for you to talk, Cimarron." She took his hands and placed them over her breasts. "You do want me, don't you? I couldn't stand it if you turned away from me."

Cimarron kissed her again. But he didn't close his eyes. He continued to search for signs of Jesse's presence. He found none.

Belinda thrust her left leg between his legs and moved it slightly, tantalizingly.

Cimarron released her and, drawing his gun, moved cautiously toward the willows. He ducked in among them, ignoring Belinda's faint and plaintive wail from behind him, and darted from one tree to the next until he had searched the entire grove and found it to be empty. Only then did he return to Belinda.

Disregarding her pouting expression, he reached out and began to unbutton her shirt and jeans, which he pulled down. He took her nipples between his thumbs and index fingers and gently massaged them.

"Let's lie down," she whispered. She placed her hands on his shoulders and drew him down to lie on the thick grass beside her. She reached for him, found him, and began to massage him through his jeans. Then her fingers were tearing at the buttons on his jeans, and a moment later she had him out and her hands, one on top of the other, encircled him.

"Take it off," she whispered. "Your gun."

Cimarron was about to protest but then decided not to. Arching his back, he let Belinda unbuckle his cartridge belt and then slide it out from under him.

He sat up, took it from her, and placed it on the ground beside him. Then, straddling her, he sat on her thighs, his jeans down around his thighs, his shaft looming rigid above her loins. He reached out and covered her mound with one hand.

His hand moved slightly, moved slowly, and Belinda, her neck arching and her breasts rising, their nipples erect, moaned. As the middle finger of Cimarron's right hand entered her, she cried out, a faint sound, and then she was gripping him, stroking him, and begging him to take her.

"I want it," she cried, forcing his shaft down between her legs. "Oh, Cimarron, I need it! In me! Now, Cimarron!"

With one hand, she pushed his hand away from her and with the other, which still grasped his erection, she tried to force it inside her.

Cimarron let himself enter her but only partially. Bracing himself on his hands, palms flat upon the ground, he knelt over her and watched her face as her head swung fitfully from side to side and she continued to try to force him to enter her. Soft mewling sounds were coming from between her lips as she raised her pelvis from the ground in an eager effort to absorb his entire length.

"You really want it?" he asked, his voice husky.

"*Yes!*"

"You want it real bad?"

"Cimarron—"

"You want it bad enough to beg me for it?"

Belinda's eyes snapped open. She stared up at Cimarron, an unreadable expression on her face.

He thrust himself all the way into her then, forcing her pelvis down upon the ground, before abruptly withdrawing from her.

Their eyes met.

"Well, do you?" he asked her.

She hesitated as he knelt above her, and then, as her eyes lowered to his shaft, her lips parted. No words came at first, but then, with a sigh that told of her defeat at his hands, she whispered, "I'm begging you for it, Cimarron. Give it to me—all of it. *Please!*"

He smiled and seized his shaft in his right hand.

Belinda's eyes closed and her lips parted. Her chest heaved as she waited for him to enter her again.

But Cimarron's hand was at work and the intense pressure

that had been building within him quickly exploded and he shuddered in the ecstasy of release, spurting wildly to wet Belinda's exposed belly and breasts.

He seized his cartridge belt, rose, and quickly buttoned his jeans.

"Cimarron!" Belinda cried, propping herself up on her elbows, her eyes wild as she stared down at the white fluid streaming down her torso.

"I've heard it said," he remarked laconically as he buckled on his cartridge belt, "that what's sauce for the gander's sauce for the goose too."

Belinda flopped down on the ground, her naked torso glistening wetly in the moonlight. "I was so close to . . ." Her words trailed away and she turned her head to one side, clenching her eyes shut.

"What you did to me that night—you nearly drove me wild and then you went and left me. I couldn't even do for myself on account of the way my hands were tied. You're better off on that score right now than I was then. You want satisfaction, use your finger. You won't use me."

"*Damn* you, Cimarron," Belinda cried, springing to her feet. She pulled up her jeans and started for him, but then she apparently changed her mind. She turned and ran into the willows, her shirt flapping loosely behind her.

When she had disappeared, Cimarron grinned. But his grin vanished as he heard the sound of a horse fording the creek behind him. He turned, expecting to see Becker coming toward him, which he did; but he was surprised and simultaneously alarmed to see another mounted rider enter the creek behind Becker, a rider whose features he could not make out because of the distance separating them and the thin light of the moon.

His hand went to his gun. He was about to draw it from its holster, his eyes on Becker and the other rider approaching him, when someone behind him slapped his hand away and pulled his .44 from its holster.

"Don't turn around," a man said from behind him. "Hands high."

Cimarron's gaze, as he raised his hands, shifted from the man coming out of the creek behind Becker to the fat man who had stepped around in front of him. It dropped to his revolver, which was now tucked securely in the man's waistband.

A second man emerged from behind Cimarron and came to stand beside the first one. Like the first man, he also had a six-gun trained on Cimarron.

"Who the hell are you?" Cimarron barked at the pair.

It was Belinda who answered his question as she appeared suddenly from behind him to take up a position to the left of the two silent men, buttoning her shirt, her eyes angry. "They're friends of mine."

"They're my friends too," said the rider who halted his horse behind Becker's as both men reached the group facing Cimarron.

"Good for you, Jesse," Belinda cried. "You got him!"

Cimarron stared up into Jesse's eyes for a moment, aware of the gun he was holding on Becker and of Becker's revolver in his waistband. Then he looked at Becker, who said, "He got the drop on me, Cimarron. I was kneeling down to picket my horse. He came up behind me and disarmed me."

"You did real good, Belinda," Jesse told his sister proudly. "You kept Cimarron busy so I could sneak up on Becker over there across the creek."

"We spotted the pair of you long before you got here to the creek, Cimarron," Belinda declared, a note of exultation in her voice. "We saw you separate. That's when Jesse went after Becker once I'd gotten your attention."

"Who are these friends of yours?" he asked.

Jesse said, "They found us back on the trail where you'd left us all tied up. We told them we'd make it worth their while if they untied us."

"You told them about the bounty," Cimarron said, his stomach seeming to sink within him. Becker doesn't stand the chance of a small puddle in hell now, he thought. Neither do I, looks like. Four against two.

"This is Cory," Belinda said, pointing to the man with the grizzled beard and side whiskers. "This is Hal," she announced, indicating the other man.

Cimarron glanced briefly at Hal—at the man's obese body, his chins, his stubbled jowls, lank hair, and lackluster blue eyes. He turned his attention to Cory then, deciding that Cory was probably more of a man to be reckoned with than Hal. Cory was lean but muscular. His face was as rawboned as his body and his brown eyes had iron in them.

"I'm sorry, Cimarron," Becker said softly. "I should have been more careful."

"Too late to lament that you weren't," Hal said in an oddly shrill tone of voice, as if there were laughter behind his words just waiting to burst forth.

"Let's kill Becker and be done with it, Hal," Cory said, his thin lips barely moving, his words as crisp as the glint in his eyes.

"Then we can take his body back to his wife," Jesse said.

"And split the bounty four ways," Belinda chirped.

"Three ways," Hal amended.

"Wait a minute," Jesse said. "We agreed on a four-way split when we met. We've done our share. More than our share. Belinda and I, we've seen to it that we got Becker. We led you to him just as we promised we would."

"We were taking a chance on you two," Cory said, stepping back a few paces. "You could have been telling us a cock-and-bull story about the bounty."

"We weren't," Belinda cried. "We told you the truth."

"Cory and me," Hal said, "talked things over while we were hiding out back there in the woods. We decided that you and your brother were entitled to one share between you."

"There'll be no bounty," Cimarron said. He proceeded to tell them about what had really happened to Jim Morris, concluding by stating that he intended to arrest Harriet Becker for the murder of her lover.

"I don't believe you," Belinda cried when he fell silent. "You're lying!"

"He's not," Becker said. "A left-handed man couldn't have hit Morris on the head from behind the way it actually happened. I didn't kill my wife's lover. She killed him."

"And I mean to see to it that she pays the price for what she did," Cimarron added flatly.

Belinda let out a roar of frustration as Jesse and Becker dismounted. Hal, turning to Cory, remarked snidely, "That sure was some performance Belinda was putting on with this loose-living lawman we watched from back there in the woods."

"She ought to go on the stage with her act," Cory said, grinning widely to reveal his crooked yellowed teeth.

"That's a shameful thing to say, Cory," Hal remarked with feigned disgust. "Sometimes I don't know what you or this wicked world we live in is coming to. A sorry state, that seems certain enough. Why, look at him! He don't show the least little bit of remorse for what he done, and him a lawman here in the Territory like he told us he was when he was talking about Morris' murder."

"You think he's repentant, Hal?"

"Repentant? He looks like a cougar savoring a mouthful of mountain goat. But maybe we can make him repent."

"Shoot him in the knee, Hal," Cory said, licking his lips. "Lame him."

"Light a fire, Jesse," Hal ordered, "and be quick about it."

As Jesse gathered wood and started a fire, Cimarron turned to Hal, who seemed to be the more dominant of the two men who had taken him by surprise, and said, "I'm tired of reaching for the clouds."

"Then put your hands down," Hal said, "but if they make one wrong move, I'll put a bullet in them and then one or two in the rest of you for good measure."

Cimarron put his hands down as Hal said something he didn't hear to Cory.

Cory moved into the trees, and when he reappeared several minutes later, there were two coiled leather bullwhips in his hands. "The tools of the freighter's trade," he crowed, holding them high above his head. "These is guaranteed to make any mule or man move, and move right sprightly."

Hal smiled faintly. "Hand one of those whips to Becker, Cory. Give the other one to our good friend Jesse here."

Cory did as he had been told.

"What are those whips for?" Belinda asked.

"For chastening this lawman we caught," Hal answered.

"Jesse and Becker are going to whip him?" she asked, beginning to smile, her eyes glowing in the light of the fire, which was now blazing and driving back the darkness.

"It'll be a pure pleasure," Jesse hooted happily, and snapped the braided leather whip he was holding, which had, like the one in Becker's hand, a hickory handle and a buckskin popper on its tip.

"Cory!" When Hal had the man's attention, he said, "Rip the lawman's shirt off!"

Cory strode up to Cimarron, his gun cocked and rammed against Cimarron's groin. He obeyed Hal's command, letting

Cimarron's torn shirt drop to the ground before turning slightly and asking Hal, "Why don't we just shoot this damned deputy and be done with it?"

"Maybe we'll do just that," Hal said, "once we've had some fun with him. He's a shifty son of a bitch, this here lawman is. Talking about there's not going to be no bounty for Becker on account of it was his wife who did the killing and not him. Now, that may be the way the law sees it, but I see it different altogether."

"How do you see it, Hal?" Cory piped nervously, frowning his puzzlement.

"Your brains must have gotten fried when we were freighting down Sonora way, Cory. Maybe it's true like Cimarron said that it was Harriet Becker who killed Jim Moris. But that don't alter one bit the fact that she wants her husband dead and is willing to pay to see him in that sad state. Once Jesse and Becker have trimmed a little hide off the lawman, maybe we will kill him right along with Becker. It'd serve him right, seeing as how he was so shamefully rutting with lovely little Belinda here."

Laughter rumbled from between Hal's lips and then abruptly died. "Lawman, you stand right where you are. Jesse, move out a ways. You too, Becker—on the far side of Cimarron."

Jesse eagerly took up a position on Cimarron's right, but Becker stood without moving on his left, the whip motionless in his hands.

"Becker, pick up that whip and lay it on the lawman," Cory yelled as he hunched over, prepared to watch the spectacle.

When Becker didn't move, Hal frowned and said, "You don't whip him, Becker, you'll take his place."

"No!" Jesse protested. "I don't want to whip Becker. It's Cimarron I want to cut. I told you Hal. He killed our pa."

"Simmer down, Jesse," Hal said in a grating voice that was meant to be soothing. "You'll get what you're yearning for where the lawman's concerned. Now you, Becker—you'd best do as you're told or you'll regret not doing it."

"You said you were going to kill me," Becker said in a low tone. "You might as well do it and get it over with. I'm not going to whip Cimarron."

"Yes, you are, Becker," Cimarron said sternly, and Becker's face assumed a startled expression. "You're not dead yet."

He stared steadily at Becker, hoping the man would realize he was playing for time even if his stalling meant that he would have to endure a whipping.

"The lawman's right, Becker," Cory cried. "You're not dead yet. But you soon will be if you don't start cracking that whip and cracking it real smart the way Hal just told you to do."

Cimarron, his eyes still on Becker, didn't see Hal's signal. His body jerked as Jesse's whip struck his chest and curled twice around his bare upper arms and torso.

"*Becker!*" Hal shouted furiously.

With obvious reluctance, Becker drew back his arm and then, an agonized expression on his face, sent his whip whirling through the air toward Cimarron, who stood stolidly and took the blow from the braided leather. Becker's was not nearly as painful as the one Jesse had just given him, because Becker had put so little effort into what he had done.

"Don't *tickle* the bastard," Cory screeched at Becker. "Put some muscle into your swing next time."

Becker did, squeezing his eyes shut in order not to see the results of what he was doing.

The result was a series of welts on Cimarron's body, pink at first and then an angry red as the whips in the hands of Jesse and Becker *thwapped thwapped* as they struck him, one after the other in a painful rhythm.

Moments later, Becker did open his eyes, and when he saw the blood staining Cimarron's biceps, chest, and back, he winced and dropped his whip.

Hal fired a single shot and Becker cried out as the bullet went harmlessly past him but close enough to cause him to begin to tremble. Hal pointed with the barrel of his revolver to the whip on the ground and Becker slowly bent down and picked it up. As Hal's gun barrel rose again, Becker took a deep breath and sent the slender length of leather flying through the air to circle Cimarron's upper body, its popper slicing the skin on Cimarron's chest, sending more blood flowing down into his navel.

Jesse continued drawing his whip back and then letting it fly. Each time he jerked it hard the moment it struck, almost toppling Cimarron once, spinning him around in a circumscribed circle several times before the whip unwound and finally freed him.

Cimarron's chest, back, and upper arms were a crisscrossed series of welts now, most of them bloody, all of them excruciatingly painful; and it seemed to him, as the minutes passed and Cory urged Becker and Jesse on, that his world consisted of only three things—two leather whips and pain so strong it seemed to be shattering him.

"No more," Becker suddenly screamed. "I can't hit him again!" He let his whip fall and slumped to the ground, his head dropping into his hands.

Cory strode toward him menacingly but stopped when Hal gave a shout and ordered him to leave Becker alone.

"The lawman's had enough," Hal announced. "For now," he added ominously.

But Jesse's whip was already snaking through the air again, and this time it knocked Cimarron's hat from his head and slashed his face, almost blinding him as the buckskin popper hit the corner of his left eye, drawing blood.

Cimarron let out an enranged roar and seized the end of the whip with both hands. He jerked it hard and it flew out of Jesse's hands. He swung it in a wide arc above his head, and then, aiming carefully as he judged the distance between himself and Jesse, he smashed the heavy hickory handle against the side of Jesse's head, bloodying it and sending Jesse pitching forward onto the ground.

"*Lawman!*"

Cimarron's hands tightened on the whip as fury tore through him and Hal took a step toward him. He dropped the whip and stood there, bleeding profusely, his upper body racked with pain.

"Now that's sensible, Cimarron," Hal said, halting his advance. He paused a moment and then asked of no one in particular, "That was entertaining, now, wasn't it just? "Real arousing." His eyes flicked toward Belinda. "I never have understood why seeing somebody suffer makes me so horny, but it always does."

Belinda, as she stared back at Hal, stood without moving, seemingly transfixed.

Cory, noticing Hal's interest in Belinda, said, "You promised me, Hal."

"And I'm a man who keeps his promises, Cory. You can have her, sure you can. But only after her brother's had her. Get the boy up on his feet."

As Cory hauled the dazed Jesse to his feet, Belinda, her eyes widening and her head moving slowly from side to side, turned and then began to run.

Cory brought her down before she had covered more than a few yards. Lying on top of her, he turned his head toward Hal and whined, "I never get to go first."

"You can be next in line right after Jesse. He'll warm her up for you."

"Hal, you're loco," Jesse cried in a strained voice as he held one trembling hand against the side of his head where the whip's hickory handle had struck him. "I couldn't! She's my sister!"

"She's a woman," Hal countered. "Never you mind about the niceties."

Jesse took a step backward and went for his guns, but Hal's gun swung around, aiming at him.

"Drop them," Hal barked, and as Jesse reluctantly did, Hal said, "Cory, you get her ready. Jesse, you get yourself ready. Open up your jeans and be sure to open them wide enough so as they won't bind you. That way you'll be able to enjoy yourself."

Jesse, his eyes on Hal's gun, which was aimed at his midsection, reached down and with trembling fingers began to unbutton his jeans.

10

"Hal, I *can't!*" Jesse's face was contorted in an anguished grimace as he stood with his jeans down around his thighs.

"He's as limp as overcooked Eyetalian spaghetti," Cory said, snorting. "Hal, he'll never get it up, so why don't I slip it to Belinda?"

Cimarron watched Belinda struggle to get out from under Cory and his face remained impassive as he saw Cory give her a vicious slap with his free hand.

He turned his head and saw that Becker had gotten to his feet and was standing rigidly, his face frozen in shock and horror.

He looked back at Hal, who was moving forward to stand in front of Jesse, who cringed away from him as Hal's gun barrel raised his flaccid flesh and then let it drop.

"Jesse, you treat it right, it'll pop right up all ready and raring to perform," Hal said brightly. "Go ahead. Do it, boy!"

Jesse took himself in his hand, but after several minutes of trying, he remained limp, a look of desperation on his face as Hal frowned and said thickly, "Looks to me like it's good for nothing but pissing through. But maybe your sister can help you out of the sad spot you're in. Cory, get up and bring Belinda over here."

When Cory, holding tightly to Belinda's right arm, stood beside Hal, Hal said, "Show a little sisterly love for your brother, Belinda."

Her wordless response was to claw at Cory's face with her free hand, causing Cory to hit her on the side of the head with his gun barrel, momentarily stunning her and almost causing her to fall.

Hal reached out. He seized Belinda's left hand, thrust it against Jesse's groin, and held it there.

Jesse closed his eyes, from which tears began to slide.

"Now, you do him good, Belinda," Hal demanded. When he released her hand, she jerked it away and placed it behind her back.

Hal made a grab for her, and as he did, Belinda raised one foot and buried it in his thick paunch, doubling him over. She swung on Cory. He cursed when her fisted hand hit his jaw, and he threw her to the ground.

Cimarron, as Cory tried to grab Belinda, bent and quickly retrieved the whip Hal had earlier forced him to drop. He raised it high above his head and snapped it smartly, sending it slashing out and away from him to firmly encircle Hal's thick neck.

He jerked the whip toward him as Hal, gagging, dropped his revolver and clawed with both hands at the whip that was choking him.

Cory released Belinda, whom he was dragging to her feet, and turned to fire at Cimarron, but Cimarron let go of the whip and sprinted swiftly forward to seize Hal and shove him toward Cory.

As Hal fell heavily against Cory, Cory's gun flew from his hand and then both men hit the ground hard.

Cimarron quickly picked up Hal's and Cory's guns. From the corner of his eye, he saw Jesse pulling up and buttoning his jeans. Not far from Jesse stood Belinda, a dazed expression on her face. At his feet, Hal and Cory were untangling themselves and starting to rise.

"Stay put," Cimarron commanded, and both men went rigid.

Jesse moved up and stood beside Cimarron. "Are you going to kill them?" he asked.

Before Cimarron could reply, Jesse gave him a shove, and as he stumbled sideways, Jesse kicked him in the shins. Cimarron let out a howl of pain.

Before he could regain his balance, Jesse slammed both fists down on his left wrist, knocking the gun from his hand, which Cory scrambled to retrieve.

Jesse kicked Cimarron a second time, shoved him again, and then wrestled the second gun from his hand as Cory's fingers were about to close on the first gun Cimarron had dropped.

Cimarron threw himself to the ground, seized the gun Cory was about to retrieve, and sprang to his feet before Jesse could get his hands on the other dropped gun.

Hal pulled Cimarron's Colt from his waistband and was about to fire when Cimarron fired first. His bullet entered Hal's body just above his waistband and Hal screamed as it did, dropping the gun he had drawn.

Cimarron put out a boot and covered the gun as Hal screamed a second time and Cory scuttled backward along the ground away from Cimarron.

Then Cory was up on his feet and running. He grabbed Belinda and, using her as a shield, backed toward the spot where the trees were thickest.

Belinda's eyes widened and she seemed to suddenly realize what was happening to her. She jammed both of her elbows backward, and as they struck Cory, he yelped and lost his grip on her. She ran, sobbing, toward her brother, but he was running toward the spot where he had earlier dropped his guns in obedience to Hal's order.

Cimarron fired, deliberately missing Jesse but causing him to halt, turn, and hold up his hands.

Cimarron raced past the still-paralyzed Becker in pursuit of Cory, keeping Jesse in his sights as he did so, and when he caught up with the fleeing Cory, he seized him by the shoulder. But Cory tore free. And then stumbled over a rock. He screamed as he fell facedown among the flames of the campfire Jesse had kindled earlier. Still screaming, Cory got to his feet but lost his balance and went down again, his clothes and hair causing the fire to blaze more brightly.

He jumped up and Cimarron backed away from him as he ran screaming dementedly in a ragged and directionless manner to unwittingly fuel the flames that were now feeding on his flesh and rapidly charring it.

Cory ran on—first one way, then another—a second fire illuminating the dark night until a rifle round hit him, causing him to lurch, scream wordlessly one final time, and then fall, to lie burning and writhing helplessly on the ground.

Cimarron, when the rifle shot had sounded, raced to where his Colt lay on the ground, picked it up, and spun around to face the direction from which the round had come.

Fire flashed from that direction and Cimarron fired in among the trees, but he turned swiftly when Becker screamed. He saw Becker drop to his knees, clutching his right arm. "Run, Becker," he yelled. "Your horse—get it and get out of here." When Becker didn't move, Cimarron raced toward him, vaguely aware of Jesse and Belinda racing into the woods as they fled the unseen attacker.

When he reached Becker, he practically threw the man into the saddle of his horse. "Go to your woman in Honey Springs," he muttered. He slapped the horse's flank, and when it went racing across the creek with Becker holding tightly to its reins and leaning against its neck, he ran to the left and dived for the only cover available to him—Hal's fat corpse.

He rolled the corpse over on its side to form a low battlement and waited for the attacker's next shot, the barrel of his Colt propped on Hal's lifeless body.

"I may have missed getting Becker," a man shouted from the cover of the trees, "but I'll get you, Cimarron."

Cimarron recognized Nick Hammond's voice.

"The undertaker in Boggy Depot," Hammond shouted, "said he saw you two head north. Heard from the man in the restaurant in Limestone Gap that a scar-faced man had eaten heartily at his place and then rode north. Cimarron, you and your friends sure do make the night noisy—and yourselves easy to find."

Hammond fired again as Cimarron lay low behind Hal's corpse and thumbed cartridges out of his belt and into the chambers of his .44.

As he rammed the final cartridge home, Hal's body bounced against him as several rounds that had been fired in rapid succession struck it.

Not Hammond, Cimarron thought. These were shots from a six-gun. *Jesse!* Somewhere out there in the woods not far from Hammond.

He suddenly realized that the night was brighter now, and an instant later he knew why. The grass to his right was ablaze, a fire that had been set by Cory's burning body. The crackling flames were racing toward him, and his horse, he realized, was on the far side of them. So was his Winchester in its boot behind his saddle.

And facing him but unseen among the trees were two men

bent on killing him. Belinda might be joining forces with them, he thought bitterly, once she's got her hands on a weapon.

He bellied down on the ground parallel to Hal's body and scurried crablike along the ground until he was only a foot from the rapidly approaching wall of flame. He sprang to his feet and hurled himself into the flames. As he emerged from them on the other side, he hit the ground and rolled over several times to put out the tiny fires that were beginning to consume his jeans.

He was up then and running, his torso and arms seared in places, causing the still-flowing blood—the result of the whipping he had endured—to bubble frothily.

He ran past the blackened bones that were all that was left of Cory, and when he reached his horse, he holstered his Colt and leaped into the saddle. He galloped into the creek and then through it, heading north.

He looked back over his shoulder several times as he rode, but he was unable to see or hear anyone pursuing him, which he was uncomfortably aware did not necessarily mean that he was not being trailed. When the sight of the burning grass behind him dimmed and then finally disappeared, he rode on for some time before dismounting. Kneeling on the bank of the creek, he washed away as much blood as he could from his chest, back, and arms, stifling the groans that fought to escape his lips because of the pain his actions were causing him.

When he had done what he could to cleanse himself, he got back in the saddle and rode on over an expanse of slablike projections protruding from the ground in an effort to hide his trail.

When the first predawn light appeared to gray the sky, he searched for a suitable place to stop and safely sleep in order to end the fatigue that was like a giant leech within him, draining away even his will to keep moving farther away from Nick Hammond, who would, he knew, surely continue searching for him.

But he found no satisfactory place on the high plain across which he was traveling, so he kept doggedly on, keenly conscious of the fact that he was visible to any rider within the radius of a mile or more.

The sun had not yet cleared the horizon when he spotted

the small herd of pronghorns grazing up ahead of him. Automatically, he reached behind him, but as his hand closed on the stock of his Winchester, he withdrew it, deciding not to risk a shot that might be heard by Nick Hammond if the man was on his backtrail.

He dropped the reins, and as the black beneath him slowed to a trot, he fastened a honda on one end of the rope that had been hanging from his saddle horn and slid the other end through it. Then, raking his horse with his spurs, he galloped toward the antelopes, all of whom, when they heard him coming toward them, performed their characteristic dance. Each animal pranced nervously in a circle, and as they did so, the bright white hairs along their rumps rose and became clearly visible, which was their instinctive means of displaying a danger signal that other pronghorns as far as a mile away could see and act upon.

Whirling the lariat he had made above his head, Cimarron guided the black with only knee pressure. As he neared the animals, they began to run from him. They were fleet, and because of the long strides they took, they threatened to outdistance him, but he continued to spur his horse and then he turned it and cut out one of the pronghorns. His lariat looped out, came down over the animal's head, and settled around its neck.

Cimarron drew rein and took several turns with the rope around the saddle horn before sliding from the saddle. He ran up to the animal he had roped, as his black, rearing backward, kept the rope taut. Bending down, he pulled his knife from his boot and with his left hand seized the antelope's right ear and jerked its head up. The knife's blade glinted in the first rays of the rising sun as it bit into and then along the pronghorn's throat, which geysered blood over Cimarron's jeans and the ground below.

When the animal slumped lifeless to the ground, Cimarron dragged it by means of the rope around its neck back to the black and he tossed the carcass over the horse's withers.

After removing the rope from the animal's neck, he rewound it and hung it from his saddle horn before boarding the black and moving out.

The sun had not yet reached its meridian when he came to a place where the flat country over which he had been riding gave way to a region of low rounded hills. He chose the one that was most thickly covered with junipers, which were interspersed with occasional aspens. He rode up its gentle slope, weaving in and out among the trees, many of which towered above him, until he reached the summit, where he halted and dismounted. After scanning the area on all sides, he selected a site that suited him—one that gave him a good view of all the approaches to the hill on which he stood.

He removed the antelope carcass from the black and dropped it to the ground. He led his horse to a thick patch of clover growing beneath the trees and picketed it there to graze. Returning to his kill, he got down on one knee, pulled his knife from his boot, and proceeded to skin the animal, after which he methodically cut away a large quantity of tallow. He spread some of the tallow on the ground in a rough rectangle and then lay down, letting his back rest upon it. The remaining tallow he rubbed on the burns on his chest and arms, and then, as his black nickered softly, he closed his eyes and let the tallow soothe his seared skin, wishing it could do more than temporarily soothe him, wishing it could completely eliminate the pain his burned body was experiencing while knowing that it could not.

But it's a comfort, he thought dreamily as he lay in the shade shed by the junipers, thinking of his encounter with Hammond and wishing he had been able to take the man then and there. But I've got bigger fish to fry, he reminded himself. Harriet Becker. Thinking of her brought his thoughts back to Hammond, the man she had hired to kill him along with her husband.

Hammond tried, he thought, recalling Hammond's reference to the man in the restaurant who had mentioned "a scar-faced man."

His hand rose to touch the scar on his face. It marks me as sure as if I wore a sign around my neck with my name and address written on it. The touch of the dead flesh brought back to him a memory that became a dream as he dozed: he was once again a boy helping his father to brand and castrate calves and he was trying his best, but his best wasn't good enough and the calf he was kneeling on threw him and bolted; his father, who was holding a red-hot branding iron, swore and swung the iron in anger, and it raked his son's unmarked face to scar it forever . . .

He snapped awake.

The pain he was feeling came not from the scar that marred his face but from the burned flesh on his arms, back, and chest despite his earlier application of tallow to the seared spots.

He lay there staring up through the branches, and he slept a deep and refreshing sleep that was not invaded by dreams.

When he awoke the following afternoon, he was ravenous.

His eyes rested on the carcass of the dead antelope and his mouth watered. But he would not risk building a fire: the breeze had died, and smoke from a fire just might find its way up through the branches into the open air to signal his presence on the hill.

He got up, drew his knife from his boot, and sliced off a piece of the antelope's haunch. He gnawed on it, blood running down his chin, and although it was tough, he managed to tear it to shreds with his teeth and swallow it. He ate another piece and then still another before his hunger no longer rumbled within him. He cut off another portion of the haunch and sliced it into thin strips that he hung over a juniper branch to dry. Then he cut off more tallow and rubbed in on his seared flesh.

While waiting for the sun to complete its descent, he took a tattered copy of *Hamlet* from his saddlebag and sat down to read it.

It was dusk when he finished the book. He closed it and returned it to his saddlebag along with the antelope jerky that the sun had dried. After boarding his black, he rode through the trees and down the northern slope of the hill into the gathering gloom.

In North Fork Town the following morning, he tethered his horse to the hitch rail in front of a dry-goods store and went inside the building, causing a shocked gasp from a woman customer standing at a counter near the door.

"I apologize for the sorry state I'm in, ma'am," he said. "But, you see, I went and lost my shirt and hat and had myself a speck of trouble down south."

The woman, flustered, seized the parcel the desk clerk behind the counter handed her and promptly fled the store.

"I'm in need of some new clothes," Cimarron told the clerk. "A pair of jeans, a shirt, and a good hat—let me have a look at those Stetsons you've got stacked up on the shelf there behind you."

"Yes, sir," the man said, his uneasy eyes on Cimarron's bare torso and arms.

When he had handed over the hats, Cimarron tried on several before choosing a black one that fit snugly. He squared the crown and nodded approvingly at his reflection in the hand mirror the clerk held up to him.

After completing his purchases, he carried his new clothes across the street to the barbershop, where he spent the next two hours gingerly bathing his battered body and then being shaved and shorn by the barber.

When he rode out of North Fork Town, bathed and barbered and wearing his slightly stiff new jeans and blue cotton shirt, and with his equally new black Stetson cocked at a jaunty angle, he was feeling, as he silently put it to himself, almost as brand-new as Adam when he first woke up in Eden.

Later, as he forded the north fork of the Canadian River, he took some of the antelope jerky from his saddlebag and ate it as he rode along and the sun glared at him, causing sweat to trickle from under his arms and run down along his ribs.

He slowed the black to a walk when he first sighted the buildings of Honey Springs in the distance. He found himself wondering if Becker had made it safely back to town—and to Nell Cooper. He wondered, too, what Harriet Becker would do when he arrived to arrest her. Whatever it was—and he was sure she would try something—he'd be ready for her.

A thought crossed his mind and he frowned. Was she still in Honey Springs? Or was she a running kind of woman? He doubted it. Harriet Becker, he felt sure, was the kind of woman to stand and fight. The kind of woman who, once on the trail she had chosen, would follow it to its end.

There was the matter of the Becker's Mercantile business. If Becker were out of the way, it would be hers. Hers and Otis Shepherd's. But Becker had said something about believing that Harriet would sell her share of the business if he had died or been killed. She'll not be abandoning it, he thought. She might not want the business, but she will be wanting the money her half-share would bring her when she sold it. And she couldn't sell it legally until it was hers, and it wouldn't be hers until she could prove that her husband was among the late lamented.

A smile appeared on Cimarron's face as he came closer to Honey Springs. Harriet Becker was not going to get her hands on the Mercantile. What she was going to get was her neck in a noose. His smile vanished and was replaced by a grim expression that grew grimmer as he saw the three riders leave the town and head toward him.

He had wanted to enter the town unnoticed, and if these were townsmen, he was about to be noticed. He turned his horse and headed due east toward the Katy's tracks. When he reached them, he crossed them and then rode around a string of empty freight cars that were parked on a siding so that they were between him and the three riders he had seen.

He slowed the black, judging how long it would take the men to pass him on the opposite side of the cars. When he felt certain that the men must be behind him by now, he walked the black toward the end of the siding; he had almost reached it when two men rode around it and halted their horses a short distance away from him, six-guns in their hands.

He drew rein and studied the faces of the two men he had never seen before.

"Get rid of your sidearm!"

The man's voice had come from behind him and Cimarron hesitated only a moment before unholstering his Colt and dropping it to the ground.

"Your rifle too," the man behind him ordered, and Cimarron unbooted the rifle and dropped it beside his Colt.

The two men in front of him moved toward him, neither of them speaking, both of them expressionless.

"I've got no quarrel with you gents," Cimarron told them. "Why're you gunning for me?"

Neither man answered him.

The man behind him said, "Get down off your horse, Cimarron."

"You mind telling me who you three are and how you know me?" Cimarron asked, stepping down from the saddle and taking up a position not far from his Winchester and Colt.

The man behind him suddenly appeared and moved his horse up beside the other two men. "We're your welcoming committee," he said.

"Harriet Becker hired you," he said, not really asking a

question as he silently cursed himself for not having anticipated such a development.

The man who had spoken nodded. "Get inside that boxcar."

Cimarron glanced at the car and then went up to it. He unlatched its door, slid it open, and climbed into the empty interior of what was or had been a cattle car, judging by its straw-strewn and manure-flecked floor.

He was followed by the two men who had not spoken to him, and before he could make any kind of move, one of them had pinioned his arms behind his back while the other one stood facing him.

"Where's Reuben Becker?" the man facing him asked.

"Haven't seen him in some time," Cimarron replied honestly.

The man holstered his six-gun and then threw a low right that slammed into Cimarron's midsection, doubling him over.

The man's knee came up and cracked against Cimarron's chin, snapping his head up to receive the man's hard left, which almost broke his nose.

"Where's Becker?" the man asked again, and when Cimarron didn't answer him, he turned his head and, speaking to the third man, who had remained outside the car, said, "Light a fire."

"Mrs. Becker," the man said then, looking again at Cimarron, "is mighty eager to know where her hubby's to be found. She set us to watching for you because she figured you might show up here sooner or later. She's got men posted on all sides of the town. We three got lucky and latched on to you."

Because Cimarron twisted his body to the right as the man in front of him threw a left jab, the blow bounced off his forearm.

The man holding him from behind kneed him in the small of the back and turned him around to again face the man in front of him.

Cimarron smelled smoke before he saw the fire the man outside the car had built and the running iron that was resting in it.

"You're going to tell us where Becker is," the man in front of him said matter-of-factly, "or you'll have more than one scar on your face when I'm through with you." His lips parted in a parody of a smile. "Maybe you'll be minus an eye or two on top of that." He stepped sideways and held out his right hand.

The man on the ground withdrew the running iron from the fire and handed it up to his companion, who took it and resumed his former position.

Cimarron, his eyes on the iron's red end, which was only inches from his face, said, "I reckon a corpse doesn't fret about whether or not it's scarred."

"Don't follow you." The iron in the man's hand didn't waver.

"Once I told you where Becker is—now, I don't know where he is, mind—but if I did and I told you, I figure that's the time you'd set about killing me."

The running iron in the man's hand moved closer to Cimarron's throat. Then it shifted to the side slightly as the man said, "Maybe I won't scar you after all."

"I'd be much obliged to you for your kindness," Cimarron said evenly, his arms beginning to ache in the tight grip of the man behind him.

"Maybe what I'll do," the man said, "is singe your hair. Hair burns swift. You got a temper, Cimarron?"

Cimarron stared at the burning iron. "There's some who've said I do."

"Well, this branding iron I'm holding can turn you into a real hothead for sure."

As the iron moved closer to his hair, Cimarron swiftly turned his head to the side and as swiftly stomped with his right boot as hard as he could on the instep of the right foot of the man who was holding him from behind.

As his victim let out an outraged howl, Cimarron stomped on the man's other instep, and when his grip loosened, Cimarron jerked to one side. As one of the man's arms released him, he swung around behind his attacker. He thrust out his leg and then he seized the man and shoved him backward over his outstretched leg. The man landed on his back with a thick thud and an equally thick grunt as the air was forced from his lungs.

Cimarron let him go and, crouching, swung his right arm. His forearm smashed against the forearm of the startled man who had been holding the iron, and it was knocked from his hand. He leaped up then as the man who had built the fire and heated the running iron boosting himself up into the car, his gun drawn.

"Hold it!" he shouted just before Cimarron knocked the gun from his hand by viciously booting and breaking the man's wrist. He bent down, grabbed the fallen gun, and threw it from the cattle car. Then, turning, he sprang to one side as the man who had been holding the iron got his gun out, took aim, and fired. His bullet buried itself in the wooden wall behind Cimarron, who, even before it had struck, was picking up the first man he had downed and lifting him. When he had raised the man, who was wordlessly howling, high above his head, he threw him at the man who had been about to brand him.

As the body hurtled through the air, the man on the floor fired, but his bullet hit the man Cimarron had thrown. The howling of the other man became a series of strangled gasps which, when he fell on top of his companion, degenerated into the whimpering of a whipped and dying dog.

Cimarron reached out as flames rose from the straw where the running iron had fallen. He seized the collar of the third man, who was crawling across the floor toward the open door. He lifted him bodily, turned him, and gave him a chopping blow with his stiff open hand that caused a bone in the man's neck to crack. As the man went down, Cimarron leaped from the inferno the cattle car was rapidly becoming.

He ran to where his Winchester and Colt lay on the ground, picked them up, holstered his Colt, and booted his rifle. Then, swinging into the saddle of his black, he gave one last glance at the cattle car, which was blazing now, before riding toward town, the screams of the badly burned men who were fleeing the hell they had unwittingly created a wild cacophony of anguished sound behind him.

He turned the horse quickly when he saw men, women, and children running from the town, obviously attracted by the flames and the screams of the men running from the burning cattle car. He pulled his hat down low on his forehead as he rode, not wanting to be seen by any of the people who were being drawn to the carnage on the Katy siding.

But then one of the running men attracted his attention and he quickly decided to take the risk involved in the action that had impulsively occurred to him. He rode back the way he had come and then in among the ragged flow of people, cutting Foley Weeks off from them and causing the black man to collide with the black.

Weeks, stunned, staggered backward, but before he could fall, Cimarron bent down, seized his right arm, hauled him up, and threw him facedown across the black's withers.

Weeks gasped for breath as Cimarron rode on, giving the town a wide berth, until he was on its northern edge. After scrutinizing the area carefully and seeing no one around, he galloped into Honey Springs thinking that the sentries Harriet Becker had hired must have deserted their posts to go and watch the barbecue he had just left behind him.

11

When he reached Becker's Mercantile, Cimarron dismounted, tethered his horse to the hitch rail in front of the store, and then hauled Foley Weeks to the ground. The man stood shakily, his eyes wide as they stared at Cimarron.

"Inside," Cimarron said, and gestured.

He followed Weeks into the Mercantile and asked the clerk behind the counter, "Where's Otis Shepherd?"

"In the storeroom," the clerk replied, pointing to the rear of the store.

"Everybody out!" Cimarron shouted, and made a sweeping gesture that encompassed the clerk and the two startled women who were examining bolts of cloth. He pulled down the shade to cover the window in the door.

"See here," the clerk began. "You can't—"

"I can!" Cimarron shot back, and took a step toward the clerk, which caused the man to run from behind the counter and beat the two women out the door. Then Cimarron latched it.

"Mr. Cimarron," Weeks said in a faint voice, "I—"

"You'll get your chance to talk," Cimarron interrupted, and then shouted, "Shepherd!"

A moment later, Otis Shepherd emerged from the storeroom, and when he saw Cimarron, he turned to run.

"Hold it, Shepherd," Cimarron yelled. When the man froze, Cimarron said, "Now you come on back out here where the three of us can be sociable together for a spell."

When Shepherd was standing next to the still-quaking Weeks, Cimarron asked, "Why'd you run, Shepherd?"

Shepherd's mouth worked but no words came from it.

"I'll tell you why you ran," Cimarron said amiably. "On

account of you heard from Harriet Becker that I was coming after her because I found out it was her who killed Jim Morris, not Reuben Becker. That right, Shepherd?"

"No—uh, I—"

"You're a lying sonofabitch, Shepherd," Cimarron snapped. "And your lies would have helped Reuben Becker climb the Golden Stairs on a rope."

Cimarron turned to Weeks. "I know Shepherd here had his eye on the Mercantile, which I figure might have made him lie about the murder. But you, Weeks, why'd you lie to me?"

"I didn't lie the least little bit, Mr. Cimarron. I told the gospel truth as God is my witness!"

Cimarron shook his head in mock sorrow. "Men like you two're enough to make a man like me lose his faith in human nature." His eyes darted from Weeks to Shepherd. "You lied to cover up Harriet Becker's crime and I'm as curious as a cat as to the reason why. You're going to tell me, Shepherd—"

Shepherd began to shake his head from side to side.

"—or I'll put you out of business," Cimarron concluded in a casual voice. As casually, he reached out and overturned a cracker barrel, spilling its contents on the floor.

He ignored Shepherd's sharp intake of breath and picked up the tin scale that sat on the counter. "Well, Shepherd?"

Shepherd said nothing.

Cimarron hurled the scale, which crashed through the plate-glass window, and then he put out one booted foot and overturned the counter behind Shepherd.

Shepherd, moaning now, clasped his hands together in front of him and held them out in supplication to Cimarron, who merely pulled his knife from his boot and walked along the line of grain sacks in front of the overturned counter, slitting them open, one after the other, until the floor was covered with oats, corn, and barley.

He glanced at Weeks, grinned, and held up the knife. "Since you don't own a business I can put you out of, it figures that it's you I'll have to damage when your turn comes round."

Weeks' eyes clamped shut and his lips moved, his prayer a whispered plea that Cimarron ignored.

He picked up a can of coal oil, opened it, and methodically

began to pour it over the bolts of cloth the two women had been examining earlier.

"Don't," Shepherd cried. "Please *don't!*"

Cimarron reached out and dislodged a shelf, sending cooking utensils clattering to the floor. He turned to Shepherd and Weeks and said, "I'm going to arrest Harriet Becker for murder. Now, what that means is Judge Parker'll need good witnesses to testify against her at her trial. I'm counting on the cooperation of you, Shepherd, and you too, Weeks, to do just that. You both said you saw what happened." Cimarron reached into a pocket of his jeans and came up with a wooden match. "Shepherd, fifty-percent ownership in a business isn't as good, I'm willing to allow, as a hundred percent is, but it's better than fifty or a hundred percent of nothing." He struck the match on a counter.

"Cimarron, don't!" Shepherd squealed, and lunged for the burning match. Cimarron shielded it from him and simultaneously kicked him in the midsection, sending him tottering backward.

"I'll tell you the truth," Shepherd gasped, "if you'll just put out that match."

"No!" Weeks cried. "Mistah Shepherd, sir, don't or Martha, she'll—"

But Shepherd ignored him as Cimarron pinched out the flaming match. His words erupted from him in a swift torrent. "I saw Harriet kill Jim Morris, but she promised to hand over Reuben's share of the Mercantile to me all free and clear once he was dead as payment for my testimony that it was Reuben and not her who killed Morris."

"Oh, Lordy, you gone and done it now, Mr. Shepherd," Weeks cried, weeping. "Now what Miz Becker going to do to my Martha?"

The name registered in Cimarron's mind and he recalled his earlier interview with Weeks, who had mentioned having a wife and a daughter named Martha.

"What's this about Harriet Becker and your daughter, Weeks?"

"She took her, Mr. Cimarron. Right after she killed Mr. Morris. She took her and told me if I didn't say that Mr. Becker did the murder, she'd murder my Martha same as she did Mr. Morris."

So that's it, Cimarron thought, nodding. He put out a hand

and gripped Weeks' shoulder. "I'll see to it that you get your daughter back. Where's Harriet Becker hiding her? Do you know?"

Weeks sobbed and shook his head. "But she say she let my girl go once Mr. Becker he be dead."

"You'll testify against Mrs. Becker once Martha is safe?" Cimarron asked Weeks.

"Oh, I'll be happy as a lark to do that, Mr. Cimarron. You don't know what me and my wife's been through since that woman took our chile."

"What about you, Shepherd?" Cimarron asked, and when Shepherd hesitated, Cimarron struck another match.

"Yes!" Shepherd screamed, his hands waving helplessly in the air in front of him. "I'll testify. I will!"

"You change your mind, Shepherd, and I'll come back here with a whole boxful of matches and a cart load of coal oil." Cimarron dropped the match, stepped on it, and went to the door, which he unlatched. Before leaving the Mercantile, he turned back to Shepherd and Weeks and said, "You've not seen me, neither of you."

"No, suh, Mr. Cimarron, I ain't," Weeks said hurriedly.

Shepherd nodded, looked down at the wreckage surrounding him, and shook his head sadly.

Outside, Cimarron freed his horse, swung into the saddle, and rode around behind the Mercantile. He rode west between the buildings on his right and the open plain on his left until he reached the rear of Nell Cooper's house, where he dismounted and led his black into the small fenced yard.

After closing the gate, he knocked on the back door and it wasn't long before it was opened by Nell Cooper.

"Cimarron!" she exclaimed. "Oh, I'm so glad to see you again," she declared, her face brightening. Then she threw her arms around him and he winced and let out an involuntary groan.

She released him. "What's wrong?"

He brushed past her, and when she was inside the kitchen with him, he closed the door and told her, "Been burned. Beaten." He told her what had happened to him.

"I'll get some salve. Sit down, Cimarron."

As she started to leave the kitchen, he caught her wrist and turned her toward him. "Did Becker get here?"

"Yes, he did. Thanks to you. I'll be forever grateful to

you, Cimarron. I'm afraid I completely misjudged you when we first met.''

"Maybe you didn't."

"I choose to believe that I did misjudge you."

He let go of her wrist. "Becker still here?"

She nodded and then hurried from the kitchen.

Cimarron sat down at the table and took off his hat, but before he had time to get comfortable, Nell was back, followed by Reuben Becker, whose right forearm was bandaged. Nell clutched a tin of salve in her hand.

"Cimarron!" Becker exclaimed, and held out his hand. "It's good to see you again."

As the two men shook hands, Nell said, "Take off your shirt, Cimarron."

When he had done so, she gasped.

Becker dropped his eyes and said, "I'm ashamed of myself for what I did to you, Cimarron."

"You had no choice at the time. There's nothing for you to be ashamed of. These whip welts'll heal."

As Nell gently began to rub salve over Cimarron's seared flesh, Becker asked, "How did you escape from Hammond?"

Cimarron told him as the soothing salve began to draw the heat from his burns.

"What about those two Burgess kids? Are they all right?"

"I expect they are," Cimarron answered. "But I don't really care whether they are or not. Jesse wound up shooting at me along with Hammond and I reckon if I'd not gotten my ass—beg pardon, Miss Cooper."

Nell giggled and then said, "My name's Nell."

"If I'd not gotten away from there," Cimarron amended.

"You've come here after Harriet, haven't you?" Becker asked, his face darkening and his eyes dulling.

"I have." He paused and then, "I just had me a little talk with Otis Shepherd and Foley Weeks over at the Mercantile." He told Becker about the conversation.

"Then you've just about wrapped up the case against my wife," Becker observed. "You've got two witnesses ready to testify for the prosecution—"

"But I haven't got the lady herself yet. I wanted to come here first, Becker, to see if you'd made it back safe and sound."

"There," Nell said, straightening. "That salve will dry in

a minute or two, Cimarron, and then you can put your shirt back on. Are you hungry, either of you?"

"Nell baked a pumpkin pie this morning," Becker said. "It's there—cooling on the windowsill."

Cimarron glanced at the pie and then told Nell, "Pumpkin pie goes down my gullet even easier than rhubarb pie and I do dote on it."

Smiling, Nell went to the window and carried the pie back to the table. She cut two pieces, placed them on plates, and as Becker sat down opposite Cimarron, put the plates in front of the two men. She took forks from a drawer and placed them beside the plates. "I'll make some fresh coffee."

"You've got some still in the pot, have you?" Cimarron asked, and when Nell nodded, he said, "Warmed over'd suit me just fine."

"Me too," Becker said.

Nell went to the stove and removed one of its lids. She placed a small log she took from the woodbox in the low flames.

"Your wife's holding a hostage, Becker," Cimarron remarked. "Foley Weeks' girl, Martha."

Becker's eyes widened. "So that's why Foley said he'd seen me kill Morris."

"It is. And Shepherd, he admitted to me that your wife was going to turn over the Mercantile to him without him having to pay her a penny for it. That's why he lied about the killing."

"Harriet must have really hated me to do what she did," Becker mused sadly.

"That's not necessarily the way the land lies," Cimarron remarked as Nell poured hot coffee into his cup. "More likely she just wanted to save her own skin and you were handy to help her do just that."

"But that's so callous, so cynical," Becker said.

"So sinful," Nell added in a strained voice.

"Maybe it's all those things you two've mentioned," Cimarron commented, and forked a piece of pie into his mouth. "What it also is, though, is a way she found to keep herself alive and kicking. Only it didn't work."

"When I got back here," Becker said, "I had a hard time getting past the men Harriet had patrolling the town's perimeters. The truth of the matter is I thought she would

163

have fled after Rose Collins told her you were coming after her, but she's still here. Cimarron, she'll kill you if she gets the chance. I have no doubt in my mind about that, none."

"Nor do I. But I don't plan on dying any time soon."

Becker dropped his eyes and toyed listlessly with his pie.

"Becker, I expect you know that if she tries to throw down on me, I'll have to defend myself."

"I know that, Cimarron. But knowing it doesn't make it any easier for me to accept."

"I'm hoping, though, to be able to take your wife to Fort Smith alive and all in one piece."

"What about the Weeks' girl?" Nell asked, sitting down at the table. "Will you be able to free her?"

"I'll have to find her first." Cimarron turned to Becker. "You happen to have any idea what your wife might have done with Martha Weeks?"

"No," Becker replied. "But she'd have to keep her someplace where she could be sure the girl couldn't get away. Somewhere in the house probably."

"Where in the house do you think?"

"Well, if I were faced with hiding a captive, I'd probably lock her up down in the root cellar."

"I'll have a look in your root cellar," Cimarron said.

"I'll go with you," Becker said.

"No, Becker. I'm going alone. I'll do my best to handle any trouble I might run into on my own. I don't want you getting yourself hurt or maybe killed. That would fit too neatly into your wife's plans. If anything happens to me, you'll still be alive and you can go and tell your tale to the court in Fort Smith and Judge Parker'll see to it that Shepherd and Weeks are sent summonses to testify against your wife."

Nell cleared her throat and said, "We haven't mentioned the men who've been guarding Harriet's house ever since she found out that you knew the truth about the murder."

"How many men?" Cimarron inquired.

"Two," Becker replied, and added, "at all times."

"Nell, have you got some kind of a bucket I could borrow?"

"Yes, I have. But what do you want it for, Cimarron?"

"When it gets dark, I'll borrow your bucket and be on my way," he said without answering her question.

* * *

Cimarron moved through the darkness that night carrying the tin bucket Nell had given him, keeping to the shadows cast by buildings and trees as he passed houses in which lamps glowed, little islands of peace and contentment, their occupants unaware of his movement through the night toward the Becker home.

When he neared it, he stopped and, standing with his body pressed against a tree, studied the house. No lights burned, but it wasn't long before he saw a man appear out of the shadows and walk slowly along one side of the house and then around it and out of sight.

He waited and his waiting was soon rewarded by the appearance of a second man moving in the opposite direction around the house. Second man? Cimarron wondered if it was a second man or the first one he had spotted merely retracing his steps. It was too dark for him to make out the man's features, so he couldn't be sure whether there were one or two men. Maybe, he thought, there's more than two.

When the man had disappeared around the side of the house, Cimarron put the bucket down behind the tree and then struck a match. As the kindling he had earlier placed in the bottom of the bucket caught fire, he thumbed five cartridges from his belt and tossed them into the flames before running as rapidly as he could to take shelter behind a nearby woodshed that stood beside the house next door to the Becker's.

He waited, his body tense and all his senses alert, as the minutes slowly passed. Then the first of the cartridges he had tossed into the fire in the bucket exploded, to be followed almost immediately by a second sharp report and then a third explosion.

Out of the shadows surrounding the Becker house came two men. They ran toward the sound of what they obviously thought was shooting, their guns drawn. When they saw the flames, they halted and stood stiffly staring down at the small fire in the bucket.

Cimarron darted out from behind the woodshed and brought the butt of his .44 down on the head of one of the men, who slumped unconscious to the ground. As the other turned, Cimarron swung and the butt of his gun cracked against the man's skull, bloodying his ear. It took a second swift blow to down the man, and when he, too, fell, Cimarron dropped to his knees, gagged both men with their bandannas, and bound their wrists together using the piggin strings he had taken from his saddlebags before leaving Nell Cooper's house.

He was about to rise and head for the house when he saw the light appear in a second-story window just above the roof. The lithe silhouette of Harriet Becker, who had obviously been awakened by the sound of the exploding cartridges, appeared in the window. She raised the curtain and peered out into the night.

"Sam, what's wrong?" she called through the open window. "Bob, are you out there?"

"We ran off a prowler," Cimarron called back, muffling his voice by holding a hand over his mouth.

For a moment, Harriet didn't move. Then, letting the curtain fall to cover the window, she withdrew, and a moment later the lamp in the room was extinguished.

Cimarron rose and sprinted toward the house. He circled it and found the slanting double doors at ground level that led to the cellar. He bent down and tried to raise them.

Locked. From the inside.

He bent down and managed to insert the barrel of his gun under a section of warped wood. Prying it up as far as it would go, he got his right hand under it and then, after holstering his Colt, his left hand. Straining, he pulled on the door, his boots braced on the stone slab that bordered it.

He continued pulling on it, using every bit of strength he could muster. Finally, the door in his hands snapped and flew upward, knocking him off balance.

He recovered quickly and as quickly went down the steps into the gloom of the cellar below the house. He struck a match and peered about him. When he spotted the door that was kept shut by a large two-by-four set in two iron braces, he made his way to it and removed the bar. As he swung the door open, someone inside the dank root cellar let out a frightened cry.

"Martha, your daddy sent me to get you out of here," Cimarron said quickly. "Now, you hush, girl. Take my hand."

He held it out to the terrified child cowering in the corner of the root cellar among bushel baskets full of turnips and potatoes, and she tentatively reached out and took it.

"No noise now," he warned her as the match burned his

fingers and went out. "You're going out through that door up there."

He led her to the steps and gave her a slight push up them. "When you get outside, you hightail it on home, you hear?"

"I will."

Cimarron climbed the steps, and when his head emerged above the remaining door that was still in place, he watched Martha race through the darkness. When she had disappeared from sight, he went back down the steps and lit another match. Its light showed him the way to the other steps on the far side of the cellar; they led up to a landing and a closed door.

He climbed the steps and tried the door—unlocked. He opened it and stepped out into the Beckers' kitchen. He felt his way through and then he struck another match. As it flared in his hand, he made his way down the hall he found himself in and then started up the stairs that led to the second floor, listening for sounds and hearing none.

Not at first. But when he neared the second-floor landing, he did hear sounds and he recognized them immediately for what they were.

They were sounds—moans and soft cries—of two people making love, and before the flame of the match died, he made out the closed door of the room from which the sounds were coming.

Dropping the dead match, he went to the door and stood there listening, drawing his Colt as he did so.

"It's so good—wonderful!"

He recognized the faint sound of Harriet Becker's voice.

Cimarron reached out and grasped the doorknob. He slowly turned it and then eased the door open slightly. Letting go of the doorknob, he struck another match and then booted the door wide open. He darted into the room and made out what appeared to be a single figure in the bed.

"Get up, and get up nice and slow," he ordered, and the naked arms fell away from the man's bare back that glowed ruddy in the light of the match's flame.

The man's buttocks rose as he pulled out of Harriet Becker, who shoved him aside and sat up, fear distorting her features as she tried to cover herself with the sheet that lay crumpled at the foot of the bed.

The man turned and sat up on the bed, his legs splayed out before him, his erection tottering.

Cimarron reached out and lit a lamp that was on a table just inside the door. "Looks like I got lucky," he remarked. "Got me two birds with one stone. Get up, Hammond, and get dressed. You too, Mrs. Becker."

"Sam," Harriet breathed. "Bob."

"What did you do to the men guarding the house?" Nick Hammond asked. "You killed them, Cimarron?"

"Nick!" Harriet cried. "Do something! He's going to kill us both!"

"I'm not," Cimarron assured her. "I'm taking the two of you back to Fort Smith to stand trial. You, Mrs. Becker, for the murder of your lover. You, Hammond—well, I've lost count of all the crimes you've committed here in the Territory, but I'm certain Marshal Upham hasn't. Now, dammit, move—both of you! Get dressed!"

Harriet got up and reached for her undergarments as Hammond swung his long legs over the opposite side of the bed and bent down to pick up his clothes, which lay scattered on the floor beside the bed.

Harriet, instead of getting dressed, turned toward Cimarron and her hands ran seductively down her sides and then along her thighs. She smiled. "You don't really want to see me hang, do you, Cimarron?"

"I'll be happy to see you hang so high you can look down on the moon, honey."

Harriet took a step toward him, and as she did so, her hands rose to cup her breasts. "I could be real nice to a big handsome stud like you, Cimarron. I could make you"—she took another step—"feel just fine. I know I could. There's no reason for us to be enemies. We could be good friends—a whole lot more than good friends."

"The way you and Morris were?"

"Better than the way Jim and I were."

"He wound up dead from an overdose of your friendliness and—"

Cimarron ducked as Hammond threw a boot at him and the boot went over his head to thud against the wall behind him.

Harriet lunged for his gun, but he threw her to one side with his free hand as Hammond's hand came out from under the pillow where he had thrust it. He fired the revolver he had retrieved, but he missed Cimarron, who had dropped to one knee and fired almost simultaneously. His bullet went through Hammond's left forearm and buried itself in the bed.

Harriet backed away from Cimarron as he said, "Throw that gun down, Hammond, or you're a dead man, even though that'll mean I won't collect the two dollars due me once I deliver you to the court in Fort Smith."

Hammond, with a snort, tossed his gun, which struck Cimarron's left boot.

"Now, are you two going to get dressed or am I going to take you both in as naked as newborns?"

Harriet and Hammond began to dress, not looking at each other and also avoiding Cimarron's eyes.

"You beat me back here and decided to wait for me to show up, is that it, Hammond?" Cimarron asked.

Hammond nodded, holding his wounded arm, from which blood was flowing.

"We all waited for you."

Cimarron felt a gun barrel jab his spine and he realized that it was Jesse Burgess who had spoken from behind him.

"Toss your gun to Hammond," Jesse ordered as his gun barrel bit deeper into Cimarron's back.

As Cimarron threw his Colt and Hammond caught it, Belinda entered the room and took up a position in front of Cimarron. Smiling up at him, her hands on her hips, she said, "My brother and I joined forces with Nick. We knew you'd show up here sooner or later, Cimarron, and when we heard the shooting, we were sure you'd arrived. It's so nice to see you again. Especially in light of the fact that you're worth so much money to us."

"Which brings us around to Becker," Hammond growled. "Where is he, Cimarron?"

Cimarron remained silent, watching Harriet slip her dress on and button it demurely.

"Harriet," Hammond said, "you might as well hand over the five hundred you're paying to have this lawman killed. He'll be dead in a minute."

"But he's not dead yet," Harriet responded pointedly.

"Don't kill him yet," Belinda cried. "Not until he tells us where Becker is."

Cimarron said nothing.

"We can make you tell us," Jesse said, hatred alive in

his black eyes as he came around to stand in front of Cimarron.

Harriet scurried across the room to a chest of drawers, pulled the bottom one open, rummaged about in it, and came up with a fistful of paper money that she brandished at Hammond. "Do it, Nick! Do it now! Kill him and this whole thousand dollars is yours!"

"Ours," Belinda said sweetly. "The bounty money is to be split three ways. That was what we agreed to when we joined Nick."

Hammond held out his free hand.

Harriet hesitated only a moment and then thrust the money into it.

As his fist closed on it, Hammond smiled. "How much will you pay on top of this thousand for your husband, love?"

"Another five hundred—when you find him and kill him."

"He's worth a thousand, seems like to me," Hammond declared.

"All right!" Harriet had screamed the words. "I'll pay you another thousand when you've killed Reuben!"

"You'll pay *us*," Jesse amended.

"Back up, Jesse," Hammond commanded. "Step to the side so I can get a good shot at the lawman."

Jesse did and Hammond fired.

But not at Cimarron. His bullet tore into the back of Jesse's skull, splitting it wide open.

Belinda screamed as her brother fell facedown on the floor, but her scream was cut off by Hammond as he fired a second time and then a third time, both of his bullets entering Belinda's chest and causing her body to jerk spasmodically as her hands groped wildly in the empty air.

She fell against Cimarron, who caught her and eased her to the ground.

"Nick!" Harriet exclaimed in a shocked voice. "You told me they were your friends—your partners!"

"I lied," he said, still smiling. "To you and to them about that little item. I never had any intention of splitting the bounty with those two snot-nosed kids. I did figure they might come in handy somewhere along the way, and they did, but I never figured on splitting the bounty money with them."

"Bastard," Belinda breathed, and died in Cimarron's arms.

"You pegged him," he said to Belinda, although he knew she could no longer hear him as he stared up at Hammond and then at the gun in the man's hand: it was aimed directly at him.

Harriet ran toward Hammond, and when she reached him, he shoved her behind him.

"Kill him, Nick," she cried. The words had barely left her lips when the window behind her shattered and her body convulsed. A look of horror spread across her features. It collapsed quickly into one of dismay. She crumpled to the floor and her eyes stared sightlessly at Cimarron, who dropped down and flattened himself on the floor.

He seized Hammond's gun, which had been lying near his boots since he had disarmed Hammond earlier.

"Hold it, Hammond," he ordered, both of his hands on the butt of Hammond's revolver, which he held angled up toward the man.

Hammond, recovering from his surprise at the shot that had killed Harriet, spun, aimed Cimarron's own gun at him . . .

Cimarron fired. His bullet took out Hammond's left eye as it burned its way into the man's brain.

As Hammond screamed and staggered backward, he dropped Cimarron's .44. The money flew from his hand and fluttered to the floor as Becker climbed through the broken window from the roof, his still-smoking Smith & Wesson in his hand.

Cimarron got to his feet, retrieved his Colt, and tossed Hammond's gun onto the rumpled bed. "How'd you get up on the roof?" he asked Becker.

"My ladder was out back."

"Thanks for your help."

"I couldn't not come, Cimarron. But I'll admit I was afraid if I did come here I'd do more harm than good."

"The harm you did was good. If you hadn't of done it, I might well be dead now."

"Nell tried to stop me."

"I'm glad she didn't succeed."

"I didn't mean to shoot Harriet. It was Hammond I was aiming at, but he put her behind him—between him and the window."

Cimarron sighed and holstered his Colt. It's like the scene

at the end of *Hamlet*, he thought. The queen and her consort are dead. So are his two hangers-on.

Words and phrases from the last scene of *Hamlet* that he'd been reading earlier echoed in Cimarron's mind . . .

O villainy! as he looked down at Harriet, no longer beautiful in death.

He is justly served, as his glance roved to Hammond, blind forever now, although one eye still remained to him.

The sight is dismal as he looked at and then quickly looked away from the twisted wreckage that were Jesse and Belinda Burgess.

This fell sergeant, death, is strict in his arrest, as his eyes turned inward upon himself.

Someone . . . someone alive . . . speaking. To him?

He blinked and saw Becker standing in front of him. He looked down at the money that Becker had gathered up from the floor and was holding out to him.

He shook his head. "I started out as a bounty hunter. But somewhere back along the trail I changed."

"You saved my life, Cimarron. Not to mention my business and reputation. All that is worth far more to me than this thousand dollars."

"I just told you, Becker. I'm not a bounty hunter."

"This money is not a bounty. It's a payment for vital services rendered to a man who is more than merely grateful to you for all you did for him. I know you're not a bounty hunter. What I don't know is, are you a damned fool?"

"I may be damned," Cimarron said in answer to Becker's question, "but I don't think I'm a fool."

Becker, smiling, handed the thousand dollars to him.

Cimarron, grinning, took it.

SPECIAL PREVIEW

**Here is the first chapter
from**

**CIMARRON
AND THE HIGH RIDER**

**seventh in the new action-packed
CIMARRON series from Signet**

1

As he rode along the northern bank of the winding Arkansas River, Cimarron took off his flat-topped black Stetson and wiped his forehead with the back of his hand. It came away sweaty.

He clapped his hat back on his head and used the blue bandanna that was tied around his neck to wipe the sweat from the rest of his face.

His cotton shirt clung to him, its blueness turned black because of the sweat that was oozing from his chest, back, and arms.

In the sky above him, the early-morning August sun blazed, unchallenged by a single cloud. Beneath his horse's hooves the buffalo grass grew lushly as a result of its partnership with the hot sun and the fertile earth that had been soaked by a heavy rain the night before.

As he rode into the small settlement of Parson's Point, Cimarron's eyes roved to the small house that was set far back

Excerpt From THE HIGH RIDER

from the narrow dirt street. He found himself wondering if she were home, and as if in answer to his speculation, Jenny Marlow's head and shoulders appeared in a ground-floor window.

When she saw him, she waved wildly.

Cimarron returned her wave and then rode out of Parson's Point toward the Cookson Hills, thinking of Jenny and all that they had done together during their ardent meetings in the not-too-distant past and of how she had done it all as wildly as she had just waved at him. He smiled—and almost turned the black beneath him.

But visiting Jenny was one thing. Courting her, if that was the name for what he did when they were together, was always a rewarding experience. Cimarron's smile broadened. But courting a run-in with her father and her three burly brothers . . . His smile died.

The last time he had been in Parson's Point the four Marlow males had almost caught him with Jenny as they dallied in the thick clover growing in a secluded spot near the river. That had been a close one, he recalled. A whole lot too close for comfort. He was sure he could take on two of the Marlows at a time if that ever became necessary, but he was just as sure that he couldn't take on more than two at a time. Every one of them—the old man, Case Marlow, and the three brothers: Bart, the eldest, Jamie, the middle one, and Sooner, the youngest—was built as big and as broad as a four-seated outhouse.

Cimarron rode on, reminiscing about Jenny, letting the black set its own slow pace, for he was in no particular hurry to get back to Fort Smith, where Marshal Upham would, no doubt about it, have some new assignment to hand him.

But would he? Cimarron suddenly wondered. Maybe Upham wouldn't want him working as a deputy marshal because of the way he had set out to collect the bounty Harriet Becker had offered him without so much as a by-your-leave. Marshal Upham, he knew, could be testy. At times temperamental.

Cimarron absently patted the pocket of his jeans, which held the thousand dollars in bounty money he had collected. He nodded thoughtfully, thinking that the money would help him hold out for a time if Upham asked him to turn in his badge.

The money was a consolation, no doubt about that. But Cimarron was aware that his thoughts had made him uncomfortable. Why? The answer was obvious to him. Because he liked being a lawman—an officer of the District Court for the

Excerpt From THE HIGH RIDER

Western District of Arkansas. Being a lawman made him feel—how? Like I've got me a place in the world, he decided finally. Like I'm not just some fiddle-footed drifter dreaming dreams that probably won't ever come true while wandering all over creation looking for the pot of gold that's supposed to be sitting at the end of a rainbow somewhere.

He rode on, decidedly uneasy now and on the verge of regretting his earlier hasty departure from Fort Smith to set out after what had been, he now clearly realized, his own particular version of the pot of gold at the end of the rainbow.

By midafternoon he was in sight of Fort Smith, which sat sprawled on the far bank of the river. He touched his black with his sunburst spurs and the horse broke into a trot.

But he suddenly drew rein when he saw the two men come tumbling out of the willows that were growing along the bank of the river. He sat his saddle, watching as the pair, locked together like some bizarre puzzle, rolled over and over on the ground.

One of the men managed to disengage himself. He leaped to his feet and kicked the man on the ground, who then got to his feet and threw a right that his opponent easily deflected by thrusting his forearm forward.

Cimarron watched the fight for a moment. He was about to move on when one of the men went for his gun.

"Hold it, you two," he shouted, and rode up to the men, who had been momentarily immobilized by his words.

"You two want to go at it knuckle and skull," he said when he drew rein beside them, "that's just fine with me. But there'll be no killing."

"This matter's private between Billy and me, mister," the taller and older of the two men shot back.

"You were going to gun me down, Charlie," Billy cried in an awed tone of voice as he stared fixedly at the gun in Charlie's hand. "And me, I'm not even armed!"

"Gunning you down's too good for a bastard like you," Charlie countered. "What I ought to do is I ought to stake you out on the ground and cut your eyelids off so the sun can blind you. A man who'd steal from his employer deserves no better!"

"I didn't steal from you," Billy insisted, his voice rising.

"Cows you stole. Money of mine."

"I never stole a damned thing from you or your cattle ranch."

Excerpt From THE HIGH RIDER

"Put that gun away, Charlie," Cimarron ordered. "Before it goes off and you drill somebody."

"Mind your own business, mister," Charlie growled, his gun swiveling around to point in Cimarron's direction.

Without another word, Cimarron slid his right boot from its stirrup and kicked out. His boot struck Charlie's hand, and the gun, as Charlie's finger convulsed on its trigger, fired. Cimarron kicked out a second time and this time he knocked the gun from Charlie's hand.

Enraged, Charlie seized Cimarron's boot and pulled hard on it.

Cimarron made a grab for his saddle horn but missed it. A moment later, he hit the ground and a moment after that Charlie was kneeling on the ground straddling him, his fists pummeling both sides of Cimarron's head.

Cimarron brought one knee up and rammed it into Charlie's groin. As Charlie yelped in pain and clutched his genitals in both hands, Cimarron seized both of the man's wrists and, getting up on his knees, hurled him to one side.

Charlie's body struck a deadfall and he lay dazed for a moment before getting to his hands and knees and shaking his head groggily.

Cimarron heard the sound of splashing behind him and he turned to find Billy racing through the shallows of the river. When Billy came out of the river on the opposite bank, he kept on running without looking back.

Cimarron's knees buckled as he was suddenly struck on the shoulder from behind. He turned and saw the limb that had been broken from the deadfall in Charlie's hand. It was rising...

Cimarron unleathered his gun in one swift movement and fired, shattering the dead wood. He reached out before his startled attacker could make another move and placed his gun against the base of the man's throat.

"I'm a deputy marshal and you, mister, are under arrest as of this minute," he announced. "Now put your hands on top of your head."

When Charlie had obeyed his order, Cimarron backed toward his black, and when he reached it, he fumbled about in his saddlebag, finally coming up with a pair of handcuffs. He bent down, picked up Charlie's gun, and placed it in his waistband.

Excerpt From THE HIGH RIDER

"Now, then," he said stonily, "I'm going to put these cuffs on you and you're going to walk ahead of me to Fort Smith."

"I didn't shoot Billy," Charlie protested. "I was just trying to scare him." He smiled warily. "You can't put a man in jail for fistfighting like Billy and me were just doing."

"I can put you in jail for assault with a deadly weapon."

"I didn't draw on you," Charlie protested.

"That branch you broke off the deadfall is the deadly weapon I'm talking about, not your gun. You're under arrest, like I just said, for assault with a deadly weapon with the intent to kill or maim. That charge'll get you not less than one nor more than five years. At hard labor."

Cimarron moved toward Charlie, his gun leveled at his attacker's midsection, the handcuffs clinking in his left hand.

He halted when he heard the sound of hoofbeats behind him. Shifting position so he could keep Charlie under his gun and also see who was riding toward him, he stared uneasily at the six riders bearing down upon him.

Case Marlow was leading the pack. His three sons were right behind him. And behind them rode Jenny. Beside her rode a man who was wearing a black suit and carrying a black book.

Four Marlow six-guns were aimed at Cimarron.

"Throw down your iron," the elder Marlow barked as he drew rein in front of Cimarron.

Cimarron dropped his gun to the ground.

"Sooner," Case said to his youngest son, "go get his gun and then get around behind him."

As Sooner got out of the saddle, Charlie held up his hands and, waving them nervously in front of him, said, "Don't shoot! Please, don't none of you shoot!"

Case ignored him, and when Sooner had picked up Cimarron's .44 and jammed it into his cartridge belt, he motioned with his gun and Sooner stepped around behind Cimarron.

Cimarron felt the barrel of Sooner's gun pressing against his spine. "Case, what's this all about?" he inquired.

"Me," Jenny said cheerfully as she walked her horse up beside her father's. "Me and you, Cimarron."

Cimarron frowned. He hooked his thumbs in his cartridge belt and stood his ground, wondering, waiting.

"You're a trifling man, Cimarron," Case said, his lips barely moving.

Excerpt From THE HIGH RIDER

"Our sister's paid—she's paying the price for your trifling with her," Bart Marlow snarled.

Jamie tilted his Stetson back on his head with the barrel of his gun and said, "But we aim to set things right between the two of you."

"I don't have the least little notion of what it is you boys are talking about," Cimarron lied, trying for a smile but promptly losing it as Case Marlow's eyes blazed in anger.

"You know damned well what we're talking about," Sooner stated from behind Cimarron.

"I don't, and that's a fact," Cimarron lied again.

"Show him what we're talking about, Jenny," Bart commanded, and Jenny obligingly got out of the saddle and stood beside her mare, both of her hands resting lightly on the bulge of her belly, which hiked the front of her dress up to reveal her ankles.

"It's yours, Cimarron," she said sweetly, smiling brilliantly. "Ours, I mean. If it's a girl I thought we could name her Dorothy. I just love that name—Dorothy. But if it's a boy, of course we'll name him Cimarron, Junior."

Cimarron, shaking his head in an effort to deny the reality of what he saw, said, "You're—"

"She's pregnant," Case shouted. "And you're the one that went and got her in a family way!"

"You're going to do right by our sister," Sooner declared ominously from behind Cimarron, his gun suddenly threatening to snap Cimarron's spine.

"You're going to marry her," Jamie declared gruffly.

"Where shall we go on our honeymoon, Cimarron?" Jenny asked. "Tulsey Town? Or all the way up to Dodge City?"

"I—you—we—" Cimarron gave it up and fell silent.

"Preacher," Case said, and beckoned to the man on the horse behind him. "Come along up here and let's get the ceremony over and done with."

As the preacher, his book in his hand, got out of the saddle, Jenny skipped up to Cimarron, took his arm, and stood with him facing her father and two of her brothers.

"Wait a minute," Cimarron said suddenly. "Now, just hold on a minute. How the hell do you know I'm the daddy?"

"Jenny told us you were," Jamie replied as if that settled the matter.

"Maybe she's been with other men besides me," Cimarron pointed out.

Excerpt From THE HIGH RIDER

"So you admit to what you did to her," Case roared, his face suddenly aflame.

"Cimarron, there never was anyone else," Jenny declared fervently and squeezed his arm. "There was always only you."

"You can't railroad me into marriage," Cimarron protested, knowing full well that the Marlow clan could and, it looked like, would do just that. "I'm not fit to be the husband of such a fine woman as Jenny here. I'm never to home. Hell, I haven't even got a place I can call home. I'm broke most of the time, and when I'm not, I—I get drunk! I gamble. I forni—" His lips snapped shut just in time.

"You're going to make an honest woman out of my daughter, Cimarron," Case said sternly. "When Jenny told us she'd spotted you riding through Parson's Point a while back, we got the preacher and rode right out after you. We've been trying for some time to get our hands on you and now we have. You're going to marry Jenny because she has got to get herself married now that she's got herself in the fix you can plainly see she's in. Preacher, get a move on!"

The preacher, a solemn expression on his round face as he stood in front of Cimarron and the still-smiling Jenny, opened his black book. "Dearly beloved—"

"I tell you, Case," Cimarron interrupted, "I'd be hopeless as a husband. You just can't go and do a thing like that to Jenny—saddle her with me, is what I mean. Now, if you'll just give this matter some serious thought, you'll see that—why, this man standing next to me has a whole lot more character than I'll ever hope to have!"

An idea suddenly occurred to Cimarron, and desperate, he decided he had nothing to lose by trying what he had in mind. And if it worked he had a lot to gain. Namely, freedom.

"Charlie here," he said, "owns a ranch. Cattle. He's not a wealthy man, but he makes do and gets by. He makes more money by far than I do in any given year, I'll wager. He could give Jenny a real good home. Couldn't you, Charlie?" Cimarron jabbed Charlie in the ribs with his elbow.

"I'm not a marrying man," Charlie snapped. "You got yourself into this, mister, you get yourself out of it." He snickered. "In," he said knowingly. "Out," he added, and burst into loud laughter.

"Case," Cimarron said soberly, "just give me a minute to talk to my friend Charlie here. Will you do that, Case?"

Excerpt From THE HIGH RIDER

As Case hesitated, Cimarron seized Charlie's arm. Leaning close to the man, he muttered, "Not less than one year and not more than five years is what you'll get by the time Judge Parker's through with you. *At hard labor!* I'll make a deal with you, Charlie, old son. You marry Jenny and I'll forget all about charging you with assault with a deadly weapon with the intent to kill or maim me."

Charlie remained silent.

Cimarron turned to face Case Marlow and said, "Charlie here would be right proud to marry Jenny, Case. He just told me he's never laid even one of his eyes on such a comely woman before."

"Well," Case drawled, "I don't see that it matters all that much who she marries just so she does marry somebody so she'll be respectable when her time comes."

"No, Pa," Jenny shrieked. "I don't want Charlie, whoever he might be. I want *Cimarron!*"

"Shut your mouth, girl," Case bellowed. "You got no say in this. It's your damned waywardness that caused us this problem in the first place, so you'll marry whoever I tell you to marry."

"Pa, you just can't go and do this to me. Look at him!" Jenny pointed to Charlie. "He's skinny as a snake. He's got arms like an ape!"

"It's most likely you'll draw closer to five years than just one, Charlie," Cimarron muttered, jabbing Charlie in the ribs a second time. "Judge Parker's a harsh man. Some say a mean man. Think on all that hard labor you're going to have to endure—if you can endure it. Rack that up against you and Jenny living together in bedded—I mean, wedded bliss, and there's just one conclusion you can jump to."

"No!" Charlie yelled at the top of his voice.

"I'll lie and say you murdered Billy," Cimarron snarled in a vicious whisper. "I'll say I saw you rape a woman. You won't go to jail, Charlie, old son. What you'll do is hang!"

"Yes!" Charlie yelled at the top of his voice.

"No!" Jenny cried, and threw her arms around Cimarron's neck. "It's you I want to marry, Cimarron."

Cimarron gently disengaged her arms and moved aside so that she was standing next to Charlie.

The preacher looked back over his shoulder at Case, and

Excerpt From THE HIGH RIDER

when Case nodded curtly, he turned to Charlie. "May I know your last name, sir? For purposes of the ceremony?"

"Lendell," Charlie said glumly.

"Hope you two have a real happy honeymoon," Cimarron said. He handed Charlie the gun he had taken from him and pulled his own gun out of Sooner's belt and holstered it.

Jenny began to wail as Cimarron returned the handcuffs to his saddlebag and then swung into his saddle.

"Dearly beloved," intoned the preacher, his eyes on the words printed in the open book he held in his hands. "We are gathered here together in the sight of God to join this man and this woman . . ."

Cimarron raked the black with his spurs and went galloping across the river toward Fort Smith.

As he emerged from the river just north of Belle Point, a whistle shrieked and he turned his head to see a round canvas tent standing on the bluff where the Poteau River joined the Arkansas.

He sat his saddle, marveling, as a man wearing black trousers, a black broadcloth coat, elastic-sided black shoes, a boiled white shirt, a black string tie, and a black top hat appeared from around the tent, a beribboned baton in his right hand. Stepping high, the man marched in an easterly direction and a moment later a calliope mounted on a brightly painted wagon appeared to spill its steam and unique music into the air.

Behind the calliope marched two more men carrying a long banner that was stretched between them. It bore the words, white on black velvet: SIMPSON'S COLOSSAL CIRCUS AND MENAGERIE.

Next in line was a cavorting clown wearing a baggy white suit and a pie plate of a red hat, his face whitened and dotted with glittering spangles.

Cimarron watched as the procession lengthened to include two elephants, each of them ridden by young women with veils over the lower halves of their faces and filmy garments covering their bodies. Behind the elephants came wagons drawn by teams of horses, their sides decorated with carved and gilded female figures discreetly draped. Perched atop the bandwagon were five men wearing scarlet uniforms richly adorned with gold braid who began to play their brass instruments in competition with the man seated at the keyboard of the calliope.

Children appeared from everywhere to march beside the gaudy parade. Men and women lined the sidewalks, gaping

Excerpt From THE HIGH RIDER

and pointing, their mouths open in undisguised awe as cages bearing lions, a rhinoceros, and monkeys rolled by on sturdy wagons.

Behind the cages were four young men who went tumbling and cartwheeling down the street, leaping into the air to land on the shoulders of their companions—a blur of movement that caused the growing crowd first to gasp and then to break into appreciative applause.

Cimarron, when the last of the parade had finally passed him, fell in behind it. He rode down the street after it, past the cemetery, and then he turned left and headed for Rogers Avenue.

He turned left again at the intersection and then entered the stone-walled compound within which was the federal courthouse and the gallows.

As he passed the macabre platform, he nodded to George Maledon, the hangman, who stood nonchalantly on one of the several traps set in the floor as he carefully examined the noose that dangled from an I-beam. " 'Morning, George."

"Nice day," Maledon responded, running his slender fingers almost lovingly along the hemp.

"For a hanging?"

"Just one this morning."

"Who's the unlucky sonofabitch this time?"

"Ernie Wilcox."

Cimarron felt a sinking sensation in the pit of his stomach as he sat his saddle staring at the noose in Maledon's hands. He felt queasy partly because he recalled all too well the time several years ago when he had nearly become a victim of the gallows and partly because he was sorry to hear that eighteen-year-old Ernie Wilcox was to be its next victim.

"The jury convicted Wilcox of murdering Labrette, did they?" he asked, knowing it was a foolish question while vaguely wishing that Maledon would reply in the negative.

"They did, Cimarron. You can carve another notch in your gun. You were the one who brought Wilcox in, weren't you?"

"I was the one. Well, have yourself a good day, George."

As Cimarron headed toward the courthouse, Maledon called out, "I always have a good day when I've a hanging to oversee."

A shudder passed through Cimarron's body. He had suddenly grown cold, although the sun still burned in the cloudless blue sky above him.

Excerpt From THE HIGH RIDER

He dismounted, tethered his horse to the hitch rail in front of the courthouse, and then went inside and made his way to Marshal Upham's office.

Upham opened the door in response to Cimarron's knock and said, "Oh, it's you, is it? I was expecting someone else."

Cimarron followed Upham across the office after closing the door behind him and sat down in one of the two leather chairs facing the desk.

Upham, once he was seated behind his desk, began to shuffle papers. "I wasn't expecting to see you, Cimarron. I find it's a rare occasion when I have to welcome a bounty hunter to my office."

"Marshal, I'm not a bounty hunter."

"The last time you were in this office you declared yourself to be one. Maybe not in so many words. But—"

"I'll tell you what happened." Cimarron proceeded to do so and he had just finished speaking when there was a tentative knock on the door.

Upham rose and crossed the office. He opened the door and said, "Ah, it's you, Miss Powell. Come in, please."

Cimarron turned in his chair to watch Upham bow the young woman he had called Miss Powell into his office.

He took in her heart-shaped face, her slim figure, and almost nonexistent waist. His eyes rose from her full hips to her equally full breasts and then to her very attractive face. Her eyes were blue. Her skin was rosy. Pert little nose she's got, he thought. Nice full lips too.

"This deputy, Miss Powell, is named Cimarron," Upham declared.

Cimarron sprang to his feet and took the hand Miss Powell held out to him. He shook it, finding her grip surprisingly strong. "I'm pleased to make your acquaintance, Miss Powell."

"You look exactly the way a Deputy United States Marshal should look, Cimarron," Miss Powell said in her slightly husky voice after giving him an appraising look. "So self-confident and—virile." She sat down in the empty chair beside Cimarron's and turned to face Upham, who had seated himself behind his desk. "I hope I didn't interrupt anything, Marshal."

"Not at all, not at all. And if you had—why, I must say that an interruption by such a lovely young woman as yourself would be nothing but most welcome."

"What a charming man you are, Marshal." Turning to

Excerpt From THE HIGH RIDER

Cimarron, who was seated again, Miss Powell asked, "Isn't he charming, Cimarron?"

"Well—" Cimarron caught the glare Upham was giving him. "Oh, he's charming all right. Never met a more charming man than the marshal."

Upham's glare faded and was replaced by a beatific, almost idiotic smile as he turned his attention to Miss Powell. "Judge Parker told me before he left town yesterday that you would be here to see me this morning. He also asked me to do whatever I could to help you. What can I do to help you, Miss Powell?"

"Judge Parker was more than kind to me when we met yesterday. He said he felt sure that you would see your way clear to provide our circus with the protection we shall most sorely need as we journey west through Indian Territory on our way to California."

"Protection?" Upham regarded his visitor quizzically.

"We've all heard how perfectly dreadful conditions are in the Territory, Marshal, so we petitioned Judge Parker to help us. He said it was your province to provide protection and he didn't want to interfere with the operation of your office. He referred me to you. I hoped that you would provide us with a—is it called a posse?"

"Is what called a posse?" Upham asked, obviously puzzled.

"I'm talking about an armed guard to escort Simpson's Colossal Circus through the Territory," Miss Powell explained. "A dozen or so men should do quite nicely."

"A dozen or so men—" Upham fell back in his chair.

"You ought to be able to manage that easy, Marshal," Cimarron commented. "A dozen of your deputies ought to be able to keep all those wild animals in their cages and all those wild Indians who're roaming around in the Territory out of the circus tent."

"That's enough, Cimarron," Upham snapped angrily. And then he began to smile. A moment later, he was beaming. "All of my deputies, Miss Powell, are at present on the scout in the Territory." He cleared his throat. "All but one, that is."

"Now, wait just one damned minute, Marshal," Cimarron almost shouted, half-rising from his chair.

Upham scowled at him and he sat back down.

"Cimarron, I'm sure," Upham said to Miss Powell, "will be happy to escort you and the other people in the circus until you reach northern Texas."

Excerpt From THE HIGH RIDER

"I'm not riding shotgun for any circus," Cimarron declared hotly.

Miss Powell gave him a disappointed look.

Upham gave him another fierce scowl. "Now that you've got bounty hunting out of your system, Cimarron, I assumed—I hope, not mistakenly—that you were ready to accept another assignment from the court."

"I am ready. I want another assignment, but—"

"I've just given you one. You will guide Simpson's Circus across the Territory. You will be responsible for the safety of its people and its property. As an officer of this court, you will uphold the fine reputation its deputy marshals have earned and carry on in their tradition of selfless service in the protection of the lives and property of innocent people in the Indian Territory."

"You will help us, then, Cimarron?" Miss Powell inquired tentatively. She leaned toward him and Cimarron found himself staring down at the provocative cleavage that her square-necked gown revealed.

"I will," he was surprised to hear himself say.

"Oh, I'm so glad," Miss Powell exclaimed, reaching out and squeezing his hand. "I'm sure I'll be safe in your strong and capable hands, Cimarron."

"I'm not so sure you will be," Upham muttered in a barely audible voice, his eyes on Cimarron, whose eyes were still on Miss Powell's cleavage.

"We all will be," Miss Powell added, and then, "Did you just say something, Marshal?"

"Nothing of any import."

"Well, I'd better be getting back to the lot," Miss Powell announced, rising from her chair.

"You might as well go right along with her, Cimarron," Upham suggested. He stood up and rounded his desk. Taking Miss Powell's arm, he led her to the door, where he bowed and kissed the hand she extended to him.

"Thank you ever so much for your cooperation, Marshal," she said. "And do be sure to thank Judge Parker as well."

Cimarron ignored the sly wink Upham gave him as Miss Powell left the office. He followed her out of the room and later, as they came out into the compound, he freed his horse and began to lead it toward the gate.

"Whatever in the world are all these people doing here?" Miss Powell asked him as more and more people streamed

Excerpt From THE HIGH RIDER

through the gate to join those already gathered in front of the gallows platform.

"They've come for the hanging," Cimarron answered.

"Hanging?"

Cimarron pointed to the noose dangling in the air.

"Oh, how dreadful!"

"When do you circus people perform?"

"At night. Why?"

"Well, it's a good thing it's not in the morning. You'd sell few tickets if you performed this morning. Everybody'd come instead to see the circus that's about to take place here."

"Circus? I'm afraid I don't understand."

"People do seem to enjoy hangings. They come from miles around to see one. It's them that turn the proceedings into a circus of sorts." Cimarron pointed.

Miss Powell gazed at the family group that was noisily picnicking near the stone wall. "You Westerners must have a terribly warped idea of what constitutes entertainment."

"We Westerners aren't much different at bottom from Easterners or Northerners or Southerners, I reckon. Most people dote on death—somebody else's. That's why a lot of them go to the circus."

"I don't follow you."

"They may not know it, but a bunch of them're hoping to see a trapeze artist fall to his death. Or a lion tear his tamer to pieces."

"Is that the man they're going to hang?"

Cimarron glanced in the direction Miss Powell was looking and saw Ernie Wilcox being marched from the jail that was in the basement of the courthouse. Preceding him was a preacher. Following him were two armed jail attendants.

"That's the man."

"Hurry. Let's get out of here. I don't want to witness what's going to happen."

Me neither, Cimarron thought as he followed Miss Powell through the gate.

"The circus lot is on the bluff by the river," Miss Powell informed him. "We'll be there in no time."

"What is it exactly that you do in the circus, Miss Powell?"

"Call me Lucinda, Cimarron. I'm sure we're going to become the very best of friends during our upcoming journey together.

Excerpt From THE HIGH RIDER

To answer your question, I'm what circus people sometimes call a high rider."

"What's that?"

"I ride a Lipizzaner stallion, which I control by using only my wrists, calves, and by subtly shifting my body's weight. The method is called high school riding or, in French, *haute école*. One can make the Lipizzaner—one that has been high school-trained—do all sorts of things: trot, waltz, sidestep, pirouette, and much more. Have you ever seen a high rider perform, Cimarron?"

But Cimarron was no longer paying attention to Lucinda. He was staring, a frown on his face, at the woman who was standing across the street from the compound gate, her arms at her sides, a forlorn expression on her face.

"Lucinda," he said, "you go on along to the circus lot. There's somebody over there I've got to have a word with. I'll catch up with you later."

He led his black across the street and stopped in front of Esther Lane. She didn't look up at him as she continued to stare into the compound.

"Miss Lane," he said softly, "you oughtn't to be here." When she did not respond, he gently touched her arm.

She looked up at him. "Cimarron."

"I'll take you someplace where you won't have to see—"

"I hope you're happy now," she said, her voice colorless. "You brought Ernie to jail and now he's going to—they're going to hang him!" She began to weep, her hands covering her face.

"It's not my doing," Cimarron argued. "He had himself a jury trial and was convicted of murder."

"I know that," Esther cried, uncovering her tear-stained face. "I was at the trial. I hired a lawyer to defend Ernie, but the man—all he could do was—he couldn't do anything. Not in the face of all those eyewitnesses who testified that they saw Ernie kill Mr. Labrette."

Cimarron turned and stared through the compound gate at the noose resting loosely—but not for long, he thought—around Wilcox's neck as the preacher read unheard words from his Bible.

"Everyone was against Ernie right from the start," Esther continued, fighting back her tears. "The people in McAlester, the newspaper there. They wrote in the paper that it was men

Excerpt From THE HIGH RIDER

like Ernie who had to be rooted out—that's what they wrote, 'rooted out'—and hanged before the Territory could ever hope to become a place for decent people to live.

"They wrote that guns in the hands of men like Ernie were lethal and that the forty-four-caliber bullet that took Mr. Labrette's life was a symbol of the evil of men like my poor Ernie. They—"

Cimarron spun around to face Esther. "Did you just say a forty-four-caliber bullet?"

She nodded dumbly, her tears beginning again.

Cimarron's thoughts raced. He recalled apprehending Wilcox in Esther's bedroom that dark night. He remembered the gun he had taken away from Wilcox.

"That gun I took from Wilcox. Was it the only one he owned?"

"Yes. He wanted to buy a better—a newer one—but he never had enough money at any one time."

An image of Wilcox's Model 1849 thirty-one-caliber revolver flashed in Cimarron's mind. He saw it clearly—its five-inch octagon barrel, its five-chambered cylinder, its blued finish.

He leaped aboard his black and went galloping across the street and into the compound, where he circled the boisterous crowd until he reached the steps at the side of the gallows platform. He let out a whoop, and when the two jail attendants guarding Wilcox turned toward him, their guns in their hands, he yelled, "Stop the hanging!"

"Cimarron," the attendant nearest him responded, "what the hell are you talking about?"

"George," Cimarron yelled, gesturing wildly, "get that noose off Wilcox's neck."

Maledon merely stared at Cimarron in surprise as the preacher spluttered and twitched nervously.

"Do it, George," Cimarron shouted. "Stop the hanging!"

The other jail attendant shook his head and said, "Only Judge Parker can stop a hanging, Cimarron. You know that."

"And the judge is out of town," his companion reminded Cimarron. "He's giving a speech over in Van Buren."

Cimarron swore and said, "All I'm asking you to do is postpone the hanging. When Judge Parker gets back to town, I'll talk to him. I'll take the responsibility for delaying the hanging."

"No, sir, Cimarron," Maledon said firmly. "We're going ahead with this. You must have gone crazy or something. Stop the hanging, he says. Nobody stops one of George Maledon's hangings. Judge Parker never even did."

Excerpt From THE HIGH RIDER

The words had a galvanizing effect on Cimarron. He leaped from the saddle, but as he bounded up the steps, both jail attendants aimed their six-guns at him and he halted halfway to the platform.

"We'll shoot you if we have to," one of them said.

"If you force us to," the other one said.

Cimarron held out his hands in a helpless gesture. "You've got me dead to rights, boys. But let's us talk this thing over like the reasonable men we are." He climbed up onto the platform.

The jail attendants both took a step backward.

Cimarron suddenly reached out and seized the preacher. Using the man as a shield, he edged around the attendants and then reached out with his free hand and removed the noose from around Wilcox's neck.

"Cimarron," Wilcox exclaimed. "I never in my life thought I'd be glad to see you again!"

"Get down from here and up behind the cantle of my saddle, Wilcox."

Wilcox fled from the platform, and when he was on Cimarron's black, Cimarron drew his .44. "You two," he said to the attendants, "drop your guns. On the trap."

When they had done so, Cimarron said, "George, you go down and around back and pull your little lever."

Moments later, as the crowd stared in shocked silence at the four men remaining on the platform, Maledon sprung the trap and the two revolvers fell through it to the ground below.

A man in the watching crowd suddenly fired at Cimarron.

He spun around as the bullet zipped past him, the preacher still held in front of him and obviously terrified, and fired a shot over the heads of the people in the crowd.

As women screamed and a baby began to bellow, he yelled, "I've got me five shots left. Now, who else wants to try to be a hero?"

No one answered him.

The crowd began to shrink away from the gallows. Then, as if responding to some unseen signal, people began running for the gate of the compound. Some of them fell to the ground in their haste, only to be trampled by the frantic people behind them.

Cimarron released the preacher and leaped from the platform as Marshal Upham's head appeared in his open courthouse office window. Once he was in the saddle, he turned his black and galloped toward the low stone wall of the compound because the gate was blocked by the fleeing throng.

"*Cimarron!*"

Cimarron didn't look back at the sound of his name, which had been shouted at the top of Marshal Upham's voice.

"Just what the hell do you think you're doing?" Upham roared as Cimarron's black leaped over a partially crumbled portion of the stone wall and went galloping toward the river.

"Where are we going?" Wilcox asked breathlessly.

There was a grin on Cimarron's face as he replied, "You and me, Wilcox, we're running away to join the circus!"

ABOUT THE AUTHOR

LEO P. KELLEY was born and raised in Pennsylvania's Wyoming Valley and spent a good part of his boyhood exploring the surrounding mountains, hunting and fishing. He served in the Army Security Agency as a cryptographer, and then went "on the road," working as dishwasher, laborer, etc. He later joined the Merchant Marine and sailed on tankers calling at Texas, South American, and Italian ports. In New York City he attended the New School for Social Research, receiving a BA in Literature. He worked in advertising, promotion, and marketing before leaving the business world to write full time.

Mr. Kelley has published a dozen novels and has several others now in the works. He has also published many short stories in leading magazines.

JOIN THE CIMARRON READER'S PANEL

If you're a reader of CIMARRON, New American Library wants to bring you more of the type of books you enjoy. For this reason we're asking you to join the CIMARRON Reader's Panel, so we can learn more about your reading tastes.

Please fill out and mail this questionnaire today. Your comments are appreciated.

1. The title of the last paperback book I bought was:
   TITLE:_____ PUBLISHER:_____

2. How many paperback books have you bought for yourself in the last six months?
   ☐ 1 to 3 ☐ 4 to 6 ☐ 7 to 9 ☐ 10 to 20 ☐ 21 or more

3. What other paperback fiction have you read in the past six months?
   Please list titles:_____
   _____
   _____
   _____

4. My favorite is (one of the above or other):_____

5. My favorite author is:_____

6. I watch television, on average (check one):
   ☐ Over 4 hours a day ☐ 2 to 4 hours a day
   ☐ 0 to 2 hours a day
   I usually watch television (check one or more):
   ☐ 8 a.m. to 5 p.m. ☐ 5 p.m. to 11 p.m. ☐ 11 p.m. to 2 a.m.

7. I read the following numbers of different magazines regularly (check one):
   ☐ More than 6 ☐ 3 to 6 magazines ☐ 0 to 2 magazines
   My favorite magazines are:_____

For our records, we need this information from all our Reader's Panel Members.

NAME:_____

ADDRESS:_____

CITY:_____ STATE:_____ ZIP CODE:_____

8. (Check one) ☐ Male ☐ Female

9. Age (Check one): ☐ 17 and under ☐ 18 to 34 ☐ 35 to 49
   ☐ 50 to 64 ☐ 65 and over

10. Education (check one):
    ☐ Now in high school ☐ Graduated high school
    ☐ Now in college ☐ Completed some college
    ☐ Graduated college

11. What is your occupation? (check one):
    ☐ Employed full-time ☐ Employed part-time ☐ Not employed
    Give your full job title:_____

Thank you. Please mail this today to:
CIMARRON, New American Library
1633 Broadway, New York, New York 10019